CHRIS

THE GUZZI
LEGACY BOOK 3

BETHANY-KRIS

www.bethanykris.com

Editor: Elizabeth Peters

Proofreaders: Tracy A., Mia B., Tori W. and Felicia F.

Cover Design © Under Cover Designs

Interior Design: Under Cover Designs

ISBN - 978-1-988197-98-2

CONTENTS

For Peppen.

CHAPTER

1

Beautiful distractions hid the worst of crimes.

The table, draped in silk, and filled with food cooked by a renown chef, welcomed their guests, in a dining room with walls covered in expensive art. It proved to Valeria that the other people sitting down at the table for dinner would forget the young lady—who was barely a woman—across from them had been in the papers just a few months ago.

They wouldn't remember her face had been on the news after her mother's murder—the wife of a prominent Mexican politician. They didn't seem to remember how just months later she walked down the aisle, not yet sixteen at that point, forced to marry the son of the man who had invited them to this dinner.

None of it mattered to them.

Money *talked*.

And it apparently said very nice things.

Like the silk linen, the coveted art, delicious food, and beautiful people dressed in their best with glittering diamonds showcased on their bodies to prove their status and wealth. All of it became a promise to them. Should these people keep quiet about the other issues at the table, like Valeria, then the Lòpezs would make a deal.

They liked that.

Deals.

Better known as bribes, or blackmail. It depended on her

husband, and his father's, preference or their need. When it had been her father on the other side of this table, they had wanted a promise he would help them smuggle their illegal drugs into the United States where he had connections to border control.

Her father said no.

They killed his wife.

Her father then agreed.

And so, they took her, too, and forced her to marry the oldest son of the Lòpez cartel's leader. A way to drive the point home, she figured. Because that's all she had been.

And now, she was a trophy.

A beautiful *thing*.

Something to own.

"*Sonreírse*," Jorge said to her left, his Spanish order for her to smile coming out dark, and harsh, even under his breath. He watched her constantly, and when she didn't behave as he wanted her to, he made her aware. His fingers curved around her thigh under the table, flexing enough to make her draw in a quick breath. "*Now*, Valeria."

Her gaze swept the people at the table, a *business* meeting, they told her. Right, more like a way to manipulate and gain what the Lòpez family needed to do their work without trouble. Tonight, it was cops in high positions of power. Officers that controlled the subordinates under them, which corrupted the system further, but allowed the cartel to breathe a little easier.

This was how it worked.

She smiled when the wife of one officer turned her attention away from Valeria's sister-in-law, Abril, to the ones at the other side of the table. The whole damn family sat there— from her father-in-law, Martín, to Jorge's younger brother, Samuel. They pulled out all the stops to draw these people into their traps without using violent means first—the cartel's usual way.

When someone denied them things turned bad. Valeria's family was a good example of that.

"Martín," the woman said to Valeria's father-in-law, smiling a little too widely, "you must be pleased, *sí*?"

What was her name again?

Missy?

More American than Mexican. A dual citizen of both countries, if she trusted what her husband told her about their guests earlier, which kept the conversation drifting back and forth between English and Spanish for most of the dinner.

Not that Valeria cared to engage.

"Pleased about what?" Martín asked, tipping his wine glass up for a drink.

Out of all the people at this table, Valeria hated Martín the most. A difficult task for him to accomplish, considering she married his son, a man who beat her to keep her in line. He had *suggested* the marriage after killing her mother, like they should have expected it.

Still, she blamed him.

For all of this.

Across the table, Missy nodded at Valeria with a subtle tilt of her chin. Her grin reached to her eyes, as though she held a secret, but for now, she was only hinting at it.

Martín seemed to understand.

"Ah, *el bebé*," Martín said, chuckling. Setting his glass to the table harder than necessary, proving just how much he had imbibed over the course of the dinner, he smiled and nodded. "Very pleased. We hoped it would be a *niño* for us. A *boy*. And yet, it seems it will be a girl, but that's okay, too."

Valeria had done her best throughout the dinner to not draw attention to herself. For the last several months, they had not allowed her out of the Lòpez's compound after her marriage. This was one of the first dinners she attended, and her greatest fears would be that someone would ask about her father, apologize for her mother's death, or even, like now, want to discuss her current life.

Valeria's hand lifted from the table to rest upon the swell of her stomach. Under her palm, she felt the baby girl shift from her mother's touch, but like the good baby she already seemed to be, the child settled, allowing Valeria little discomfort from the movement.

"Congratulations," the woman said to Valeria. "Babies are gifts."

"Blessings," the man next to her added.

Right.

Her husband created this baby through violent means and pain, but she wouldn't say so. Was raping her a *blessing*? And besides, she loved her daughter. She loved her enough that she sat at this table, kept her smile on, and shut her fucking mouth so that Jorge wouldn't beat her later in the evening when everyone left. Then, the baby wouldn't get hurt, too.

"Thank you," Valeria whispered.

Her first words at the dinner.

No one seemed to notice.

Next to her, Jorge gave Valeria a tight smile. Another warning, she figured, but without him speaking it out loud. She didn't need him to do that at all—she was aware what he expected of her, and what the punishment would be if she failed.

It used to scare her.

He terrified her.

Now, she just … *worried.*

For this child she carried, mostly. Because what would happen to her once she made her presence known in the world. Valeria, all of sixteen years old, but she would be seventeen before this baby was born. Not that it mattered because what control did a girl of her age have against a man like her husband. Six years her senior, a criminal who had only taken her because of the status it would provide him, and far too power hungry for his own good.

What could she do?

How might she protect this baby from him?

From the rest of them?

"Val, would you like another drink of water?"

At the soft question from a familiar, kind voice, Valeria came out of her thoughts to see her sister-in-law standing from the seat on the other side of hers. Abril gave Valeria a small smile, but in her eyes she found the truth.

Concern warred in Abril's gaze.

Older than her by a few months, Abril was the only person in the Lòpez family that Valeria had made friends with, and sometimes, she even questioned it because she no longer trusted anyone. Abril had done nothing to prove she deserved that hesitation though. She helped.

And she had promised to help more.

"Water?" Abril asked again.

Valeria nodded. "Yes, thank you, that would be nice."

Abril passed Valeria's chair, her hand coming to rest on her shoulder as she bent down to whisper, "The plan happens tonight—I received the message."

As quickly as Abril had told her the words, ones that might promise her freedom, she was leaving the dining room and the rest behind. Valeria looked to the man at her side, finding her husband distracted, and grinning at the young wife of an official across the table from him.

That grin meant he wanted to fuck the woman.

Valeria didn't care.

The promise of freedom would make a person smile, no matter how dangerous, crazy, and even if there was no guarantee her plan to run away would work.

Still, she had to try.

For this child, she *had to*.

"Valeria."

She hoped the guilt didn't show on her face when she met Jorge's gaze. He never missed her distractions. Now didn't seem like a good time to play with fire. The blank expression he wore said she was the last thing on his mind.

Good.

"Yes?"

"I'm sure you won't mind going home to the compound alone tonight, will you?" he asked.

He posed it like a question.

It wasn't.

"Of course, not," she said.

"I'll be home for breakfast. Take care of my baby. You got me?"

Better than he understood.

~

Valeria did her best to soothe the nerves running wild as she brushed down the colt, *Butter*, in the stables. Butter, only two months old, had given Valeria a reason to visit the stables on the compound more often over the last couple of months.

The compound itself, set on a good twenty acres of secluded, desolate land protected by armed guards, allowed the Lòpez family privacy. To the east, one would find cliffs leading out to choppy, dangerous ocean water. The guards and an electric fence secured the only road leading out of the compound. Two larger barns, used like warehouses and full of drugs to smuggle, sat further west of the compound, while their homes and stables made up a small village right in the center.

There was no way out.

Or so they thought …

One simply needed enough time, and the means to make it happen. Not that they ever gave her the opportunity to run before. She could rarely do anything without a guard or her husband nearby to watch her do … whatever.

The stables, however, were her free time. Or, that's how Jorge liked to put it. He didn't have much interest in the horses, it was more of a pet project for his siblings, and some guards that stayed on the property.

Valeria took a liking to the horses *because* her husband didn't care. He wouldn't follow her into the stables to look after the horses, and he didn't mind her taking one out for a ride—like she did after arriving back to the compound that night—as long as someone was with her to keep an eye on her.

But when she looked after the horses in the stables?

No one cared.

No one watched her, then.

The sound of boots crunching against dried grass, and the hay that fell around the outside of the stables during the last delivery, made Valeria slow the strokes of her brush against the colt's hind end. She peered up over the back of the colt in just enough time to see Abril slip into the stables.

Dressed in riding boots, a helmet in hand, jeans molded to her legs, and a shawl that would keep her warm on a ride, Abril looked ready to take a horse out.

"Ready?" she asked.

Valeria swallowed hard. "Did they see you?"

"One or two."

God.

That just made Valeria nervous. Her heart threatened to jump into her throat. Was this possible? Would this even *work*?

She didn't know.

But she had to try.

"Stop worrying," Abril whispered, coming closer to the colt, and Valeria. "We have it all worked out, right? You went out on a horse and came back with a guard. They saw you do it. And like usual, you're in here taking care of the horses—nothing strange."

Right, right.

"But—"

"But nothing. They'll see *me* go out on a horse," Abril said, shrugging, "and they won't think anything strange when they see you go into the house."

Valeria nodded.

Except it wouldn't be Abril taking a horse out, and it wouldn't be Valeria heading back to the house. The girls were close enough in age, and in some ways, appearance given their olive-toned skin was the same, their stark, straight black hair both reached mid-back, and as long as someone was looking at them from behind while they sat on a horse, no one would tell the difference.

Abril had an inch of height on Valeria. Her eyes were a shade deeper brown than Valeria's russet gaze. Her sister-in-law took after her family in appearance. Sharp, angular jaws, elongated features. Whereas Valeria had a softer, rounder face, and lower cheekbones that always showed the apples of her cheeks when she smiled.

Looking at them face to face, it was clear the two looked nothing alike. But from behind, and on a horse, at a distance?

No one would be able to tell.

"Someone has to see *you* come back, though," Valeria pointed out. "Or they'll believe you helped me get away."

Abril shrugged as she dropped the riding helmet to the floor of the stables and kicked off her riding boots. "And they will."

"How?"

"You know Juan?"

"Samuel's guard?"

Her brother-in-law had a friend—*friend* being a loose term because Valeria wasn't sure any of the people in this family had someone they cared about, except for Abril. Point was, Samuel preferred one guard amongst the many that looked after them at the compound.

"What about him?" Valeria asked.

Abril smirked up at Valeria. "He'll do me a favor, okay? Tit for tat, I gave him something he wanted, and he'll make sure someone *saw me* come back tonight on foot after the horse threw me off. Now, are you going to get dressed and switch clothes with me, or keep wasting time?"

Valeria had so many more questions.

What kind of favor?

What had Abril done?

"All right," Valeria muttered.

The two of them stepped into a stable corner and made quick work of shedding their clothes. Abril dressed in the clothing from Valeria, and she took her sister-in-law's stuff to slip on. Before long, they came out of the corner, and Valeria turned to head for the horse she preferred to ride on toward the end of the stables.

"No, take Maple," Abril said, "he's my horse, and that's the one they expect me to ride."

"But he won't come back."

And Abril *loved* Maple.

"It's okay," Abril said, "he will be taken care of once you get to where you're supposed to go. I know that."

Valeria hesitated to move for the other horse who was blowing them his special kisses because his favorite human was close, and it meant a ride was coming. Turning to Abril, Valeria let the first tear fall, and she didn't bother to brush it away.

"Thank you for doing this."

She understood well just how much Abril was risking.

What it could mean if someone caught them …

"Take care of my niece," Abril replied, "and stay away so he can't hurt you anymore, Val."

"I will."

Or she would try.

It was all going to fall on a hope, a wish, and a damn prayer, though. She didn't doubt for a second that once Jorge knew she had run away, he would come after her. He would never stop tracking her down.

She was his trophy.

His thing.

He *won* her.

She belonged to him, and only he decided when to toss her away like trash on the sidewalk. But that was okay because Valeria would keep running. As long as it meant her baby was safe, and Jorge couldn't hurt their child, then she would keep going.

To the ends of the fucking earth.

Abril checked the watch on her wrist, and said, "You only have three hours, now. Do you remember the spot where you're supposed to meet Cruz? He has the fake papers you'll need with him, and he can get you across the border, but only for a small window of time, Val."

"Can I even trust him?"

"Papá killed his father—he'd do anything that went against my father or brothers. It's only because he was my ... it doesn't matter," Abril whispered, shaking her head. In a flash, the emotion she had showed speaking about her lost love, something she guarded even from Valeria unless she slipped up like now, to cold in a blink. "He will be at the meeting place, but he will not wait past the time we agreed. You need to go, so *go*."

"Right," Valeria said. "Now or never."

"Good luck."

Those words—*good luck*—echoed in Valeria's mind long after she had taken Maple from the stables and headed out toward the cliffs to the east of the compound. Two hours later, when her back ached, her legs felt like pins and needles had settled into her bloodstream, and her stomach cramped, she still thought about those words.

Maple never slowed.

The darkness turned black.

Valeria thought about those words.

Good luck.

Luck hadn't found her yet.

And while she could taste the promise of freedom with every gallop of Maple's hooves against the ground, it still felt temporary.

How long could she run?

How long would it be before Jorge found her?

CHAPTER

2

For a man like Christopher Guzzi, comfort came easy. *Usually*. He was most comfortable when surrounded by people he trusted—or better, those he loved. His family, for starters. When it was just them, his brothers and father or mother, and him, then Chris didn't put on his mask.

The one *all* Guzzi sons wore.

The Don's child.

A made man.

A proper Guzzi.

It never failed to amaze him that from the outside looking in, people had a perspective of his family that they shaped and perfected over the years. Untouchable. Vastly wealthy. *Dangerous*. They needed to be that way to everyone else, a formidable wall of a mafia Don and his army of sons lined up to protect their organization and legacy.

Because otherwise, they all realized what would happen. If someone couldn't have what they had, then they needed to be what they were. *Famiglias* like theirs didn't stay on top being weak, and God knew the Guzzis were anything but that.

Unless they were all alone, the doors closed, and it was just a father and his sons in private, the rules shifted. The masks left, and the walls dropped. Chris, at only twenty-three years old, enjoyed his position as a young made man in his father's Cosa Nostra, no doubt about it.

He also liked this.

Easy conversation with his father about *anything* but business. His oldest brother, Marcus, laughing where he sat on the corner of their father's oak desk—because fuck, it was rare for Marcus to let loose anymore, not when he was too busy being their father's understudy.

Sometimes it seemed like the Mafia took over every aspect of their lives, controlling how they needed to behave even with each other, and blurring the lines between business, and blood. And then there were moments like these when they were all brought back down to earth, reminded of why they were all here.

They were *family*.

And this was when they were at their best.

God save the soul who thought to ruin it.

Gian's—his father—laughter faded at the joke Marcus told before his gaze turned on Chris at the other side of the desk. "Have you talked to your brother?"

Chris had four brothers, and yet, when someone asked him a question like that, it meant they were asking about his identical twin, Corrado. Out of all his brothers, his twin had been the only one who decided not to join the family business. Not that Corrado headed straight in his life when it came to the law—he still very much worked on the illegal side of their life, but it wasn't within their mafia rankings.

"I did, he was just catching his flight to New York," Chris said. "He didn't say too much, distracted, possibly."

Marcus chuckled. "I bet."

Chris shot his brother a look.

Marcus only shrugged.

"Now, now," Gian murmured.

"I'm still trying to figure out how that works, is all."

"As long as it works for them, then that's what matters," Chris returned to Marcus.

"I don't share well," Marcus noted. "Not sure that would work for me."

Chris thought about that one.

"Yeah, me either," he muttered.

Somehow, his twin found himself in love and in a relationship with *two* people. Alessio, and Ginevra. Knowing how his brother's sexual preferences followed Corrado through most of his life, haunting him because he never seemed like he fit in with the rest of his family or their life, Chris was happy he found the people with whom he belonged. What else needed to be said?

Did he understand how that three-person relationship worked?

No.

Did he want to?

Again, no.

It wasn't his life, his home, or his bed.

Simple as that.

And he didn't want other people discussing it where Corrado, Alessio, or Ginevra weren't around to be a part of the discussion. Good manners, and all.

Right?

"Besides, if there's something you want to ask Corrado," Chris told Marcus, "then you could, oh, *ask* him. Or Les— he's pretty open to talk."

Marcus blinked. "Probably not."

"Then, don't speculate."

"That's fair," Gian said, jumping into the discussion as the phone on his desk rang. He gave his two sons a look, pointing a finger at both, a silent *quiet*, before he picked up the call, and put the phone to his ear. "*Bonjour, ciao*, Gian here."

It took Gian just long enough to hear who was on the other line before he reached over, hit the speaker button on the phone, and set it back down to the cradle. The voice that filled the office was one Chris hadn't heard in a while, and he still wasn't sure how he felt when he heard it.

A mixture of things, he supposed.

Only a couple of them any good.

"Do you have a minute to chat, Gian?" Dare asked.

"A few—two of the boys are here."

"Which ones?"

"Marcus, and Chris. What can we do for you?"

Chris never asked for details about how his father came in to contact or all the finer details of Gian's business with Dare —no one seemed to be aware of his last name—but somehow, he had. Gian ended up as one investor who fronted *a lot* of cash to finance a business venture Dare and his partner now controlled.

They called it The League.

An organization which trained assassins, like his brother, Corrado, and then sold them at an auction to the highest bidder. Sure, The League also had their own teams of assassins that worked *only* for The League, and independent contractors, again, like Chris's twin, and one of Corrado's lovers, Alessio.

But mostly, they made real money in the auctions. Selling skilled individuals who could kill someone in a hundred different ways on demand.

Chris had been one of those people once—he trained with Corrado because *fuck*, he couldn't imagine leaving his twin to something like The League without someone there to watch his back. He'd always looked after his twin.

The League wasn't for him, and he realized that rather quickly, but he stuck out his contract. He did the one-year training, stayed for another year to work on a team with his brother and the others they had placed him with, and then he came back home at nineteen.

He wasn't like them.

Chris wanted to be a made man.

And so, he did.

"I have an issue," Dare said, "and I thought getting your opinion on what I should do about it might help to clear up my thoughts, Gian."

"Do tell."

"A job came in. The client isn't *new*, or rather, the family isn't."

"Who?"

"New York—Marcellos."

Gian dragged in a heavy breath and rested back in his chair to steeple his fingers together. He didn't look at either of his sons, but Chris didn't need to see his father's eyes to understand what he was thinking when that name came into play. Oh, sure, their family was on friendly terms with the Marcello Cosa Nostra in New York. The largest mafia organization in North America, it was always better to be on their good side.

His father's reaction, no doubt, was because he wondered *what* the issue was. With the Marcellos, it couldn't be something small. They went all in, or nothing at all. There was no in between for them, and it was one reason Chris respected them as much as he did in the grand scheme.

"And?" Gian asked.

"They need a retrieval done," Dare said, "which seems simple on the surface—it's my team's specialty, right?"

"It seems to be their focus, yes."

"Except there are details that make it problematic for this job. And beyond *those* issues, I have another problem."

"Which is what?" Gian demanded. "Because my suggestion, Dare, would be to give the Marcello family whatever they want, and get them off your ass. They are not the types to be fucked around, and they won't stand for you to jerk on their chains, if you understand what I'm saying here. Take it into account when dealing with them."

"I *am*," Dare muttered, "that's not the issue."

"Well, what is?"

"The auctions, Gian."

"Ah," his father said in a sigh, massaging at his temples with his fingers. "Right, those are next month."

"And the main team—the one I'd use for this job—are being sent out to Russia next month for a prison assignment. We need someone to scope the target out first, and gain as much information as we can get before we gather who and what we need. Then, we can grab the target, but not before. Maybe two months, or a little less. I don't have someone who would be appropriate for this job except Corrado and Alessio."

"I can do it," Chris said.

He didn't regret saying the words, sure. All eyes in the room turned on him as soon as he said it. And even the man on the phone quieted at the declaration.

"What?" he asked.

"You haven't done a job for The League since you were nineteen," his father said.

"It's like riding a bike," Chris returned, "you fall off, and get back on."

Right.

Like riding a bike.

Mostly, Chris spoke up because he didn't want his twin to

be bothered and that fucking ingrained need inside his being to take care of Corrado, and look out for him—even when his twin didn't have a clue he did it—was bred deep.

He blamed genetics.

And his father.

"That's … going to be my suggestion, actually," Dare said, his voice filtering through the speaker again. "Because with *your* influence and name, Gian, it would make it a hell of a lot easier to infiltrate the organization where we believe the target is located."

"What in the hell are you talking about?" Gian asked.

"When can you two get to Vegas for a proper briefing?"

Gian gave Chris a glance.

He shrugged.

"Christmas is soon," Gian said.

"Right after New Years?"

Chris nodded to his father. "After the new year is fine."

"Good. I will arrange it with the Marcellos."

The phone call ended before anyone said goodbye, not that Chris or his father seemed to mind. Marcus continued sipping on a glass of whiskey, not bothering to step in at all.

"Are you sure you want to take that assignment?" Gian asked Chris. "You have duties here to *la famiglia*, too, son. I am sure I could make do for a couple of months, but it's not about that. I want you to be certain this is what you want to do."

His father, always looking out for his boys.

Chris appreciated it.

"Why not?"

Yeah, *why not*?

That seemed to be the story of his life.

Might as well add another chapter.

~

The League ran their business out of a cluster of connected buildings deep within the desolate land of Nevada which they dubbed *the complex*. And frankly, Chris thought the name fit considering it's massive size. It had to be considering everything and anything The League needed to operate smoothly was inside the complex.

He trained here. *Broke* here. He lived here—ate, slept, and survived behind these walls. He was sure, despite the time he had stayed and worked for The League, he hadn't seen every single square inch of the place.

They also added to the place over the years, building on to the complex for whatever suited their purposes. It had been a while since Chris last visited the secluded cluster of connected buildings, so he hadn't known they added an Olympic-size pool until he stood in the doorway leading to it.

He stared across the calm blue water, unnerved by the black tiling design at the bottom of the pool. It gave the water a bottomless effect, and it sent his anxiety spiking through the roof.

If the water went over his fucking head, it was too deep. An almost drowning as a child left Chris with a paranoia and fear for water. He did his best to hide it from others, but his family knew.

And The League.

They had knowledge of it, too.

One of the many reasons he was conflicted on being back inside this building. Although he appreciated all they did for him here, and what it taught him, Chris still walked away from this place with more scars than he cared to count. Some, more than others, never too far away from his thoughts.

Their motto?

Break the body, break the mind.

They'd done that to him.

Again and again.

"Chris," Gian murmured.

For the first time, he looked away from the pool, realizing he had come to a complete stop before he passed the room to stare inside. His father, a few steps down the hall, raised a brow and waited for him to get over his ... *thing*.

"Sorry," Chris blurted, "I'm coming."

Gian nodded, but said nothing about the water, or the obvious problem Chris had by being *near* it. His father was good in that way, and Chris respected it. "Dare is waiting with the others. Let's not keep them."

Right, right.

Their reason for being here.

Knowing his father made a good point, and the Marcellos had been kind enough to allow them to hold this meeting after the holidays passed, Chris forced his attention away from the goddamn pool. He followed behind his father in silence, walking through newer halls of the complex he wasn't familiar with as the owners added them over the last year.

Before long, they stood in the doorway of Dare's office. The group inside, four in total, turned to greet them, although none wore smiles.

That serious, huh?

Chris recognized all the men, but for different reasons. Dare, standing behind his desk, because he had been Chris's boss for a time, and he was his father's business partner with this place. Cree, the Native with his hands clasped at his back in front of a row of screens showcasing an aerial view of what looked to be a map, because he was one who trained Chris here.

The other two men, Dante and Andino Marcello, he knew

from the business—*Cosa Nostra*. Rarely were they known to leave New York, but especially not to come to Nevada, so he figured this job was important to them.

"Gian, and Chris, right?" Dante asked, looking his way.

Chris nodded. "That's me."

"Not to be confused with his twin, who—"

"Isn't here," Chris interjected, giving Andino Marcello a stare that would silence the devil. He understood this man had issues with his twin, and he didn't care to hear them. Fucking *nobody*, regardless of what their last name happened to be, would bad mouth his twin, but not to his damn face. "And we have things to do, don't we?"

"We do," Dare said from behind his desk, "and we're waiting on you all before we start."

"Sorry to keep you waiting," Gian said, giving Chris a wave to enter the office first, "shall we get started?"

Dare picked up the remote on his desk and pointed it at the screen once Chris and his father entered the office. The picture changed when he pressed a button, showcasing Andino in a tux, a woman in a white wedding dress, and a little girl between them being held by a black-haired, *beautiful* woman with a wide smile.

And God, yeah, beautiful didn't do the woman justice. Her joyful smile brightened her delicate features, and her black hair had a glossy sheen under the sunlight. Tall, and curvy, the lavender dress she had picked for the day hugged her body and showed off all kinds of leg.

With only a picture, Chris thought whoever had taken it had captured the woman's beauty, her confidence, and her womanly appeal all at the same time.

Quite a feat.

"Valeria Lòpez," Cree said when Dare stayed quiet. "Formerly *Gomez*, but she changed it after a forced marriage to

Jorge Lòpez at fifteen when the cartel killed her mother down in Mexico, it became a means to blackmail her father. Or, those are the details we have."

"That's all we had," Andino muttered.

"Right," Dare said, nodding at Andino, "and so this is what we're working on. Somehow, around sixteen from what we understand, Valeria was pregnant, and ran away from her husband, and the cartel. She found her way to the States, and we don't know how. What we do know is her daughter was born in the States, and at some point, she met Haven Murphy."

"Marcello, now," Andino added under his breath.

That name rang a bell.

Chris looked to Andino. "Your new wife?"

Andino nodded. "The two happened to be roommates for quite a while before I came along, Valeria worked for Haven, and one night she came home … seemed like Val up and left and so did—"

Dare pressed a button, and the screen changed to a single picture of the little girl Valeria had been holding in the wedding picture. "Her daughter, Maria. Who is six. We cannot find anything for this little girl anywhere at the moment. No school records in Mexico, nothing for a doctor, and … yeah."

Chris let out a heavy breath as he took in the black-haired, brown-eyed child. She looked all of maybe five on the screen if that. Cute, with a wide, toothy smile, and her arms high in the air as her yellow summer dress spun around her legs.

"Jorge Lòpez is her father," Dare said, "but what's impor-tant is … Valeria ran from the cartel, we're aware she was forced into marriage, and at some point, they took her again. We have every reason to believe she is back with the cartel."

"Might she want to be there?" Chris asked.

"Possibly," the man returned, "but you must figure that out when you get inside, won't you?"

Gian hummed under his breath beside his son. "And that's why you want me here, isn't it? Being the boss of the Guzzis, I'm not affiliated to the Marcellos on paper as a business partner, they wouldn't expect me to go there for her, and I could use my status and territory as a transaction for them, correct?"

"They wouldn't suspect something's up, no."

Chris looked to the two Marcello men as this was *their* job. They had come here with it, and they wanted to retrieve the woman. "Why is she important? A cartel wife ... that's playing with fire. I'm familiar with details about the Lòpez cartel. Jorge, he's the oldest son, and has taken over more now that his father took a step back years ago. And you want to ... what, take his wife and child from him?"

Andino arched a brow, replying, "I respect the hesitance, but the woman never asked for the life they gave her. From what my wife explained, and I understood, Val stayed on the run and had been for years, which meant she had to be running from something."

"Or *someone*," Chris finished.

"Jorge, likely," Andino agreed. "Val and Haven ... she needs to know if Val is where she wants to be, is *safe*, and happy. And if she is, fine, we leave it alone. But if she isn't, and if she needs help, that's what you're here to do."

Chris cleared his throat and nodded once. "All right."

Dare passed him a glance. "The job's a go?"

"The job is a go."

CHAPTER 3

"Mamá, watch me!"

Valeria already had one eye on her daughter, but she tipped the rim of her large, pink summer hat higher so that Maria could see her. She smiled, refusing to allow her six-year-old to see her discomfort about where they were staying. Maria liked the pool at her grandfather, Martín's, mansion in Mexico City, but Valeria hated it.

Or better yet, she hated the people here.

Most of them.

"When did she learn to swim?"

The soft voice at Valeria's left didn't take her attention away from her daughter in the pool—safety first, and all—but she still answered Abril on the lounger. "Last summer. A friend and I took her twice a week to an indoor pool for lessons."

"A *friend*?"

Valeria did her best not to roll her eyes at her sister-in-law. Six years on the run, and Jorge had caught up to her. It wasn't Abril's fault, and no one had ever found out the truth about how she helped Valeria all those years ago. She had been back in Mexico, under Jorge's thumb, for a year now … and life was worse.

"Haven Murphy," Valeria said, her gaze darting to the marble steps leading to the back of the mansion's patio doors.

It was a habit for her now—she looked for Jorge if she *dared* mention anything about her time when she ran away because if he was within hearing distance, or if someone else was that would tell on her, she would suffer for it later. "She thought it was a good idea."

In her stark white, one-piece bathing suit that contrasted against her deeply tanned skin, Abril shifted to face Valeria more on her lounger. Valeria still kept one eye on her little girl in the water, just in case Maria became tired, and needed her ma to jump in after her.

"I would think you might be … *furioso*—angry—with her, after everything."

Val blinked. "Why?"

"It was because of her that he found you, no?"

"I don't blame her. It wasn't her fault that someone leaked a picture from the private wedding to the public, and it was the one that Maria and I were also in, Abril. It was the circumstance, and nothing more."

Valeria never understood how she befriended Haven when she found herself in New York a good year after taking off from Mexico, but she had never been more grateful for the friendship. For years, Haven was the only person Valeria had to rely on—they lived together, for Christ's sake. And then when Haven met someone who was maybe as dangerous as Jorge had been for Valeria, she knew it was a risk to continue her friendship.

Except, she was scared to walk away.

She *loved* her friend.

Haven married that man.

Turned out, he wasn't awful like Jorge.

The rest, from the wedding to the leaked picture, all brought Valeria right back to this hellscape Jorge liked to call *home* for her. And oh, he had been so fucking pleased to watch his men drag her through the gates of the compound, messy and fighting, while another man carried his drugged, sleeping daughter to him.

"We shouldn't talk about that," Valeria said.

"Hmm."

Mostly, because it pissed Jorge off, and Valeria didn't feel like dealing with her husband later in the evening. But also, because it hurt Valeria in her heart to think about the people she had left behind.

Haven.

Her best friend.

Chances were, she would never see Haven again. That would be to Haven's best benefit, all things considered. Anything Valeria cared about, Jorge took note, and used it to keep her controlled, and to make her behave.

Even her daughter wasn't out of bounds for him, the bastard. Valeria had learned over the last year since her forceful return that it was better to do what the asshole wanted from her than to fight him every step of the way.

One hurt less.

"Well, at least he allowed you out of the compound for this weekend," Abril muttered, rolling to her back on the lounger, and tipping her matching white sunhat down enough to hide the sun's rays from her face. "That's a start."

Yes, but for *what*?

Jorge did nothing without reason.

Valeria assumed this was the same.

"Not too far, now," Valeria called to her daughter as Maria dared to head for the deep end. She could swim in it, but it still made Valeria a little too nervous for her liking. "Come back where you can still touch your feet, Maria."

"Okay, Mamá," her girl replied.

She watched as Maria swam closer to the edge of the pool on the shallow side, her tanned legs kicking up a storm and splattering the tiled edge with droplets of water. It was only then that Valeria noticed the man approaching, and because Maria happened to splash him with water from the pool.

Not that he seemed to care.

Dressed in beige slacks, his leather shoes hit the tiles soundlessly as he rolled up the sleeves of his silk dress shirt around his elbows, showing off skin darkened by the sun. He'd left the top two buttons of his shirt undone at his throat and seemed comfortable approaching them.

Roberto García.

Son of a rival cartel leader.

Enemy of *theirs*.

In peace talks.

And also—

"Ah, dove, you're getting too much sun," Roberto murmured as he came to a stop beside Abril's lounger.

Abril took a deep breath, but didn't move her sunhat to peer up at the man who should be her intended husband sometime over the next few months. Or, that's what Valeria had understood. According to Jorge, it was one of the many attempts at making peace between the rival cartels. Although, she wasn't sure they should trust anything that came out of his rotten mouth.

"I am fine, but *gracias*," Abril replied, not unkindly.

Still, a bite lingered in her tone.

Roberto didn't miss it if the slight narrowing of his eyes was any sign to his lessening patience. His gaze darted to Valeria, and he offered her a tight smile. "You two look like twins today—*almost*."

Yes, her in a pale pink one-piece.

Abril in her white one.

Valeria shrugged. "Only from behind, though."

That made Abril laugh.

Roberto didn't understand.

Valeria grinned.

Her amusement didn't last long when a familiar figure came to stand on the marble steps. She swore she distinguished his gaze nailing into her from thirty feet away. She couldn't see his eyes from behind the dark aviator sunglasses he wore, their weight was still palpable.

"Valeria, clean Maria up and come inside," Jorge called out to her, "we're about ready to sit down for dinner."

She didn't reply, simply moved to do as she was told, slipping off the lounger to approach the side of the pool. As she pulled Maria from the water, a towel already waiting for her to dry her daughter off, and get her dressed, Roberto murmured something to Abril behind her before he headed for the mansion.

Valeria turned around with a towel-wrapped Maria in just enough time to watch Abril *glower* at the man's back as he walked away. "Be careful," she told her sister-in-law, "because they won't like seeing your face looking like that about him."

Abril's jaw tightened before her hateful expression morphed into a blank slate. "I refuse to marry that man."

"He isn't a bad man."

"He isn't the man I want, Val."

Yes, well … she knew how that worked.

How this life of theirs worked.

Look at her.

Valeria said nothing.

Abril didn't seem to mind.

~

Spanish flowed around the table between the men, but the women at their sides kept quiet, and focused on the meal. It was what the Lòpez men expected from their wives, or sister, in Abril's case. They weren't interested in hearing a woman's perspective on their business, and they didn't want opinions.

Valeria didn't care.

She used that time to make sure Maria ate enough of her food that she wouldn't be asking for a snack every five minutes after dinner ended. And when her attention was on her daughter, which she didn't get often because Jorge was an asshole, no one seemed to pay any mind to Valeria.

She considered that a win.

Right?

Maria sat between her mother, and Jorge. She called him Papá because Jorge refused to answer to anything else, but God knew Maria didn't like the man who had helped to give her life. It didn't help that the child had a front-row seat to the horrible treatment her mother received from her father daily.

Not to mention, until this last year, Maria hadn't known her father at all. So, they forced the girl out of America, put her in front of some *man* who behaved like a monster, and expected the six-year-old to love him.

Okay.

Valeria did her best to make sure Maria behaved and gave her father the attention he wanted. It was easier on all of them that way, but in private, she let her daughter hug her tight, cry, and beg to go back to America, and Haven. Away from these people who she said were mean and hurt her mom.

What else could she do?

"Is it good?" Valeria asked.

Maria nodded. "I like it."

"Good."

"This will be a good deal," Martín, her father-in-law, said with a pointed finger moving between Abril and Roberto sitting side by side across from Valeria and Jorge. "It is a good match, and it will bring our organizations closer … more money, more power, *sí*?"

Jorge smiled tersely. "Absolutely, Papá."

Across the table, Roberto chuckled. "The Garcías never thought we would see the day when we made peace with the Lòpez family, but as they say, all wars must come to an eventual end, right?"

"That's what they say," the man next to Roberto muttered.

Samuel.

The other Lòpez son.

No one paid him any mind.

Valeria was a little distracted by trying to ignore the hand that came to rest behind her chair. Jorge's fingers curved around her shoulder, his fingers digging in painfully. Still, she managed a smile across their daughter between them, just enough to make him assume she was fine with his touch.

She wanted to *puke*.

Still, Jorge's hand flexed against her shoulder again when his father smiled at the man who was now arranged to be his future son-in-law because of the upcoming marriage to Abril. Even if she didn't sense that tension in her husband's hand, she would know the truth. In private, Jorge didn't *shut up*.

His father had taken a step down from running the cartel a while back. Jorge was the one who had the major control of the operation, but that didn't stop his father from stepping in occasionally, to remind everyone that the king wasn't truly dead.

Like this deal with their enemy.

This *marriage*.

Jorge despised it all.

"Good things are happening to us all," Jorge murmured to the table, lifting a glass of red wine for the others to follow his lead. He tipped his glass toward his father, "To power, Papá, by whatever means we can get it, no?"

Martín smiled and raised his own glass. "To power."

Jorge tipped his drink back and swallowed it in one gulp. Valeria knew if he kept that up, by the time they got up to their room later, he would be drunk and unpleasant. To say the least ... more like *violent* and wanting her.

Something else to make her sick.

"And we have more things to look forward to," Jorge added, setting his glass down to the table hard. "More business—starting next week. Everyone will benefit if it goes right."

Across the table, Roberto asked, "*Everyone?*"

He meant their side of things, too. Because now, if the two cartels merged, even if Jorge didn't like it, what benefitted them should also benefit Roberto's father's organization. That was how it should work, but Valeria didn't believe for a second Jorge would agree.

Jorge didn't reply.

Valeria doubted the other man missed it.

Valeria tightened the silk robe around her body, using the ties to cinch the fabric at the trim curve of her waist. She sensed his presence the moment he opened the bedroom door.

Jorge had that effect.

"Why would you dress in *that*?" he asked.

It was by his tone she knew he had polished off the bottle of red wine from the table after dinner. *Great.* He was always worse when he was a little too drunk, and his lips were loose.

Not only did she have to deal with his pawing in bed but also his fucking mouth which never shut the hell up. It was a losing battle.

"*Val*," he mumbled.

She turned around to face him, only to find him circling the foot of the bed to come closer to her. Maybe her attention should have been on the door because she always found it easier to handle him when she could see him coming.

Valeria hated being surprised.

Like now.

As she assumed, he was drunk. *Thoroughly.* Bloodshot eyes, a slack mouth, and a sheen of perspiration dotting the lines in his forehead as his gaze narrowed in on her. Not that she had much time to react because she didn't.

He reached for her before she might refuse him—*lie* and say she was on her cycle, which turned him off like nothing else. Pulling the robe she had just tightened away from her body with his rough hand, it allowed him access to the silk short and camisole set she wore underneath.

He picked her clothes, too.

"Jorge," she started to say.

His hand found her breast, sliding under the silk before clamping down tight enough to take her breath and words away as he muttered, "Next week, when the Canadians come down to make that deal, we won't need the fucking Garcías for *anything*. And then my father will understand that I can do this without merging. Smart, aren't I?"

Valeria swallowed hard, ignoring the bile rising in her throat as his hand slid from one of her breasts to the other, and then climbed higher on her neck to rest against her throat.

If she flinched, he would become rough. She didn't need more bruises to hide with makeup.

It never worked, anyway.

"Of course, you are," she lied. "But might he be mad?"

"I don't *care* what he'll be!"

She flinched.

Except, the high level of his shout made their daughter wake up in the room she used across the hall from theirs inside the mansion.

Maria's tired cries were muffled, but Valeria still heard them. She fixed her sleep clothes, but Jorge didn't remove his hand from her body.

"She's *six*," he snapped, "and is fine—she'll go back to sleep on her own."

"It's a new place, and it might scare her."

"You can't *baby* her forever."

No, but she would right now.

Maria needed her.

And she needed to get away from Jorge.

Win-win.

"Please," Valeria whispered, "I'll just get her back to sleep, and then I'll come to bed."

Jorge sighed, and rolled his eyes, letting his hand drop from her throat as he took a step back. "*Fine*. Whatever. Go."

She didn't need to be told again. Hopefully, by the time she got back to bed, he would be passed out. Sometimes the universe worked for her, and other times, it only seemed to want to laugh in her face.

Valeria didn't glance back as she exited the bedroom and crossed the hall. Once she was inside her daughter's room, Maria reached for her from the sheets that were nothing like the ones she had loved so much in her pink bed back in New York.

Nothing here was like New York.

"Mamá," Maria breathed, "someone *yelled.*"

"It's okay," Valeria murmured, slipping under the blankets with her daughter, and holding her tight. "Mamá's here, *bebita.* I love you."

CHAPTER

4

Chris checked the watch on his wrist as the jet jumped when the landing gear first touched down on the ground. He found that was the most nerve-wracking part of flying. He didn't mind takeoff, or even being in the air. It was landing that always had his heart jumping into his damn throat.

Their flight was on time, according to his watch. Across the aisle from his seat on the private jet, his father cleared his throat as the pressure in the cabin became bearable, and their voices didn't sound like an echo to each other's ears.

"Not anymore settled about this, are you?" Gian asked.

In a tailored suit, unbothered and relaxed sitting in the white leather seat, Gian smirked in Chris's direction, like he had known the whole time what was running through his quiet son's mind. His father always seemed to have a good grasp on the complexities of his boys although Chris never understood why.

Sometimes, it felt like a curse.

Others, a gift.

"I don't see the point in *you* coming along for this," Chris replied, shrugging his broad shoulders under his own suit. He was thinking his choice of attire would be a mistake once they stepped off the temperature-controlled jet into the dry, Mexican heat. Not that it mattered. Guzzis were who they were, suits and class included, even when the weather called for board shorts and a dip in the ocean. "All I'm saying, is I can do this all without you needing to come along, Dad."

Gian nodded and turned to stare out the port window as the plane slowed. Soon, it would taxi into the private gate at the international airport. According to their contact, guards would greet them although they arrived at a public airport.

It showed how far the cartel reached, and Chris refused to allow that thought very far from his mind. When people forgot who they were dealing with, they underestimated them at the same time.

He wouldn't be doing that.

Not here.

They couldn't afford to.

"It is a show of faith for me to be here for this first meeting," Gian said, never turning back to give Chris his full attention as he spoke, "and you know that. In this life, this *business*, it is better when bosses sit down for a proper face to face, and then we go from there. It extends a friendly hand, and people are less likely to question our intentions. That is what we need here, isn't it?"

Gian made all good points.

He wasn't wrong.

Still, Chris watched his father from the side, and all he thought about was his mother back home in Canada. They were all at a rather comfortable place with *la famiglia*, and the family business. It had been a good while since the mafia touched their family violently, and Chris didn't want this cartel job for The League to be the first thing in a while to remind their family—but especially not his mother—that this was dangerous.

They knew.

All of them did.

It didn't change the fact that, sometimes, people became

relaxed in their positions, and believed nothing would touch them in their lives.

Cartels were notoriously vicious, and risky, when doing business with them. A true statement whether someone learned it firsthand, or not. That, more than anything else, was what kept Chris on edge since they were using business as a front to get their *in* to the goddamn cartel here. Not only was he looking for a woman he wasn't sure wanted to leave Mexico, but he also had to consider his father's safety.

Like fuck would he leave here needing to tell his mother that her husband wouldn't be coming home to her alive. That just would not happen. Not if Chris had any say.

Chris could have done this job alone without his father, but yes, it would be easier with his presence here to defer to until the leaders of the cartel trusted him. But as soon as that fucking happened, Gian was gone.

No questions asked.

"Did you call Ma?" Chris asked.

Gian's lips lifted with a small smile. "I will call her once we're off the plane, Chris."

"You should call her now."

"Stop worrying. You sound like her."

Right.

Chris forced himself to shut up and let his annoying thoughts stay tucked away in his mind. There were a lot of reasons he could think of for why he shouldn't have taken this job, but it was too late to back out now.

The phone in Chris's pocket buzzed, and he took it out to check the text rolling across the screen. A simple message from his twin, but it calmed his overacting nerves. Corrado's text only read, *Call me if you need anything.*

Chris would keep that in mind.

He might need it.

The private jet took a good twenty minutes to taxi to the correct gate where they could finally unbuckle and grab their bags from the cupboards at the front. Chris grabbed his own, a larger bag, than his father's overnight travel duffle. If all went right, the overnight bag was all his father would need here, because Gian wouldn't be staying more than a day or two.

They had to play their cards right.

"*Merci*," Gian thanked the pilot at the front in French.

It was a toss-up with his father, and even his twin, or their oldest sibling, Marcus, which language they might use to talk. Chris was handy with English and Italian, but he had never picked up on French, for whatever reason.

Chris exited the plane after his father, giving the pilot a nod as he passed. He didn't know where the flight attendant had disappeared to, but he didn't care, either. At the bottom of the stairs, assault rifles in hand, stood three men dressed in matching outfits of denim jeans, and black shirts.

"Ah, good," Gian muttered under his breath, "the cartel followed through."

Chris swallowed the discomfort in his throat. "Good."

It was unnerving when someone realized just how much control the cartels in Mexico— there were two major organizations that had long been in battle against one another—had in the country. From the government, to small businesses in the towns they used to make or smuggle their drugs through, it didn't matter.

Blackmail.

Bribery.

Violence.

Cartels were not a game.

And here the Guzzis were, ready to play one with them.

Fun.

"Gian Guzzi?" the man standing ahead of the other two asked, his accent heavy.

"That would be me," Chris's father returned.

The man nodded. "We'll walk you through customs, sir, and take you to the drop."

The drop.

Huh.

They weren't even calling it a meeting today.

Good to know.

"This is not the compound."

Chris's declaration to his father was quiet and said before the guards who had already stepped out of the vehicle opened the back door for them to exit the car. He had to say it while he had the chance because he wasn't sure what to expect here. Sure, the Lòpez cartel had not offered many details about where or how they would do business, but that didn't mean he was comfortable going in blind, either.

"Let's get the pleasantries out of the way first," Gian said quickly, "and then we'll worry about what is going on here, *oui*?"

Chris sighed. "All right."

He only knew the yellow brick mansion with the terracotta roof, surrounded by a large stone fence where armed guards stood staring down at their vehicle, wasn't the Lòpezs' infamous compound because of The League. The aerial views The League had provided of the cartel's home base was neither in the middle of a busy city, nor were there any mansions on the property. Small homes, stables, barns, and a few other buildings out in the middle of nowhere, but not *this*.

"Step out," one of the guard's said when he came to open the rear passenger door for Gian and Chris. "And they will open the gate for you to enter the grounds."

Chris had a million and one questions to ask, but he stayed silent because this wasn't *his* show. His father was the one who had come here as the front man, so to speak. He was the boss, the one wanting to make a deal with the cartel, and Chris was nothing more than muscle at his father's side.

For now.

He needed to keep the act up.

The guard hadn't lied.

Chris stared up at the almost white-blue sky, the sun so bright, it still hurt his eyes behind the dark sunglasses he wore. His distraction only lasted as long as it took for the creak of metal to bring his attention back to what was important.

The guards stepped aside as the gate opened.

Gian moved forward first, but Chris was fast to follow behind. Just beyond the wrought metal gate, a pathway made of red stone and lined with towering trees led them toward the front of the mansion. Waiting on white marble steps were two men, both of whom Chris recognized, although he kept that to himself.

Still needed to keep up that act …

"Gian Guzzi, and … son, correct?" the man standing just beyond the other asked.

Jorge Lòpez.

In his head, Chris did a mental inventory of the man and also what he knew about him. From the yellow silk dress shirt he wore, with the sleeves rolled up around his elbows, to the black slacks that looked pressed from an iron. This was the man they forced Valeria to marry, according to the information they had, and he was also the oldest son of the cartel's former leader.

Well, that's what they assumed. No one had a clue if the former leader was a *former*, but from all public appearances, Jorge ran the show now.

"Chris," Gian said, "my son's name is Chris. We were not sure what to expect today, but this home is a lovely spot for a meeting."

"Our father's," the man just behind Jorge stated.

Samuel.

Second son of the Lòpez leader. Brother to Jorge. Chris wouldn't concern himself with Samuel, except for the fact he was a Lòpez, and *there*. Part of it all and possibly keeping Valeria hidden somewhere.

Or was she even hidden here?

Yet to be determined.

Gian continued his greetings with the Lòpez brothers while Chris took in his surroundings. He blamed that on his training at The League, and not so much the fact he was a made man. They had taught him to find what he needed to deal with first. To take in his surroundings, and everything else, too.

Then, there were as little surprises as possible. Although, should a surprise come up on him, he would handle that knowing everything else around him. It was all in the details, really.

"And," Gian said to Chris's left as he noted the white trim around the windows of the mansion, "once we hammer down the main details, I will take a step back because I have business to attend to at home. I can't leave it for long."

"Which is where your son will come in, *sí*?" Jorge asked, his accent thickening his English.

"Chris will take over whatever you need here for my side

of things. I intend to involve myself in all of this, even if it is from afar and I want to understand how things will work, where everything will be held, and how you intend to smuggle the cocaine over. I hope you understand, but I am a *details* man."

Jorge chuckled. "As am I, Gian."

"*Oui*, well, when I am guaranteeing you the ability to supply to all of Canada through my organization and contacts, I am sure you won't be uncomfortable with allowing us a stay here, and time to understand your business, and process, Mr. Lòpez."

"We'll make it work," Samuel muttered, "although we're not accustomed to someone who wants *all* the details. We rarely work that way."

"Except we will in this case," Jorge added, "a deal with you ensures we will be the largest producing and supplying cartel in Mexico."

Chris didn't miss the way the two brothers passed a look between them, something unsaid lingering in their stares. He tucked it into the back of his mind and returned to surveying the grounds.

"And you won't take issue with my son doing the majority of the work and passing word back then?" Gian asked.

"Is that why he's currently scoping us out?"

Chris didn't miss the sharpness of Jorge Lòpez's tone. He came back to the conversation, smiling carefully to make sure the man didn't think he was malicious in his perusal of the grounds.

He was all too aware in that moment of certain things he needed to be careful to do for this plan of theirs to work. Things he needed to portray to allow him inside the cartel's top echelon to get closer to Valeria—wherever she was here, because no one saw her yet.

They needed to trust him, at all costs. He was to be no better or worse than them, in their eyes, and willing to indulge in whatever they asked of him to make sure they didn't question his reasoning for being here. "It's a beautiful home. Almost reminds me of my parents' mansion."

Jorge eyed Chris for a moment, his silence stretching on a beat too long before he said, "Large, is it?"

"Two wings. More acres than someone cares to count."

"Not as protected, I bet."

Chris shrugged. "Better not to make a show, in our part of the world."

Jorge nodded. "I can understand that, I suppose."

Gian cleared his throat. "Shall we begin this process, then?"

"Yes, let's get comfortable inside. We figured … a quick lunch, and then maybe a drink later in the back by the pool before a proper dinner. If that works for you, Gian?"

"It does," Gian replied.

"Good. Lunch will be ready soon. Later, the rest of our family will join us for dinner."

Oh?

Chris kept that question inside, but barely. Did the rest of the *family* mean Jorge's supposed wife—Valeria—and his daughter, Maria, too? Because that would answer a lot of things that were still unknown here.

"I hope you like bourbon," Jorge said, "as that is our drink of choice for *business* deals."

"I do," Gian said.

Chris smiled when the men turned their backs to him and his father. The Guzzis were *in*.

For now.

~

Lunch went well, and as Chris assumed, his father took over the majority of the conversation with Jorge. Chris and Samuel sat at opposite ends of the table, enjoying their meal and sharing a word when asked for it, but otherwise, staying out of the dealings between the other two.

Not that Chris minded.

He enjoyed being the silent one in a conversation more than he liked to be the one who talked. It allowed him to learn a hell of a lot more when he wasn't concerned about what might slip out of his mouth.

Once lunch finished, and Jorge and Gian seemed fine with the *specifics* of their arrangement, with one supplying the other cocaine, the four moved outside.

Well, three, he supposed.

Samuel disappeared after lunch. He stepped outside with them for a moment, but left soon after, re-entering the mansion through the back without as much as a word why.

It didn't matter.

Chris had other things on his mind.

The *pool*, for starters.

His anxiety picked up as he, his father, and Jorge walked along the side of the pool, each with a glass of bourbon in their hands to sip from. He wouldn't enjoy the drink this close to water even if the fear seemed unfounded.

Chris could *swim*.

He learned to do that.

The pool on one end was not deep.

He could touch the bottom.

Even hearing those thoughts in his mind, a constant mantra that played on repeat whenever he faced water, it only helped a little. Not enough for him to forget what it felt like to have water rushing into his lungs with every breath he attempted to take in. It didn't stop the memory of his garbled shouts as he tried to call for help as the water pulled him under the docks at his uncle's vacation home.

"Chris," his father said quietly.

His gaze snapped away from the pool, drifting to where his father had stepped out of his conversation with Jorge to bring Chris out of his head. A knowing glint in his father's eye—that familiar concern—stared back at him.

"Do you like the bourbon?" his father asked.

Jorge, who seemed confused at the question, not to mention hadn't noticed Chris's distraction, glanced between the two men. Gian brought him out of a state of panic but also did it without making the other man aware of his son's deepest fear.

It was never good to hand someone your weakness.

They used it when you did that.

"Yes," Chris said, keeping the nerves out of his tone, "it's fine."

"It better be," Jorge muttered, "I paid enough for the import."

"Forgive me for being forward," Gian said, bringing Jorge's attention away from Chris for the moment, "but I can't help noticing this is your father's home, and yet, we haven't seen him. They told me, although I don't trust everything said in passing, that your father stepped back from the cartel a while ago, yes?"

Jorge raised a brow and brought the lit cigar between his fingers to his lips for a heady drag. Grey smoke lifted toward the darkening sky, telling them night would fall soon.

"He has stepped back," Jorge said, passing the house behind them a look, "but he still puts his opinion and influence in whenever he wants."

A bite colored his tone.

Gian didn't miss it.

"And what, he doesn't agree with us being here?"

Jorge tipped his cigar in Gian's direction. "*Almost* correct —not quite, though. He's of the opinion the business will be good, but he's currently attempting a merger between our cartel, and the only rival we have. Something I think is a mistake, and with you Canadians on my books, we won't need to merge at all."

"Is he aware?"

"He stepped back."

"But did he?"

"It doesn't matter once it's all said and done, does it?"

They didn't get the chance to reply to the man because a door closing had Jorge's attention turning away. His brow lifted in contemplation before he smiled. Not a *fond* smile.

"Ah, there they are. Which means the rest have already arrived, and we can begin a proper dinner." Jorge lifted a hand to wave, and called out, "*Hermosa*, bring the *princesa* over for a proper hello to our new friends."

Chris turned to see who had come out on the back steps of the mansion, not familiar with Spanish but having heard just enough in his lifetime to understand those affectionate terms that left Jorge's mouth. In a white dress, holding the hand of a small girl at her side, Chris found the answer to one of their unknowns standing on marble steps.

Yes, Valeria was very much alive.

Yes, the cartel had her.

And yes, she was beautiful as that picture of her at the Marcello wedding had shown. Shockingly so. The image on the screen he had seen before now had not done the woman justice.

Tanned, golden skin. Pin-straight, black hair that fell to

her mid-back. Tall, and womanly. Her soft features, accentuated with a touch of makeup, seemed more natural than dolled up. The dress she chose draped over her curves loosely, yet still allowed him an appreciation for her body.

None of which he had any right to notice. Nor should he.

"My wife, and daughter," Jorge said to them, although Valeria had not yet left the stairs with little Maria at her side. "Val is shy, so don't mind if she doesn't talk a lot. It's her nature."

Or, Chris wondered, could she not talk? That's what he was here to find out.

CHAPTER 5

"*Hermosa*, bring the *princesa* over for a proper hello to our new friends."

Valeria heard Jorge's call to her, but her attention was on someone far more important. Surely, he could wait two minutes. Maria attempted to pull the bow from her dark ponytail, and as much and Valeria sympathized with her daughter's annoyance, she was still quick to kneel and fix the ribbon. She gave her girl a smile and winked.

"Remember what I said?" she asked.

Maria sighed, her dark gaze darting to the side as two kids came out of the back of the mansion, their squeals chasing them down the steps. Valeria thought they were the children of Jorge's men—the ones privileged enough to dine with them during business, or otherwise. She couldn't talk to people on the payroll, unless it was Maria's nanny, and so she couldn't say for sure.

"Maria," Valeria murmured, letting her fingers twist into the ends of her daughter's soft curls. "What did I say this morning, huh?"

"To be good today. We must look pretty. *Be quiet.*"

God.

She hated this.

Those weren't things a child Maria's age should have to worry about at all. Valeria knew, however, if her child misbehaved that she wouldn't hear the end from Jorge. He'd given her more than enough warnings leading up to this dinner for the last week about what he expected from her, and Maria.

Sure, she could handle his moods, even if it was the last thing she wanted to do, but it wasn't fair for her daughter, either. Even if Jorge didn't shout and smack Maria around, she would still have to watch the asshole do it to her mother.

Valeria tried to avoid that.

"Mamá, can I go play with them?" Maria pointed at the kids running down the grassy pathway leading away from the pool. "Please?"

Frankly, Valeria couldn't find a reason to tell her daughter no. At least, playing with the kids would keep her out from beneath her father's feet for a while, or until dinner. It wasn't like the girl could find trouble when there happened to be a small army of guards all around the damn mansion to look after them.

Jorge had asked for her to bring Maria over, but what did it matter?

"Sure," Valeria told Maria. "Be kind and don't get your dress *too* dirty."

Maria grinned and swished the skirt of yellow dress like she had when her mother put it on her earlier. "I'll *try*."

"That's my girl."

"Val!"

She tensed at Jorge's shout for her, gave Maria a quick kiss, and stood up when her daughter raced down the steps to chase after the other children. Air filled her lungs in a heavy inhale, the one extra second she needed to be ready to face her husband, and put on that fake smile he seemed to like so much for his guests.

Everything was fake here.

Nothing was true.

Settled enough in her heart that Valeria thought she might

pretend to give a fuck about what Jorge wanted, she turned to see her husband still staring expectantly at her—although, with annoyance tugging his lips down at the edges. *Great.*

It wasn't Jorge that her attention turned to though. He was a background thought, never leaving and always a reminder for her to behave. Rather, it was the two men standing near Jorge, one ahead of him, and another behind him at the wet bar beside the pool.

A father and a son, maybe?

Valeria thought the older gentleman, and younger—but he had to be close to her age, at least—shared a lot of similar features. Their strong, square-cut jaws, brown, short-cropped hair, dark eyes, and high, defined cheekbones. The slight differences in the shapes of their faces didn't detract from the fact it was obvious they were family.

What had Jorge told her today?

Business meeting—new partners.

Right.

Valeria was hyperaware of the men's gazes locked on her as she came down the stairs and walked along the edge of the pool to approach them. She was careful in her heels not to step on any wet spot, lest she slip, and fall into the water. Wouldn't that be just perfect?

It was the man ahead of Jorge by a step—the younger of the two—that didn't drop Valeria's stare as she came closer. He was handsome, strikingly so with his piercing gaze, and rugged features that seemed carved from stone. He didn't smile, but he also didn't have to considering his lips naturally curved in such a way they pulled into the hint of a smirk, anyway. His form, fit under a tailored suit, rested confidently in his stance.

Valeria shook her head, turning her gaze away from the man that was still watching her with every step she took closer to him, her husband, and the other unknown gentle-man. God knew she didn't need Jorge thinking she was staring a beat too long at another man even if said man *was* decent to stare at.

That was her first thought about him, too, which was strange. Looks were the last thing Valeria noticed about a man. His appearance only hid what was beneath the hand-some package. A lesson she had, unfortunately, learned first-hand, and not one she cared to learn again.

"I wanted you to bring Maria over to say hello," Jorge said, nothing hiding his displeasure in the slightest once Valeria was close enough for him to speak. He reached for her, and while it killed her to put on this act for the newcom-ers, she allowed his arm to snake around her waist, and pull her into his side. Cigar smoke clung to the air, and it became worse when Jorge lifted the lit cigar in his other hand for a heady drag. "And now look at her."

Valeria's gaze searched for her girl, and she found her. "She's having fun with the other children, let her play. She's a child."

"It's good for children to play," the older gentleman said, "because it lets them burn out all that energy they can't seem to get rid of otherwise."

Jorge tipped his cigar in the man's direction and nodded. "You make a good point, Gian."

Gian.

Was that Italian?

She thought so, but the man had a strange accent. It had a hint of Italian, but also something else, too. Something as equally smooth, maybe. French?

Valeria couldn't be sure.

Gian chuckled. "Been a while since any of my boys were that young, however. Isn't that right, Chris?"

"It is, Papa."

So, she had been right.

Father and son.

Jorge's hand tightened on Valeria's waist, bringing her attention back to him. Heaven forbid her eyes weren't always on him, waiting for the next moment when he would snap his fingers, and demand something new.

"Valeria," he said, "meet my new business partners. Gian and Christopher—although, he likes Chris, they told me—Guzzi. From Canada."

Business partners.

Right.

The cartel had one business.

Jorge tipped his head toward her, saying to Gian, "And this is the wife I may have mentioned once or twice."

"Yes, Valeria, correct?"

She nodded. "That's me."

Gian smiled, but said nothing.

Jorge didn't notice, continuing with, "We had a rough patch for a while, but somehow, Valeria found her way home, didn't you, *hermosa*?"

Her heart thundered in her throat. Yeah, *she* found her way home. As though it had been her choice to come back to Mexico, and not like Jorge hunted her down as though she were an animal that deserved what it got. She wondered if her choosing to come home also meant watching Jorge's man point a rifle at her daughter's head, and calmly explaining that if she didn't go with them, they would kill Maria?

She swallowed those words, knowing damn well nothing good would come from her letting it slip out of her mouth. Instead, she took the safe route, even if every single part of her screamed to do the opposite.

So was her life, now.

"Yes, right where I belong," Valeria agreed.

All lies.

The younger man—Chris—had said nothing at all, and he didn't then, either. Gian chuckled as though he understood Jorge fine.

"You should go watch Maria while I discuss details here," Jorge told her.

Fine with me.

"Sure," Valeria replied.

He didn't let her go, so she didn't move. She understood what Jorge expected; she gave him a quick kiss on the corner of his mouth, swallowing back the bile that flooded her tongue, before giving the other two men a smile. One she had practiced time and time again in the mirror. That way, no one had a clue it was a fake.

"Very nice to meet both of you," Valeria said.

The men greeted her in kind, not that she cared for small talk, or whatever business they had come here to do. She still counted down the seconds when she could get away from her husband for the evening though. Jorge had that effect on people.

Tiptoeing out of the room Maria would use to sleep in for the night at her grandfather's mansion, Valeria carefully closed the door without making more noise that might wake her daughter up. She could stay upstairs for a bit—a few minutes more, safely—and Jorge would know nothing different, but she wasn't stupid.

He expected her to put their child to sleep after dinner and come right back down. He would send someone up after her, if he figured she was taking too long, and no one needed that problem.

Mostly, dinner had gone well. The Canadians kept conversation on everything *but* business, although Jorge hadn't seemed to mind indulging their chattiness, for once. She figured because he banked on being able to supply their territory in order to get out of the arrangement his father had made with the García cartel. If they wanted to talk about the sky, he would probably do it as long as it got him what he wanted, no doubt.

Valeria didn't care either way. She liked it when Maria didn't have to hear about all of that nonsense, anyway. Wasn't it bad enough that the girl had a front-row seat to her father being horrible against her mother, did she also need the cartel spelled out for her, too?

Maria wouldn't be young forever.

Eventually, she would understand.

Not now, though.

Valeria navigated the halls of the upstairs, walking down the grand spiral stairs where at the bottom, she listened to the echoing voices of the men inside the large sitting room. She edged closer to the doorway, but stayed hidden beyond view to peek inside.

With dinner over, business took its place.

"You expect to need that many kilos a *month*?" Jorge asked.

Gian stared at Chris. "*Oui?*"

"We can supply Canada-wide through our connections with the gangs, and other organizations. We've had the stronghold over most organized crime in Canada for … longer than I have been alive," Chris added.

"He isn't wrong," Gian added. "So yes, monthly."

"The smuggle runs will have to go in through several ports of entry," Jorge muttered, his gaze narrowing on the glass of liquor in his hand, "to avoid detection. We'll have that covered, but once it gets over the border, it's your problem."

"We can handle that."

"Now, on the *money* side of things."

Valeria tuned their conversation out. What did it matter? She concluded that anyone working with Jorge, or the cartel, was likely no fucking better than him at the end of the day.

Did they understand how the family built the cartel?

How they became so strong?

On the backs of the weak and the ignorant, breaking down a country's justice, legal, and political systems piece by piece until nothing was left but *corruption*. With the blood of innocents, spilled across crate after crate of every shipment of cocaine that crossed the borders.

There was nothing good here.

Even thinking these Canadians couldn't be any better or worse than her husband and his family, her gaze still drifted to the younger of the two.

Chris.

She didn't understand why, but she enjoyed looking at him, even if she had no business doing it, and that would be a dangerous game for her to play. He was just another *good-looking* man, nothing special, right? He'd barely spoken two words to her, so she didn't need to be staring at him, not like she might want to know more *about* him. She didn't get curious about men, not when she had neither the time, the give a damn, nor the ability to do something with it.

Valeria was going crazy.

Yet, as she stared across the room from her hidden position in the shadows of the doorway, it seemed Chris recognized someone was looking at him. His attention left the conversation, and his gaze drifted upward, finding the spot where Valeria hid, watching him and the others. She stiffened, her heart picking up pace with its beats, as his stare lingered her way. A heat danced over her skin when those thin lips of his twitched before curving into a sensual smile.

Did he see her?

"Careful," a soft voice said behind her.

Valeria jerked in her heels. "Jesus, Abril. Make a noise."

Her sister-in-law laughed under her breath, a single dark eyebrow lifting in what seemed like a challenge. "Like you're doing?"

"Well …"

She had a point.

Abril stepped in beside Valeria in the shadows but didn't glance her way. Instead, she stared across the room, looking at the men, and specifically, the one man who still had his attention focused in their direction.

"Don't let Jorge see you staring at one of his new friends," Abril said under her breath, "lest he get in his feelings about it, and wonder if something is going on, *si*?"

"What might go on?"

"Nothing. He only needs to think there is. We both know what happens then, Val."

Right.

Valeria stepped back from the entryway, needing five minutes to breathe alone, and far away from her confusion. "Tell Jorge I wanted to take a walk outside—it's hot in here, and I'm not feeling well."

She might as well take the chance to get away even if her husband would come looking for her soon enough. He always did; it was one thing she counted on with Jorge although she wished he would find someone else to focus his attention on.

Well, he did that, too.

Any woman pretty enough he wanted to stick his dick in,

he did exactly that. Not that Valeria complained. If he fucked someone else, then he wasn't raping her night after night.

Win some, lose some.

"Tell him for me, if he asks," she said again.

Abril nodded. "Sure."

Valeria sensed the presence join her on the back stairs of the mansion before he even said a word. She hadn't heard him open the door, or his steps as he came to stand next to her while she stared up at the stars dotting the inky sky, but she felt him.

Somehow.

"Christopher," she said, not *unkindly.*

"I prefer Chris," he returned.

Valeria did her best to keep her gaze on the sky overhead, and not the handsome man next to her. She wasn't sure why he had come out here. Had he seen her in the shadows and followed her?

If so, what did that mean?

Nothing decent, she imagined. Her heart stuttered at the idea, and she liked it too much. *Not good.*

"Care to take a walk?" he asked.

Valeria looked at him then, surprised at his offer. Earlier, when they met, and even at dinner, she hadn't spoken more than a few careful sentences to him. It wouldn't be enough for him to assume they were friendly, or otherwise. And yet, he smiled at her as though he already had her answer.

"As long as it's where the guards can see," she finally replied.

Chris nodded, peering around to survey the grounds where they could be seen. His gaze lingered on the walkway around the pool for a second, and then two. "Sure. How about around the pool?"

Was that a walk, then?

What did it matter?

"Sure," she said.

Chris remained quiet as they strolled down the pathway and stayed alongside the pool. Valeria noticed the way he continued to glance towards the calm water at the surface, but not in a way that said he cared for the pool.

"Swimming isn't your thing?" she dared to ask.

His head snapped in her direction. "Pardon?"

"You stare at the water like it might bite you."

She didn't miss the way his throat jumped at her statement, or how his Adam's apple bobbed reflexively.

"I almost drowned as a child," he murmured, his tone terse, "and it's followed me throughout my life. Water makes me nervous, that's all. Nonsensical, considering I can swim, but I swear I can taste the water in my lungs when I'm close enough."

Huh.

She wouldn't have guessed that.

"I'm sorry that happened," she whispered.

Chris shrugged and smiled again. "A long time ago, I suppose."

And yet, she bet it seemed like yesterday to him. Because he trusted her with the truth, Valeria would never breathe a word about it to anyone else.

Everyone needed their secrets, no?

That little detail about Chris made Valeria take a second glance at him, not that she needed to be doing that at all. Still, it made him seem different to her and almost easier to ignore the fact he was here to do business with her husband.

Their conversation during the walk around the pool

stayed on safe topics, and she still looked for the guards to make sure *they* kept an eye on her. That way, later when Jorge no doubt asked where she left to, he would confirm nothing nefarious had been going on when his back was turned.

The paranoid *bastard*.

Although, Chris kept a distance between them. He didn't get too close to Valeria throughout their stroll, and his hands remained clasped at his back while he did his best to ignore the pool beside them.

"Do you like it here?" he asked.

Random, she thought.

"What do you mean?"

Chris shrugged under the nice fit of his suit jacket. "Here, *Mexico*. Being the wife of a cartel leader, tucked away from the rest of the world, you know? All these beautiful things surrounding you, and you must have status in your position. Do you like it?"

Not at all.

Not one fucking bit.

Valeria asked for none of those things, and instead, they forced it upon her regardless if she wanted them. When she made it clear, this was not the life for her, she faced the wrath of a man she didn't think was worthy enough to kiss her shoes.

What choice did she have, though?

"People who live in gilded cages," Valeria said, tone soft, "often forget that's where they are after a while. Or we learn we need to forget it to survive."

Chris looked her way, but she was already staring ahead at the man who had come out to stand on the back steps. Like when Chris had joined her on the steps earlier, she sensed his presence the same way she did Jorge's now. Except his had been fine, and her husband's was not.

Jorge looked her way, his face a mask of calm, and his arms folded over his broad, silk-covered chest. He said nothing, but she saw the tilt of his head, a silent demand for her to come his way, and not to say a thing about it. He was famous for his silent commands, and she had learned to fear those more than his outbursts. It was when he was quiet she didn't know what might come next.

"Thank you for the walk," Valeria told Chris, "but I think this is the end for me tonight."

Chris noticed Jorge then, too. "Thank you for indulging me."

"Of course."

As much as Val wanted to look over her shoulder as she left Chris behind to head for Jorge on the steps, she didn't. Jorge hadn't once looked away from her, after all. While he appeared fine outside, she doubted that he was on the inside.

"Head inside," he told her as she climbed the stairs, "and stay there for the evening, Val."

"I only needed a breather."

She attempted to move past him, but his arm struck out fast, and he caught her at the elbow. To anyone else, she was sure his hand on her body would appear innocent from afar, but his fingers dug in hard, leaving marks behind. Tomorrow, she would have to wear something with longer sleeves to hide the bruises he was creating on her body, not that it was anything new. She had become good at hiding things Jorge didn't want the rest of the surrounding people to see.

Valeria swallowed hard, knowing better than to tell him to let her go. He would only hurt her worse later. "Do you want me to go inside, or not?"

"*Just* a breather?"

His gaze burned into hers, searching for the lie.

He would find none.

Not yet, anyway.

"Just a breather," she echoed. "The house was getting stuffy."

Jorge let her go. "Head inside, as I told you."

Like she had a choice?

Valeria went.

CHAPTER

6

"Papa."

Chris slid in beside his father where Gian seemed comfortable to stand next to a window overlooking the garden on the north side of the property. Quite a large garden, too, and one his mother would appreciate, had she been here to see it.

"Chris," Gian replied in kind.

"Did they leave you on your own?"

Gian raised his brows, and lifted the drink in his hand for a sip. "I wandered off, but no one bothered to follow me. I figured something else must have taken their attention for a time."

Possibly.

Or, at least Jorge's attention.

"I approached her outside," Chris said, lowering his tone to above a murmur. If he believed Jorge to be paranoid, then even if they assumed they were alone, they likely were not. "We took a walk around the pool."

Gian cleared his throat. "Do you think that's smart at this moment?"

"We have to know, don't we?"

"Know what?"

"Whether this is where she wants to be," Chris said, shrugging. "I know all signs point to her being taken by force, given what we know, but there was still a possibility that she wanted to be here with him."

"Was," his father noted. "Past tense."

Right.

"She's controlled here, isn't she?"

"To be fair, they all are," Gian replied. "Fear is the first tactic a cartel uses to keep people in line, even their own."

"Sure, but so much so that to take a short walk with me, she asked that we stay in view of the guards?"

"Some women don't want even a suggestion of impropriety, Chris."

His father wasn't wrong, and he knew Gian was playing the devil's advocate for him right now. Gian was of the mindset that Valeria didn't want to be here, and there was nothing to figure out. Chris wasn't as simple, and needed to be one-hundred percent sure before he started this plan of theirs, and did something crazy.

"I asked her if she liked it here," Chris added, "and while her response was … meant to distract me, I still heard what she didn't say."

"Hmm. What, then?"

"The husband came out. She went back in the house."

Chris didn't mention how, while it may have seemed like he was staring at the sky when Valeria joined Jorge on the steps earlier, he had been keeping one eye on them. He saw it all—the way Jorge grabbed her, like she was property to him, and even the flash of fear in Valeria's face before she slipped inside the house.

"Tell me," Gian said, turning to face Chris, but keeping his head tilted down, "why, even with all the details we had on this situation, that you thought the woman might be here willingly, son."

That seemed obvious enough, didn't it?

"I don't pretend to understand the complexities of other people's relationships," Chris replied, "and if people think she would be the first woman to fall in love with her captor, then they would be wrong. I wanted to be *sure*."

Gian sighed, nodding. "And you're convinced now?"

"Undoubtedly. She's not here because she wants to be."

Which meant, it was time for them to get to work. Or rather, for Chris to get to work. He needed to get his father out of this country, and work out a plan to get Valeria, and little Maria, out of here, too.

Without Jorge coming after them.

That would be the hardest part.

Jorge chased after Valeria once—hunted her down like a dog. He took years to find her hiding out in New York, but patience and perseverance paid off. That's what would happen the next time, too. Chris wanted to make sure that wasn't a possibility for the man when it was all said and done.

So, what did that mean?

Someone would have to die, likely.

It was the approach of footsteps that had Gian and Chris turning to see who found them away from the rest of people at the mansion. Samuel, the youngest Lòpez son, came to stand at the end of the hallway, but didn't come closer to intrude on their space. Out of the two brothers, Chris preferred this one.

In the single day they had been in the Lòpezs' presence, Samuel seemed like the easier, more rational of the two that he would need to deal with. Appearances were also deceiving, and Chris wasn't stupid enough to trust the man, either. He would also keep that in mind.

"Yes?" Gian asked him.

Samuel smiled. "Jorge made your accommodations for the night at a hotel in the city."

"Thank him for me."

"Of course. Jorge would like to complete any last details —he hears you want to head out tomorrow, Gian, and won't have time to do it before you leave. So, if we could do that soon, then we can end this night on a good note."

"Right, well, we'll be out in a moment."

The man gave them a nod before he turned, and left them in private once again. Chris turned to his father, giving him a look.

"What?" Gian asked.

"What are these last *details*?"

His father chuckled. "A contract, is all."

Ah, yeah.

Because even criminals took their contracts seriously. It was something Chris had never understood because despite the honor they toted in their oath to Cosa Nostra, there was little amongst the men in the underworld of crime.

"What will happen with that contract once this is over, and we've fucked them around?"

Gian grinned, and tipped his glass up to swallow the last of his drink before sitting it down with a loud clink to the nearby stand. "Deal with that when we come to it, *fils*."

That sounded easy.

Chris doubted it would be.

Standing next to his father, just beyond the iron wrought gate that had given them entrance to the Lòpez mansion, Chris tried not to be unnerved by the amount of guards standing around. Sure, he had seen the men over the course of the day, and even when they first arrived, but he didn't remember there being *so many*.

Or, perhaps more came out to play when nighttime fell.

Not that it mattered.

He noticed them now.

A good ten guards stood on the stone wall, and some behind Chris and Gian on the sidewalk as they waited for the car Jorge had sent for them. They said nothing and given neither of the Lòpez brothers had come out to wait with them while they left, it put Chris on edge.

He wondered if that was the point.

To his benefit, Chris did his best to ignore the guards, and instead, stared up at the inky sky overhead. There was nothing like looking at the sky when you were in a country that wasn't your own. He swore it allowed a person a different view—this time was no different for him, watching the stars streak the sky with their brilliance against a dark backdrop.

If anything, that settled him.

But not by much.

Gian checked his phone, unbothered about their current circumstances. "Your mother has been messaging me all day."

"Worried, I bet."

"No, she wanted me to bring her back a special treat she likes here. I'll grab it before I head for the jet tomorrow morning."

Chris rolled his eyes.

Typical.

His father spoiled his wife to the ends of the earth and back. All his mother had to do was speak, and she would have whatever she wanted in the blink of an eye. No questions asked. Gian had made sure his sons understood that nothing less was acceptable for their mother, and he expected them to treat their future wives, or *spouses*, in his twin's case, with the same respect.

A pair of headlights flashed at the end of the street, and a black car crawled to them. The guards all around them shifted their positions, letting Chris know the vehicle was theirs. Once the town car stopped at the curb, Chris didn't bother to wait for the driver to get out and open his father's door for him.

Chris did it for Gian.

"Ah, good, I didn't miss the two of you leaving," came a voice from behind.

Chris kept one hand on the back passenger door, ready to close his father inside the vehicle should he need to, as he turned to greet the approaching man. Jorge slipped through the slight opening in the gate, his smile friendly as he nodded to Gian in the car.

"I look forward to working with you, *amigo*," Jorge said.

Gian replied in kind. "And you, as well."

Jorge came close enough to clap a hand on Chris's shoulder, grabbing tightly when he added, "And I am sure your son here can take care of all the details you need, but I will keep you informed in the meantime."

"*Perfetto.*"

"Have a good night, Gian, and a safe flight tomorrow."

"Thank you," his father replied.

Gian gave Chris a glance, and so, he closed his father inside the vehicle. Jorge had let go of Chris's shoulder, but when he moved to round the vehicle and get in his side, the man blocked his path.

Jorge's smile dissipated. In its place rested a blank mask,

and cold eyes. He stared Chris down like he meant for it to be intimidating, but it was merely annoying. Not that he showed it.

"Yes?" Chris asked. "Is there something I can do for you?"

Jorge's lips quirked up at the edges.

A *hint* of a smile.

It wasn't kind, though.

No, it kind of felt threatening.

"There is," Jorge said.

"Do tell."

Chris didn't wonder *what* people saw in Jorge Lòpez. He didn't assume what the man had done, or was capable of, that made people terrified of him. Hell, his family had control of a good thirty percent of Mexico—from small businesses, to entire towns, and even the goddamn government.

No one became *that* powerful by being nice or playing fair. This man had spilled a lot of blood to get here and would spill as much as he needed to get whatever he still wanted to go.

That, primarily, was what made Jorge more dangerous than people could understand. His unstable mindset, his uncaring attitude, and his willingness to be irrational to get what he wanted made him tricky to deal with. Chris needed to consider all those things on this job, or it would be his life that ended before his time was up.

Chris understood fine and well why he should be afraid of this man, and yet, he still figured … Jorge Lòpez was just a man. Another man in this criminal world of theirs with a big fucking ego, and a gun to match it. And like all men who assumed they couldn't be beat; it only took the right man coming up against him to get it done.

Chris would be that man.

Just not tonight.

"Well?" Chris asked when Jorge stayed silent.

"I tried to find the right way to phrase this, but perhaps being blunt is the better option, *si*?"

"I prefer a man who is frank rather than one that hides his issues or intentions behind the guise of politeness."

Jorge nodded. "I will remember that, then."

"And?"

Because he didn't think this man had approached him for *that* exchange, to be honest. He wasn't disappointed.

"For future reference, Christopher, if I catch you with my wife where the guards cannot see you, I will cut off your hands, and have them delivered to your mother in a box lined with satin. I hope I have made myself clear."

Well, okay.

He always had appreciated a good threat, even if it was leveled on him. Maybe there was a broken part of him, but he always took them as challenges. Undoubtedly, his twin would tell him to be careful here, to be mindful of where he stepped with the man in front of him. His twin wouldn't be wrong, either.

"That so?" Chris asked.

"It is."

"Hmm."

Jorge arched a brow. "Are we *clear*?"

Chris's jaw tightened.

Jorge never looked away.

"Crystal clear," Chris murmured.

"Perfect. Have a good night, and I look forward to working with you in the coming weeks when we get things settled for you to come in again. Next time we meet, I suspect it'll be at the ranch, although most of us call it the compound."

Yes, and he looked forward to that.

Not that Chris said it out loud.

"Of course."

All at once, Jorge stepped back from Chris, that kind—but *fake*—smile firmly back in place as he gestured at the car. "Safe travels to the hotel, *amigo*."

Friend.

Right.

They wouldn't ever be friends.

Chris didn't reply, simply nodded to the man, and turned his back to him. The one and only time he would ever put his back to Jorge, all things considered. Rounding the car to get in the back with his father, he looked over the roof of the vehicle in just enough time to see Jorge head back through the gate.

He swallowed hard, realizing something.

Jorge would go to Valeria.

Chris could leave, but she could not. Her torment continued. What would happen to her tonight? Had his little trick of taking her on a walk caused her more pain?

The idea made his heart ache.

Fuck.

Feelings didn't work well in business, or a job. It would be hard to turn off. He was human, after all.

So was she.

Yanking open the back passenger door, Chris climbed in the vehicle, and before he had even buckled up, tires squealed against the pavement. Next to him, his father looked his way.

"And what's that about?" Gian asked.

"A pissing contest—what else?"

Gian made a noise under his breath. "If you think

someone else might be better to do this job, then I am sure we can come up with a solution to make it happen, son."

"No, I'll do it."

That, he understood for sure.

Not even a question.

At all.

CHAPTER 7

"Maria is still asleep, then?"

Valeria had expected no one else to be in the kitchen when she walked in, but at least it was just Samuel. He wasn't as difficult to deal with as Jorge, but she also didn't feel like she could trust him very much.

"She is—thought I should check because it's been a long night," she said.

Her brother-in-law nodded and lifted a bottle of wine. "A drink?"

"Sure."

Not that she would say it, but that was why she had come down here. Once the late dinner, and party after, died down, the guests had left, and the servants went to their quarters for the night, Jorge disappeared, too. Valeria wasn't sure where her husband went, but while she had the chance, she planned on taking advantage.

Or rather, five minutes alone.

Soon, Jorge would be back.

That was a guarantee.

Samuel grabbed two long-stemmed glasses from the cupboard and made quick work of uncorking the bottle of wine. Once he had the wine poured through a decanter he'd found under the kitchen island, he held a glass out for her to take.

"Here, *chica*."

Valeria took the drink, and sipped, letting the heady flavors soak her palate. "Thanks."

Samuel didn't invite her for more conversation as he drank his wine, but Valeria didn't mind, either. She had other things to worry about, and silence was better than the alternative for these men.

She was almost through her glass, enjoying the silence of the large mansion, when the hair on the back of her neck stood on end. It wasn't a good sensation, not when dread accompanied it, climbing up her spine with punishing steps.

That was how she knew Jorge was behind her.

Samuel confirmed it by looking over her shoulder and nodding at someone. His words only added to what she knew when he said, "Brother."

"The Canadians left."

"Hmm."

"The deal is good, Samuel," Jorge said, his voice coming closer to Valeria. She did her best to stay put, drink her wine, and hopefully, her husband would leave her alone for the night. Not that it had ever worked for her in the past, but she wasn't about to give up hope just yet. "And once it's done, we won't need the fucking Garcías for shit."

"And then what happens when the Garcías realize we fucked them over?"

"You're asking pointless questions."

"Or is it you don't have the answers?"

The pregnant, loaded silence stretched on in the kitchen, making Valeria wish she was anywhere but there. It was rare for Samuel and Jorge to disagree about things, but especially with the cartel. When they did, however, it rarely ended well. She did not want to be the idiot in the middle.

"Who is running this operation?" Jorge asked.

He was right behind Valeria, now. She didn't need to turn

around to *feel* the heat of his body too close to hers, or the way it made her sick just from proximity alone.

So was her life.

"Papá," Samuel replied.

"Wrong answer, brother."

Samuel sighed. "Jorge—"

"He oversees *details*," Jorge spat. "Says yes or no, or makes demands. He isn't on the front lines. He isn't making the *money*. I do all of that, and because this is the right choice, whether he likes it, then it is what we will do. The Canadian deal will get rid of our García issue, or at the least, it will negate the problem altogether. It's a win-win."

"Right," Samuel replied, "a win-win."

Satisfied with his brother conceding to his point, Jorge turned his attention on Valeria by stroking the back of her neck where she had pushed her hair over her right shoulder. It was a light graze of his fingertips along the ridge of her spine, almost daring to dip below the neckline of her dress. Nothing *violent*. Certainly not this man's usual motives, and yet, it still burned.

She didn't want his touch.

"Val," Jorge murmured.

"Hmm?"

"Would you care to tell me what happened earlier with that man?"

She closed her eyes. Honestly, she had been waiting for this, but Jorge had incredible patience at times. Hadn't six years of him chasing her taught her anything at all?

Apparently, not.

"I don't understand what you mean," she said, choosing her words carefully.

Again, his fingers drifted over her neck, along the line of her shoulder, and then he tucked in a few strands of her hair that had fallen out of place. He stepped in a little closer to her back, his mouth coming down to press a soft kiss to the side of her throat before he murmured, "You were outside *alone* with him."

The lump came back in her throat.

Across the island, Samuel turned his gaze away from them. None of Jorge's family ever cared to indulge his nonsense, but especially not with Valeria. She suspected because, if they did, they wouldn't like what happened after.

Jorge and his lessons were infamous.

"I took a moment to breathe on the steps," she said, keeping her tone level to *not* poke the monster. "He came out after and asked if I wouldn't mind taking a walk around the pool. I didn't want to be rude, and the guards watched."

She figured that was important to point out to him. The guards *had* been watching—Valeria made sure. She understood how to play this game with her husband, and she was quick enough on her feet to make sure she didn't step in any trouble with him. At least, none that would leave her with permanent damage.

Some other things, however, were unavoidable.

Jorge proved that time and time again.

Against her jaw, his lips curved into a sneer before he *bit* her. Not an easy bite—not even *playful*. His teeth cut into her skin, and she sucked in a sharp breath when his hand came up to grab the back of her neck with a rough grasp.

"And for that," he muttered against her jawline, "you are *lucky*. If not for the guards, we would have been having a very different discussion."

"I did nothing wr—"

"And you're also a lying whore, Val. You already got out of my hands once, but I promise it won't happen again. I will have you put in a shipping container and sent to the highest bidder who will keep you under lock and key until they tire of *fucking* you before you'll ever get away from me again. Do you understand me?"

She squeezed her eyes shut.

Samuel cleared his throat. "Excuse me."

Valeria didn't open her eyes again until she heard the footsteps recede from the kitchen and fade away down the hall. She might have been mad that Samuel left her alone with Jorge when, his intentions were bad, but why bother?

No one else would save her here.

She had to do that alone.

Somehow.

Jorge's hand tightened on Valeria's neck, and without a word, he spun her around so the two faced one another. He barricaded her against the island, his one hand sliding around to grip the front of her throat while his other played with the hem of her dress, twisting it between his fingers like he considered ripping it off her.

It wouldn't be the first time.

"Did you enjoy coming into the city again?" he asked.

No.

Because she was with him.

She lied. "I did."

"See, if you behaved yourself more, and showed an effort to care about this marriage of ours, and what I want from you, I might let you have more freedom."

No, he wouldn't.

Whether it was one of his vacation homes, the ranch, or the city … if she had to be with him, then it was all the same fucking prison to her.

She didn't have to say anything to Jorge because he leaned in close, and pressed a kiss that tasted like aged bourbon against her lips. His sneer deepened into a smirk that promised she would not like what happened next.

"Get upstairs," he uttered, "and make sure you're naked when I join you."

"Are you going to tell me where we're going now?"

Next to her in the backseat of the Cadillac, Jorge kept his gaze locked on the window. That didn't bother Valeria as much, seeing as how his attention focused elsewhere. What bothered her was the fact she had to dress up, leave her daughter at the ranch, and without a reason.

"Does it matter? A night out is good for you, Val."

"Curiosity, is all."

"Women are better when they're not curious," he returned, "because you're more interesting to look at that way, and less problematic."

Perfect.

Not that it helped to sedate her worries. Usually, when Jorge took her out, he made her aware of what to expect, and what he expected from her. Because those were two different things.

"It's a dinner," Jorge muttered to her left, "that's all. I thought the Canadian might like to sit down with me before he arrives at the ranch in a few days. His father headed back to his own country. He has details to share about the deal we hadn't hammered out."

Chris?

Huh.

She tried not to show how that only made her *more* curious. She didn't need to admit that thoughts about Chris Guzzi lingered in her mind more than they should since their first meeting. His question to her during that walk—*did she like it here?*—played on repeat in the back of her mind. Alongside the image of his face, that handsome profile she had no business admiring.

He didn't have to care about her, or ask about her welfare, so to speak. And yet he had, which made her wonder about him.

All dangerous things.

"So, why am I here?" she asked.

Jorge passed her a cold, dismissive glance. "Because he asked for you to come along. Thought I might enjoy bringing you. I didn't want to seem rude. Don't disappoint me tonight and do something I'll deal with later. Understand?"

Valeria nodded.

"I got it."

Better than he understood.

The rest of the drive passed in silence. That continued even after they had parked, and the driver opened their doors for them to exit the vehicle. Her husband only spoke to tell her to *smile* before they entered the traditionally decorated restaurant, one she hadn't visited before. It wasn't a business owned or controlled by her husband or one of his men, considering the woman working the front desk said they had to wait until their guest wanted them at his table.

"This *shit*," Jorge uttered under his breath. "Anywhere else would have been suitable."

Or, she thought, *he's showing you that you don't have a stronghold everywhere.*

Once they entered the back of the restaurant where Chris waited, standing next to a table spread out with a buffet of food already prepped to eat on gold-plated dishes, Jorge still hadn't relaxed.

"Guzzi," he said, gruffly.

Chris smiled, his gaze darting to Valeria even as he said, "Jorge, thank you for indulging me tonight."

"Better make it worth it, that's all I have to say. Is the food here any good? I don't trust people I am not paying to make me anything I have to put inside my mouth."

"It's a buffet. We're all eating from the same plates. A true sign of friendship, yes? And trust."

Smart again.

Valeria shouldn't notice those things.

Or the way Christopher looked in his suit.

Still, she did.

Maybe a part of her recognized … this man would be a problem for her. It didn't matter he looked at her like he was looking into her soul, searching for something she was keeping well hidden. Or that she liked his handsome features, and the way his form filled out the very expensive Armani he wore.

There was something else …

And she liked it.

"Fine," Jorge muttered. "Let's sit, and we'll—"

A sharp *Boss* from behind them had Jorge turning before he approached the table to pull out a chair for himself, likely leaving her to fend for herself.

"What?" Jorge asked the man who kept a safe distance.

The section they were dining in had no other patrons.

A private area?

What strings had Chris pulled?

"Your father is on the phone."

Jorge grunted and waved a hand. "I will call him back."

"He's adamant that—"

"*Fine.*" Jorge gave Chris a nod, saying, "I will be a few minutes. I'm sure you can entertain yourself without me." He eyed the platters on the table, adding, "Begin eating without me, hmm? We eat, and then we do business."

"Right," Chris agreed. "No worries."

Jorge pivoted on his heel, unbothered with leaving Valeria there to fend for herself. She was stunned, however, when Chris was quick to come around to her side of the table, and the first thing he did was grab a chair to pull out.

For her.

This close, she smelled the distinct aroma of his cologne. It fit his personality, she thought. Understated, but with distinct notes. Complex. Like him.

Valeria ignored the heat in her gut, never mind the way her heart raced when his hand came to rest on her waist when his dark tenor urged her to, "Sit."

Lord.

Definitely a problem.

One she didn't expect to have.

She held onto the clutch in her hands tighter as she took the seat he offered, but didn't breathe any easier when his hand left her side. In fact, she wished for it to come back. "Thank you."

"Never thank a man for being a gentleman," he said, rounding the table to take his own seat, "because then they seem to think every kind act deserves a reward, hmm? It's better not to teach men that behaving means getting something in return."

Valeria stared across the table, unsure of what to say. Chris stared back, a sensual smile curving his lips. Finally, her brain worked.

"Why did you ask him to bring me here tonight?"

Chris shrugged. "Because I find you fascinating, and he's *slightly* more interesting when you're near. Also, it might keep him in line."

"Good luck with that. Jorge is ... uncontainable."

To say the least.

"Well, he has to behave a little, if he wants my father's business. I thought I should remind him of that before I arrive at the ranch. And you, well, you can enjoy the meal. I paid a lot for this evening, but if you smile even once, it'll be worth it."

Valeria did just that.

Smile.

Chris winked back.

Damn.

~

Maria bounced at her mother's side, tugging on Valeria's hand with her excitement. "Can I ride Butter?"

Valeria smiled down at her girl. "Of course."

Butter, somehow, turned from a rowdy colt into a *very* tame riding horse. If there was one thing that had come out of Valeria being dragged back to this hell, it was the fact she put her daughter on a horse, and Maria took right to it like a fish to water. She *loved* the horses, but especially Butter.

"Come on, we have to tack them up," Valeria said, "and I bet they sense someone is coming to take them out for a ride, so they're as excited as you are."

Maria pumped a fist into the air, and Valeria let go of her daughter's hand. The girl darted down the steps, and headed for the large row of stables to the west of their home at the compound. It wasn't like she had to worry about someone taking her daughter here, considering how well-protected the family ranch was with all the guards, only one proper road leading in or out, and all the desolate land and cliffs surrounding them.

Her child wasn't going anywhere here.

Valeria followed behind Maria, but at a much slower speed. She passed the house that belonged to Abril, and Samuel. The siblings shared their one-level bungalow on the ranch until, according to Jorge, one of the two married and they moved off the property. Knowing how things were going, she suspected it would be Abril to leave first.

And she would miss her.

Jorge, having already left their two-level ranch home earlier that morning, was ... somewhere. Between the three other small homes that the guards used to sleep, and do their business, or the many barns further out that served as makeshift warehouses when drugs needed to be stored before being smuggled out of the country.

Knowing he could be anywhere around kept Valeria on her best behavior, because not only were guards likely watching her, but her husband might be, too. Sure, she preferred being at the ranch compound rather than out in public with her husband, but that was only because here, she let her masks slip.

A little.

Not too much though.

Privacy meant a lot.

Once she had entered the stables, Valeria found Maria already standing on a stool, and leaning over the gate to feed Butter a small, thin slice of apple from the pail they used as treats. She smiled at her mother while Valeria got to work on pulling down the horse gear from the walls.

Since they were already dressed and ready to go in their riding boots, she only needed to find Maria's helmet, and her own. Then, they would get the horses tacked up, and the two of them could spend their morning *away* from the ranch.

Or as far as was safely possible.

Valeria turned the corner at the back of the stables where

all the helmets sat on a shelf, and came to a full stop at the sight of Jorge leaning in the rear doorway. "Oh."

He smiled. "Going on a ride?"

"She asked after breakfast. You weren't there to—"

"I'll take her later," he said.

Valeria blinked. "What?"

Jorge shrugged. "If she wants to go on a ride, then I will take her later."

Not that Valeria wanted to point it out, but Jorge *hated* the horses. He didn't like riding, and he only kept the stables at the ranch full of horses because it kept up the appearance, and Abril would throw an unholy fit if someone took away her horses. He didn't keep the beautiful beasts because he ever took care of them or liked to ride the way the rest of them did.

"Do you want to explain to her that she can't go out when I told her she could?" Valeria asked.

"I can and will, yes. You wanted a ride, too?"

"I like riding in the mornings."

That wasn't news to him.

Riding was the one thing Jorge allowed Valeria even though it had been the way she escaped all those years ago. None of them had ever figured that out. They assumed someone smuggled her out of the ranch, likely in a vehicle. They killed a handful of guards for their troubles in an effort to figure it out.

Because her husband didn't know the truth, he never questioned allowing her to get on a horse, and go. Sometimes, she had to take someone with her, if she planned to go to the cliffs, or further out into the desolate land surrounding the ranch.

She didn't mind that.

They stayed far behind.

"You can go out," Jorge said, "but find someone to take with you. As for Maria, she can stay with me."

Anger flooded Valeria.

"Why?"

"Pardon?"

"Why can't she come with me for a ride like she does every other day?"

Jorge lifted his brow and smirked in that arrogant way again. "Because I said so. You forget occasionally, Val, that you have no control or say here. *I do.* And so, if I don't want my daughter going off with you on the horses, then she won't. Not to mention, if I want to make sure you come back, what better way to do that then to make sure you have a good damn reason to return, hmm?"

Fuck him.

She hated this man.

God knew she had a whole list of reasons to despise him. From his treatment of her, the abuse, how he enjoyed taking from her body when she didn't willingly give it to him, and *more* … so much fucking more.

And yet, she hated him the most for this reason right here. Because he used their child as a way to manipulate Valeria and keep her in line.

"I won't go on a ride, then," Valeria said, "I wanted to go with her."

It might have been childish, but if she could find one way to tell Jorge to go fuck himself, then she would do that.

Her husband clicked his tongue. "No, you will go out on your ride. And you will go alone while she watches you go."

Ah.

Valeria got it, then.

It wasn't just about controlling her, but Maria, too. This way, he could make sure his daughter saw her mother leave her behind, make a promise, and not keep it … because that's what he did.

That's what monsters did.

"Fine," Valeria murmured, "I'll take a ride."

"Have fun."

The first thing Valeria noticed when she arrived back at the stables after a quick ride to the cliffs—Jorge didn't say how long she had to stay out, after all—was the line of her husband's men walking the road as though they were meeting someone.

Maybe they were.

No one entered the gate before going through the guards.

The second thing Valeria noticed was that despite Jorge saying he would keep Maria with him, her daughter wasn't anywhere to be seen as she steered the horse toward the stables. She tried to keep the panic at a manageable level, but it was hard.

Jorge's threats lingered …

She didn't doubt that, if needed, he would take her daughter away, and there would be nothing she could do about it. It's why she shut her mouth, behaved, and did as Jorge told her to do.

Who would protect Maria?

It had to be her.

Even if she sacrificed to do it.

The panic didn't last for too long, however. She had just steered the horse to the stable's entrance when across the ranch, the front door of their home flew open, and little Maria came flying down the steps, running in her mother's direction.

It made Val smile.

Fuck Jorge.

He thought he could control the amount of love her daughter had for her by pitting the two against each other, but there was a lot he didn't know about Maria. And even her, in a way. He thought he was aware of everything about Valeria, but she kept a lot to herself.

Like her daughter.

Next to her friend, Haven, the only person Maria had for the last few years *was* her mother. It was Valeria who taught her to speak, to read, and to sing; *her* who spent long nights holding her child when she was sick.

She loved her *unconditionally*.

And no matter what Jorge tried to do, he couldn't erase those memories for Maria. Instead, every single time he raised his hand to strike the girl's mother, he was simply adding to the reasons she distrusted and disliked him.

He would have to figure that out on his own time, though. Valeria didn't plan to help him out in that regard.

"Mamá!" Maria shouted, still coming her way.

Valeria's smile dropped when a woman stepped out of the house. Maria was already halfway across the property. The *nanny*—Carla Nunez. Or, a nanny was what Jorge liked to call the woman he kept around to make sure his bed was warm with a variety when he felt the need to change scenery from raping Valeria.

According to Abril, Carla—a year younger than Valeria in age—had come around after Valeria took off years ago and had stuck around. Now, Jorge used the woman to keep an eye on Maria, and her, too. She took great satisfaction in refusing to allow Valeria choices regarding her daughter, and more.

On the ranch, Carla was always nearby.

It drove her crazy.

The woman was a rat, reporting back on her behavior, and the things she did with her daughter. Little was private when someone was always waiting to listen in, and that left her unsettled.

Valeria jumped down from the horse, grabbing the reins to steer the animal into the stables while Maria was still running to catch up with her mom. Abril came out of the stable entrance with leather gloves in one hand, and her riding boots already on.

"I would have waited for you," Valeria told her, "had I known you were going out."

Abril shrugged. "I wasn't going to, but then I heard we'll have a visitor, and I don't feel like being nice with Jorge while he plays with his friends."

"What?"

"The Canadians are back," Abril explained. "Or the one is —the younger one."

Chris.

It had been a week since that first meeting, and a few days since the dinner, and Valeria almost forgot about him. Well, that was a lie. She couldn't forget the devastatingly handsome man who seemed far too interested in her, but she knew it would be better for her if she did. So, she put him out of her mind.

"He'll be staying a while," Abril added, "because according to Samuel, they want to know how *everything* will go down for this deal."

"Huh."

"Mamá," Maria huffed, out of breath as she came to a stop next to the horse Valeria had taken out, "was the water pretty today?"

Instantly, Valeria dropped to her knees. "It was. I'm sorry Papá said you couldn't come. Later, okay?"

"What?" Abril asked.

"It's nothing," Valeria was quick to say, seeing that Carla was fast approaching, and not wanting her to hear, "but I wanted to take her out on a ride, and Jorge wouldn't let me. You know how he is."

Abril made a disgusted grunt, her gaze following Carla as the woman came closer. "Then, I will take her out with me."

"You don't have—"

"What's he going to say, Val? *Nothing*."

"Maria," Carla called, "we have to finish your studies."

Right, Valeria thought, *because you know anything about tutoring my daughter.*

"Actually," Abril told the woman, taking Maria's hand in her own to make her position clear, "she will go out on a ride with me, but thank you."

Carla scowled as she reached their spot. "Jorge said—"

"You're not Jorge."

Abril smiled.

Carla stiffened.

"And I am sure you can find better things to do for two hours," Abril added. "God knows you find enough to do at night when Valeria is the one putting her child to sleep, yes?"

Carla's face reddened. "Excuse me?"

"You heard what I said."

Valeria kept her mouth shut, knowing if she opened it, Carla would take that back to Jorge as this was her doing. She would pay for that later, so she knew better.

"Lunch is at one," Carla snapped.

"I will have her back before then."

That was that.

Valeria didn't know whether to be grateful for her sister-in-law, or terrified that in a lot of ways, Abril was the same as her brother. She was just as volatile, and twice as dangerous when she wanted to be.

Manipulative.

Cunning, and sly.

What would she do with it?

That was the real question.

CHAPTER

8

"Arms out, like a T," Jorge called, a smirk playing at the edges of his lips.

Chris gave the man on the other side of the gate cocked brow, but did as Jorge ordered. The gate opened, and two of the armed guards that had walked out the exit road from the Lòpez ranch came through to check him, patting him down and looking for any sign of a wire. It had to be that because they didn't seem to give a shit about the knife in his pocket.

He wouldn't get so irritated over being checked. It wasn't the first time he needed to do that, and God knew being who he was, he had enough run-ins with the cops over the years to be familiar with a pat down. It was more the fact that Jorge seemed to be enjoying Chris's annoyance.

The one man with the bandana covering his face grabbed the duffle bag Chris had brought along with his clothes, and other items, from the ground. He wasn't respectful about checking the bag.

"He's clean," one of the men said to Jorge.

"*Perfecto*," Jorge praised. "As I thought he would be, ah, *amigo*?"

Chris jerked his arm out of the hold of the one man who still hadn't let him go, and fixed the front of his blazer, brushing off any invisible dust. He hated being handled like he was nothing more than a *dog*. "Offensive, is all."

Jorge waved a hand, dismissing that statement. "Can't be

too safe, for one. And for two, I enjoy the show. Now, are you ready to see the ranch?"

"Which do you prefer to call it, the compound or the ranch?"

"Whichever one seems less illegal at the time."

Good point.

"I look forward to seeing it," Chris said.

"Come on, then."

Once the guards stepped back to give Chris room, he moved to follow Jorge who already had his back turned to the others as he walked down the road. Just how long was the road before they arrived at the ranch?

Chris stepped beyond the iron gate with the cursive *L* welded at the center, and a thought whispered through his mind at the same time. *No going back now.* The job had only kind of been in play before, but now it was go time. Well, his mind wasn't wrong, but he pushed it out of his head, so he could focus on the now.

From here on out, Chris would have to be careful. It was just him here—his father, as of a week ago, was back in Canada, and he didn't have a back up. Sure, he had a phone to call out if he needed help, but what good was that going to do? It would take people time to get here to him, and by then, it would be already too late.

"You'll see the barns first," Jorge said, "a couple of miles in. We use them for a lot of things, being we have actual animals on the ranch, but we also use them for storage before a drop, or if we have an oversupply at any given time. Depending on the circumstances before a smuggle run for your father, we'll be storing his on the property."

Gravel crunched under Chris's feet, and the hot sun over-head beat down on his back, reminding him why it had been a bad idea to wear his usual slacks and blazer. At least, he had been smart enough not to wear a fucking tie.

Still, as he shrugged off his jacket, he asked, "How far in is the main ranch?"

"Five miles."

"And we walk the whole way?"

Jorge chuckled. "We do."

Great.

"Has the ranch ever been stormed by officials, or—"

"No," Jorge interjected fast, "because I pay a lot of money to make sure that doesn't happen. Or, we divert their attention to somewhere else, give them *something* they want, and that's all."

"I don't understand."

The man glanced over his shoulder at Chris, grinning sardonically. "Here, it is all about who you know, and who you can blackmail or bribe. They *need* an arrest, or a bust, and so we give it to them, so they have something to flash on the news, and make it look like they're doing something important. The public thinks they're getting a hold on the cartels, the government looks good, and *la policía* appear like they're doing their job. Our main operation remains untouched, and we continue to operate as normal. Clear enough?"

More than, but Chris didn't bother to say it.

"I heard your wife was the daughter of a politician," Chris said, still keeping a few paces between him and Jorge just in case. He still didn't trust the man. "Does that play into your bribery and blackmail at all?"

"It did," Jorge muttered, "and then I had the man killed when he was no longer useful, so it didn't matter."

Yes, *after* Valeria had run off. Chris had enough information to know that. He wondered if that was because Jorge thought her father helped her to get away. He didn't ask because that wouldn't be smart, but he still wondered.

Sure enough, two large barns took form on the horizon. With the lack of animals around the fenced in sections around the barns, he had to wonder if the structures were being used to house something with a heartbeat, bricks of cocaine, or both.

Likely the latter.

"The barns are a good distraction, or … ruse," Chris noted, trying to keep up the con of why he was here in the first damn place. For *business*. "Any aerial shots would only show the barns, and any animals or whatever else. Thermal imaging would show the heat of the animals and confuse the systems. It fits well with the ranch, and nothing looks out of place."

"Exactly."

At around three miles, the duffle bag hanging from Chris's grasp became heavier. He wasn't out of shape—at home, he went into a gym three times a week, and jogged every morning on a treadmill just to wake up before jumping in the shower. He maintained his image and body because he preferred to be healthy, but no fucking human should walk in the dead heat for this long.

"And the barns are only the beginning of the ranch," Jorge said, glancing back at him once more. "There is a great deal more to see, and my men will show you around for the tour tomorrow after you've settled in for the evening. I have something else I need to handle, but I will come around to check in throughout the day. You'll have lodging here—one of the smaller houses on the property—and full run of the place to look around and see what you think. Sound good?"

Chris nodded. "Sounds fine."

Time to get this job started.

~

"Are you lost?"

Feminine laughter, two distinct tenors, rang out in the darkness. The amusement at his expense didn't offend Chris, but he took a moment to figure out where the sound was coming from.

Apparently, following the fence line would not take him back to the main pathways of the Lòpez ranch that would lead to the houses, but rather, *behind* them. Or in this case, one house. Chris wasn't told to explore on his own after he settled into the residence he would use during his stay, but he also hadn't been told *not* to explore, either.

He figured, what was the harm?

This late at night, it seemed like the only people around were the guards. He wasn't going inside any of the houses, or other buildings. This wasn't snooping, and he enjoyed a good walk in the evenings and mornings.

He found the source of the laughter sitting on the back wraparound porch of a one-level bungalow. Sitting on a hanging swing, each with a wine glass in hand, two familiar women looked his way. Only one was smiling though.

"Abril," he greeted, stepping away from the fence to approach the house, "and Valeria. I wouldn't say I'm lost, no … more like looking around."

"Careful," Abril said, tipping her wine glass up to her lips as though she might take a drink, "my brother doesn't like it when people snoop."

"Does he also take a problem with people who like to walk?"

Abril made a noise under her breath. "Depends on what you're walking *toward*."

Consciously, Chris's gaze drifted to the quieter woman

sitting beside Abril on the bench. Valeria, that was. She didn't avoid his gaze, but he could see she wasn't going to engage him in a conversation like this, either.

That bothered him.

Valeria was, after all, the entire reason for him being here. He kind of needed her to talk to him, amongst other things. Like trust him, but that was a task for another day … or evening. It wasn't something he could do tonight, anyway.

"Care for a drink?" Abril asked after emptying her wine glass. "Liquor, water, or coffee, I mean."

Chris nodded. "Water would be great."

"I'll just be a minute."

The woman was quick to stand from the bench, giving Valeria a quiet word that Chris wasn't able to hear, before disappearing into the back of the house. He walked closer to the porch, coming to a stop on the bottom step, but not moving further. It was enough for him to let Valeria know he would engage her though.

That's all he wanted.

"You like wine?" he asked.

Valeria smiled, glancing down at the glass in her hand. "Not particularly, but I *do* like getting away from my house for an hour. Abril is one of the few people I can relax with like this without … having to hear about it."

He heard what she didn't say.

Chris didn't call it out.

Shrugging, she was quick to add, "She *loves* wine, and likes to try new ones. I indulge her. This one isn't so bad."

Chris noted the color of the remaining liquid in her glass. "A white wine is good for a hot night under the stars, but hell, so is vodka."

Valeria laughed.

Freely.

She tossed her head back with a laugh, surprised by his frank statement. To be fair, the way the woman looked in the moonlight as she laughed equally shocked him. The russet tones in her golden skin were more clear, her dimmed gaze brightened, and those pretty lips of hers curved in the most beautiful way in her easy joy.

He wondered if she didn't get to do that enough.

Laugh, that was.

Not wanting to make her uncomfortable with his staring when she quieted, Chris cleared his throat, and glanced up at the inky sky. "I don't think I can appreciate the size of this place at night, but by the time I settled in after arriving, it was already dark."

"They haven't given you a proper tour yet?"

"Tomorrow."

"I'm sure you'll appreciate what they've done here. Men who visit typically do."

He didn't miss the edge to her tone.

"And that's what you assume I am, then? A man like them?"

Valeria's gaze darted to his.

Chris arched a brow, challenging her to say whatever was on her mind instead of alluding to it. Absolutes, he could work with. Hints, not so much.

"You know what my husband is—what he *does*," Valeria said quietly, "and because I know why you're here, to make a deal with him, there's only one thing for me to assume about you, too."

"Shame you think that, then."

Valeria's throat jumped when she swallowed. "Why is that?"

"Appearances are deceiving. And bad men don't always do bad things. Sometimes, they do good things, too."

"Don't they?"

How simple that question seemed.

The answer was anything but.

Unfortunately, Chris's life had taught him that no matter what he said here, she would find it most difficult to believe him. Because her experiences were not the same as his. Her life taught her one thing, and that's what she understood.

It was his duty to show her differently.

That was the thing, right?

Actions spoke louder than words.

"We'll see," he said.

Valeria opened her mouth as though she would reply, but all it took was Abril coming back out from the rear of the house for her to quiet. Abril came down the stairs, a glass of water for Chris in one hand, and a refill of wine in the other for her.

"Thank you," he said.

Abril nodded. "You know, in my experience, it's always what *motivates* a man that determines whether his actions are justifiable. What do you think, Chris?"

Huh.

Seems someone had been listening.

He smirked. "I would say you're right."

"I usually am."

Although Chris was in Mexico with the Lòpez cartel for a reason, he could still appreciate and respect the set up they had here. The ranch itself was almost a small community. In the middle, a cluster of homes sat in a large circle, all connected by pathways and gravel driveways. Another two barns also sat further in the property, along with stables.

For horses, apparently.

The cocaine, the man showing Chris around explained, they made and packaged it for shipping in Colombia where the cartel had gained control over production. They moved the substance between several locations—the ranch being one—to store before a smuggle run, which was a different story, and something Chris would get details on later.

"It's important," the man—Jesús, was it?—said as they stepped out of the house that Chris would use for his stay, "that the cartel maintains its control over territory, and distribution. Territory is the issue we've been having for a while, because of the García organization."

Right.

The cartel that controlled the lower portion of Mexico, and for a while, had tried to take control of the production in Colombia.

"We're working on that," the man said before Chris could ask further.

He wasn't *that* interested in the cartel, or their business. Cartels were complex criminal organizations, but he had a good enough grasp on the details to know how they worked. The lengths the family went to in order to maintain their privacy and control fascinated him, but he didn't really *care*.

Yet, he had to pretend to.

Fun.

Chris's entire purpose here rested on a ruse, and him being able to keep it up. The longer he could stay in the Lòpezs' presence, gather as much information about their lives and business, the better chance he had at getting Valeria and her daughter out of here alive. So, he continued to ask questions, and allow the man to take him around the ranch when what he wanted was a goddamn nap.

As far as the Lòpez family, and Jorge, understood ...

Chris was here because his father was anal on every single detail in business. Most, if not all, organizations would not be willing to indulge the demands Gian had made for this *deal*, but because the Lòpez cartel needed something from the Guzzis—the arrangement for a cocaine supply between them would be in the hundreds of millions a year—they would play along.

But for how long?

That was the real question.

As they walked along a pathway leading toward the biggest house on the property, something in the corner of his eye caught Chris's attention. A familiar woman came out of the stables with a saddle in her hands that she tossed onto a fence to hold it up before turning back to disappear inside the building.

Valeria.

For a second, Chris felt as though he could breathe a little better. Sure, he had seen her the night before, but he hadn't felt safe asking her questions about her safety here when prying ears were nearby. All week, he had worried about that woman, and what might happen to her. It left him with little sleep, and more restless nights than he cared to admit. And when he slept, images of her beautifully sad face filled his mind.

Not that he needed to be dreaming about that woman at all, or how she had looked with her curves filling out a dress, heels to show off long, golden legs, and black hair pin-straight falling down her back. Because *no*, he didn't need those images in his mind alongside the concern he already had for her.

This was a problem waiting to happen.

Obviously.

It was a little relieving for him to see her looking well and happy in the daylight. He still wanted to *speak* to her—get close, look her in the eyes, and make sure things were okay. It wasn't a game he should play, and nothing good would come out of the fact he had a growing emotional attachment to this job, but whatever.

Chris was who he was.

Someone who *cared*.

He gave a fuck.

Before he reconsidered, he asked the man ahead of him, "Can we go inside the stables?"

"Didn't you want a drink?"

"Sure, soon. The stables?"

"Why not?"

He expected his current guard to follow him inside the stables, as that had been his entire tour today in a nutshell, but someone called the guy's name just as they came up to the entrance where one could hear the horses hooves scuffing the floor inside.

"*Jesús, venir!*"

Chris had no idea what the man across the way was shouting to his guard, but whatever it was, Jesús was quick to give him a nod before he said, "I'll be back in a moment—you're good to look around, *sí?*"

"Perfectly fine," Chris replied.

Even better that he got to do it alone, now.

"Do not wander off."

"Of course, not."

He was right where he wanted to be.

As soon as Jesús's back was turned, Chris headed inside the stables. His gaze swept the space, taking in the horses, and the equipment lining one wall. A bucket of apple slices rested on the floor near one station, and the scent of animals and hay clung to the air with every breath he drew in.

Another time, and he might have admired the stables, and the beautiful creatures it housed. He always had a healthy appreciation for horses and had gone riding a time or two in the past. But as he was running low on time, and couldn't chance getting caught alone with Valeria, he didn't bother to enjoy the stables.

Instead, he found the woman in question down the corridor stepping into a stall beside a white and beige speckled horse.

"Ah, *caballo*," Valeria said as the sounds of a brush being dragged over the horse's hide echoed from the stall, "you're a *bonito* boy today. You like the brush, huh?"

Chris didn't even hesitate, simply headed down the corridor, and slipped into the stall where Valeria was brushing the horse down. Her gaze flew to him, her eyes widening as her pink lips fell open in a perfect *O* at the sight of him. No, he certainly didn't have time to admire the stables, or to have small talk, but he enjoyed the sight of this woman in front of him in her surprise.

There was something beautiful about that.

About *her*.

"You can't be in here," she blurted, her breath gone.

Chris leaned back enough to peek out the stall which gave him a perfect view of the stable doors that were still wide open. "No one is here to stop me."

His stare went back to her.

She swallowed hard.

"What do you want?"

"To talk," he replied.

Valeria took a little step back, but she didn't have very far to go. The horse next to them pranced in place wanting his attention back with that brush. "Do you understand that my husband will hurt—"

"Oh, he's made it clear what he intends to do if I get too close to you, yes."

She chewed on her bottom lip, those dark brown eyes of hers—like melting pools of russet—drifting over him like she wasn't sure what to do with Chris. "That's fine and great for you," she returned, "but I am more concerned about what he might do to me."

That made Chris stiffen.

"He hurts you?"

Valeria's cheek twitched. "I ... I shouldn't talk about it."

"Yeah," he said, taking one step closer to her as he spoke, "I'm not at all worried about your husband, Val. He's a problem—an issue for me to take care of. I'm not even here for him, not *really*."

Her gaze locked onto his.

Chris stepped close enough to her that her back hit the wall of the stall, and she needed to stare up at him. There was no getting away now, and he wanted something to be very clear to her. For one, because he needed for her to trust him. And for two, because this would only work if she understood what was about to happen.

"W-what are you doing?" she whispered.

Chris hadn't intended to crowd Valeria because he wanted to make her uncomfortable, but because he needed to make sure she wouldn't run, not when he had the chance to do this. The funny thing?

She wasn't uncomfortable.

Not in the *slightest*.

Staring at him, those pupils of hers blew wide, show-casing his own reflection back to him. Her tongue peeked out to wet the seam of her lips, the action making his chest grow tight with something unusual—*lust*. That was before he noticed the way she looked him over, curious, yet wary, and still with *interest*. He bet if he touched her pulse point at her throat, he'd find her sweet heart racing like crazy.

What are you doing?

Get out of your head, asshole.

Focus.

His thoughts brought him back to the present, but barely. Because now, he concerned himself with the way Valeria's skinny jeans molded to her shapely legs, and the low dip of her flimsy blouse that gave a peek at the valley between her breasts. Her skin, the golden sheen dotting it, pebbled from his attention, and he had the greatest urge to *touch* her, or God forbid … fucking taste her.

Wow.

Valeria made a small noise.

Chris's gaze flew back up to hers. "What's that for?"

"*Me?* What is that for?"

"I beg your pardon?"

"The way you stare at me …"

Chris's brow furrowed. "You're an exceptionally beautiful woman. Does no one tell you that?"

"*You* shouldn't."

Hadn't she learned, yet?

"But I still did."

She sucked in a shaky breath. "It has been a long time since someone looked at me like that."

"Shame, that," he murmured. "Beautiful things should be admired by the ones who care for them, and they should be told often of their worth and value."

Valeria dropped his stare. "I'm not worth very much *here.*"

"Or is it you aren't valued?"

Their stares met again.

Chris inched closer, because he wanted her pressed

against the wall, and also because something at the neckline of her shirt had caught his attention. A mark that marred her skin, but he had to be sure. Lifting his hand, a shiver that raced through Valeria when his fingertips glided along the fabric of her blouse to move it aside.

Sure enough …

He found three bruises there, a dark red that told him they were recent. He made a rough noise under his breath, though it came out thick between them and loaded with things he wasn't sure he should say yet. Perhaps a part of him had still assumed this woman might want to be here, but he doubt she wanted to also be abused.

Now, he didn't wonder at all.

"I'm not here for your husband," Chris said quietly, meeting Valeria's stare again, but not dropping his hand to stop from touching her. He liked the heat of her body, and the silkiness of her skin, and considering the way she trembled, and her breaths came out harder while she watched him, he could tell she liked it, too. "Despite what they might say, I didn't come here for them. I came for you."

"What does that mean?"

He didn't have time.

It was a long story, and they didn't have the minutes needed to tell it. Time was already running out for their little moment here.

"Who did this?" he asked, his fingers sweeping over the bruises.

"Take a guess."

"Jorge?"

"Regularly."

"Last night?"

"This morning," she breathed.

The dark, violent urge that swept through him seemed

destructive, and *reckless*. He wanted nothing more than to feed into it and hurt the man who put his hands on his wife. Whether she was property to Jorge didn't factor in at all—*no man* should hurt their spouse, ever.

Full stop.

"I'm sorry," Chris said, his thumb sweeping to the side, across her collarbone. That shiver in her body followed the same path, and her lips parted again like she might say something to him. All he wondered was what it might be like to kiss this woman—something else he had no business doing.

Well, so much for *that*.

He had broken all the rules, now.

"I want to kiss you," he said. "Can I?"

She sucked in a hard breath, but nodded once. Chris closed the distance between them in a blink, catching Valeria's mouth with his own in a soft, yet still *burning* kiss. She never hesitated to kiss him back, her lips working against his, like she found something that was pure heaven to her senses. His tongue struck against the seam of her lips, demanding more, and she gave it to him willingly.

Beautifully.

Her fist found his shirt, and she dragged him closer as a war raged on between them. It was strange, in a way. Kissing someone had never been a battle before, to hand over himself to her, and see what happened after that.

And yet, that's what it seemed like. She tasted of cherries, and vanilla. Sweetness, and sin.

Chris backed Valeria into the stable wall again, the horse shifting beside them as her palms found his jaw, and he dragged her closer with his. There was something intoxicating about this woman, and he wanted to find out what. Not that he had enough time to do it.

The sound of boots crunching against gravel had Chris

taking a wide step back from Valeria. He didn't have a clue what came over him, but as he stared at her still pressed to the wall, her fingertips hovering over her lips like she wanted to feel his kiss, he didn't regret what just happened.

Even if it was dangerous ... and *stupid*.

The questions in her eyes stared back at him. He couldn't answer them now.

"Chris?"

He gave her a pointed stare and took two steps backwards out of the stall to find the man from earlier—Jesús—glancing down the stables. He smiled at the man, thankful that he learned how to mimic his twin's, Corrado, natural ability to remain calm in all situations. Even when his heart raged out of control.

"Just admiring the horse," Chris said. "Can we get that drink, now?"

Jesús nodded. "Absolutely, and Jorge called, too. He invited you to dinner with him if you're hungry."

Chris headed for the man, forcing himself not to glance back into the stall at Valeria as he did so. "Food would be great."

And so was the flavor of Valeria Lòpez still lingering in his mouth.

Fuck.

CHAPTER
9

"Easy, *easy*."

Valeria's attempt to soothe the broken horse worked. Abril came out here in the field and worked with the horse to make it rideable, but after a bad fall from the horse throwing her from the saddle … well, she was hesitant to approach the animal so soon.

Horses were like people. Sometimes, they didn't always connect with someone else. Human, or animal. And other times, they needed a bit to come around. Valeria figured that was the problem with Duke, the horse she was trying to work with on his riding skills, so she tried to take him out while Abril took a break from working with him.

At least this way, he didn't have long spells of little to no activity with a human. Something beyond being fed, brushes, or having his stall cleaned. He would be a riding horse, and so someone needed to ride him.

Simple as that.

"That's a good boy, Duke," Valeria said, reaching down to pat his muscular neck. "One more trip around the fence line, huh? Let's go."

She pulled the reins on the right side, a silent command for the animal to turn in that direction. It took a harder tug for him to listen to her command, though, which spoke to his stubbornness. That was another issue with him. He didn't like to do what others wanted him to do when he would much rather do what he wanted.

Horses with stubborn streaks kept them even after being trained. She figured Duke would be an adult's horse, and not appropriate for children to ride. Which was fine, honestly. Some horses were better suited to adults because they needed that strong, dominant hand.

They were halfway around the fence line of the field that the horses used to graze when she first noticed *him*. Chris, that was.

It was impossible for her to ignore the way her heart raced in her chest from nothing more than sight alone. He seemed so calm, unbothered, and confident leaning against the post of the wooden fence, his gaze locked on her as she came closer to his spot riding Duke.

After their moment in the stables the other day, Valeria had done her best to avoid him because she didn't know how to deal with the strange emotions the Canadian invoked in her. Not to mention, there was just something about the way he *looked* at her. She couldn't explain what it was, but she swore he was looking right into her soul, seeing all of those secrets she tried damn hard to hide, with very little effort at all.

Chris raised a hand, a small wave urging her closer to him.

Damn.

Now, she couldn't pretend like she hadn't seen him. Although, if she were being an honest woman, she didn't want to avoid him at all. That would probably end badly for her in one way or another.

"Enjoying a ride?" he asked when Duke trotted closer to his spot at the fence post.

Valeria kept a good fifteen feet between her, and him. *Just in case*. Surely, no one would see them out here in the field and think something inappropriate might go on, but she couldn't be too careful.

Jorge had acted on lesser beliefs.

He shouldn't be tested.

Besides, *something* had happened.

In the stables …

Valeria couldn't forget it.

Neither could her body.

"Training Duke, actually," she replied. "Have you taken a horse out yet?"

"Considering it." Chris flashed her a grin one might consider sinful. God knew she did if the way her thighs clenched around the body of the horse was any sign. She was not used to *this*—to feeling attraction for someone else. Not at all. "Although, I have to say I am enjoying watching you ride a horse far more."

There was no hiding the suggestion in his tone.

He didn't even make the attempt.

Why did she like that?

Because she shouldn't.

At all.

Valeria swallowed thickly. "You shouldn't do that."

"Pardon?"

"*Flirt* with me."

Chris shrugged one shoulder, almost uncaringly even though he looked damn good doing it. "When *you* say you don't want me to, then I won't. See, telling me I shouldn't do something isn't the same as telling me not to do it because you don't like it, Val."

Goddamn him for being right.

Valeria, out of an instinctual need to be safe and nothing more, peeked back to the ranch, and stables. Here, all she ever did was look over her shoulder to see who was spying, and might report back to Jorge about her behavior. She hadn't realized how often she did it until Chris was nearby.

Sad thing, that.

"No worries, no one is watching," Chris said, amusement coloring his tone.

Valeria was quick to snap around to glare at him, then. "Don't treat this like a *joke*. I might like your attention, but that doesn't mean I can always *accept* it."

His playful smile never faltered.

God.

Why did he have to be so *cocky*?

So damn confident?

Arrogant men were not Valeria's first choice, that was for sure, and yet she found it was a good look on Chris. She was not used to the heat traveling lower between her thighs, making an ache settle deep in her bones.

Jesus.

And that *want*?

Clawing at her chest?

It was too much.

"Don't you have questions for me?" he asked.

She did.

Too many.

And yet, all she could say was, "You will get me killed."

"Quite the opposite, Valeria."

What?

Again with that *suggestion*. Like he was here for her—he said it as though that's what he meant, but she couldn't be sure that's what it was.

She didn't even trust herself.

"Would you let me do it again?"

Valeria sucked in a shaky breath, a flush traveling down

her throat. She could feel the heat crawling over her skin though she did her best to ignore it. She asked, although she was sure she knew his answer, "Do what?"

"Kiss you."

"*Valeria!*"

The shout of Abril coming from the stables had her rearing the horse back, already turning to head for the stables and leaving Chris behind.

"Will you?" he called after her.

His tone was still dark with wicked promises that made her skin pebble, and her thighs clench. She couldn't miss it, not that she wanted to.

"Not if I value my life."

He probably didn't hear her.

That was okay.

Even she didn't believe it.

The week following Valeria's encounter with Chris in the field could only be described as hell. Not because anyone had caught them, although it came close, or because anyone suspected something had happened. Rather, she couldn't help the paranoia that seemed to creep up her spine whenever the memory of Chris kissing her against that wall, or him asking her if he could do it again as he leaned against the fence, would flood her mind.

It was made worse whenever she would be close enough for Jorge to be looking at her when the memories came rushing into her mind, intent on driving her crazy, making her hot, *and* scared for her life all at the same time.

Because that's what her husband would do, she knew. Undoubtedly, he would kill her for even *thinking* about another man, let alone kissing one. Jorge was terribly jealous when a man was staring at Valeria for too long because he thought of her as a prize he had won. And not once, but twice, when he caught her after running. He was not giving her up, and instead of treating her like something prized, he behaved like she was shit under his shoe.

The more troubling part?

Valeria couldn't stop thinking about it.

About Chris.

That moment replayed in her mind daily—on fucking repeat. It woke her up at night when Jorge was beside her, and she didn't need to be thinking about it, all things considered. The taste of him seemed like it lingered on her lips whenever she sipped on a glass of water because it reminded her of him. *Crisp*, and fresh.

Like the way his kiss and simple touch had made her body light up with barely any effort on his part at all.

God.

She didn't need that.

None of it.

Worse was the fact she thought a huge part of her might want to do it again, and that was terrifying. Valeria spent her days at the side of a man who raped and beat her simply for being his wife. And a random man shows up with strange words coming out of his mouth about being there for her, and she's kissing him in a stable? Entertaining his flirting while she rode a horse?

Stupid.

That's what she was.

A stupid little *niña*.

Because only a girl would behave the way she did, so recklessly and dumbly. It was the only excuse she could come up with to justify why she had done what she did, and why she wanted to do it again.

Or you are so starved for love and affection that a kind man with care in his eyes reminded you that you are both alive, and a woman.

Fuck her thoughts, too.

Valeria had done her best to avoid Chris over the last week. He had occasionally joined them at their table for a meal, but he made a careful effort not to talk to her in her husband's presence, which she was sure Jorge appreciated, as he usually did for other men. And if there was a chance for her to speak with Chris, she was quick to take herself out of the situation so they couldn't talk.

She didn't need the trouble.

Right?

So, why did her body think differently?

"Don't let the kitten get too far from you," Valeria called to her daughter from the porch.

Sitting on the steps with her sister-in-law, she watched as Maria chased after a kitten she sneaked from a barn. It was normal for the cats to mate and have a batch of kittens on a ranch. Cats kept the vermin down with their hunting habits.

Somehow, Maria convinced her father to let her keep the kitten she had snuck away from the litter when it was big enough, and no longer needed its mother. Valeria figured Jorge had only allowed her to take the gray and white kitten because it was something for him to use to bribe their child, not because she seemed to love the kitten. Whenever he thought she misbehaved, he threatened to send the kitten back to the barn, or worse …

Valeria did her best to assure Maria that wouldn't happen, but she also seemed like she made promises she wouldn't be able to keep. And that, more than anything, killed her. She was never more aware of how little control she had over her life until it was her daughter, and nothing was for her to decide.

Even if it was just a kitten.

"Oh, no!" Maria shouted when the kitten darted away from her and went around the house. "Come back, Kitty!"

Kitty.

Yep, that's what she had named it.

Valeria let her.

What else could she do?

"Hurry and grab it before it goes back to the barn," Abril told Maria, "because that's probably what she wants to do."

Maria darted after the kitten, almost going out of Valeria's line of sight, but stopped just short. Her head tilted back as a shadow drifted over her form, and she stared up at whoever had come around the side of the house.

"Better hold on to her good so she doesn't get away again," a familiar voice said.

Valeria felt that voice through every part of her body.

Every single fucking part.

Chris.

"Thank you very much," Maria said, smiling.

They both came into view around the side of the house, standing beside a garden bed of roses that Abril liked to maintain. She had one for every house although she only lived in her own.

Chris passed a look toward the house, his gaze landing on Valeria before it went back to her daughter. Kneeling down, he handed the squirming kitten to her daughter with a soft smile. His voice lowered as he spoke to her daughter, and pet the kitten between her ears with the pad of his finger.

It didn't matter.

Maria smiled, looking back at her mom, and then nodding

at whatever Chris had told her. Pointing at a flower, he waited for Maria to give him the okay before he pulled a small pocketknife from his slacks. He cut the rose that the kitten had jumped on at the stem, dragging the blade down the length to remove any small thorns. Then, he tucked the pink rose into her daughter's hair, right above Maria's ear.

"Beautiful, like your Ma," he said just loud enough for Valeria to hear.

Her throat tightened.

In her chest, her heart thundered.

Chris must have asked Maria something else because his head tilted to the side. Her child's happy smile faded when she shrugged in her dress. She understood well enough what Chris said next because his lips moved to say, "I'm sorry, Maria."

He said something else, and Maria quickly bounced on her feet, happy all over again as though nothing was wrong. The two of them laughed, and Chris pointed between himself, and then her daughter with a firm nod. Then, he pointed at Valeria, too, and gave Maria a wink that had her smile growing wide all over again.

"You understand?" she heard him ask.

Maria grinned. "I understand."

"Good—I promise. I don't break those."

"Do you pinky promise?"

Chris shot Valeria another look from the side, but his stare didn't linger long before it went right back to her daughter. Unquestioningly, he brought his hand out, and popped his pinky out for her daughter to catch with her own. Maria hooked their pinkies and tugged.

"Pinky promise," he said.

"That's the most *important* one, you know."

"I know."

Valeria wanted to know what they talked about—so badly. What was it the man said to her daughter that had her frowning and sad, but then had her smiling like the entire world watched and loved her in the next second?

The sight was sweet, really.

Maria didn't take to strangers, but especially not men. Valeria blamed that on the fact there hadn't been a lot of men in her daughter's life when they stayed on the run for the last few years, but also because the man who should adore and treat her well made it his mission to ensure she saw his vile treatment of her mother. Her *mom*—someone she loved more than anyone else in the world. Her little girl with a heart of gold wouldn't soon forget that, Valeria knew.

For whatever reason though … Maria liked Chris.

"He's good with kids," Abril noted at her side, "and she's not even his, huh?"

Valeria let out a sigh. "Hmm."

"And stop staring, Val. You look like a woman who has found something she likes."

Well, *shit*.

She averted her stare.

So much for avoiding him.

Not that it mattered, and her attempt to look away didn't last for long, either. Chris stood, after giving Maria a one-armed hug and a kiss to the top of her head, and looked their way again. She sensed his gaze on her, even though she was trying to make it seem like she was looking out at the land beyond him, and not at him.

"Have a good day, ladies," he murmured.

That was it.

He walked off.

The confusion, and heaviness in Valeria's heart became

worse. This—whatever was happening here—would lead nowhere good.

She was sure.

～

The next evening found everyone on the ranch celebrating a successful smuggle run into Texas that had been touch and go for a good month or more due to changes at the ports of entry. Valeria wasn't interested in the flowing alcohol, or the laughter of her husband's men that filled their house, and spilled out into the backyard where they had gathered in a large group.

She hung back on the rear porch of their home, forgotten by Jorge as he swallowed back more whiskey, and laughed at whatever the man next to him had said. It wasn't like she would complain about his lack of attention, but that wasn't what bothered Valeria at the moment.

Other things stuck to the back of her mind like sticky tar, dark and *thick*, promising it would stay there forever unless she handled it, and soon. *Chris*. And his little show the day before with her daughter.

For whatever reason, it wouldn't leave her mind. Like his kiss that day in the stables, or that whenever he was within visual distance of her, he stared at her when no one else did.

All bad things.

And yet, *good*, too.

Even if it was crazy and dangerous. If Valeria were a smart woman, she would tell the man to stop. To leave her be and go his way.

Except he'd said something to her in the stables …

He came here for her.

What did that mean?

This might be one of the few times she would be able to deal with the thoughts that plagued her, so she decided to at least try. Now or never because it was likely she wouldn't get another chance soon.

And Chris came to Jorge's impromptu celebration. He hung back like she did, but never stepped in on their conversations unless they invited him, or otherwise.

He didn't want to be there.

Clearly.

With everyone's attention on the row of fireworks that Samuel was setting off, while Abril kept an exhausted Maria safely away, Chris slipped inside the house. He had to pass by Valeria to do it, and met her gaze unashamed as he did so, arching a brow before he disappeared inside.

Without saying anything at all, his silent challenge sounded like, *Well, are you coming?*

Did the man read her mind?

She would soon find out.

It was foolish, no doubt about it. At least, inside the house, Valeria would be able to slip into another room should someone come inside, or even run upstairs. There were variables that worked to her favor here, and she figured it should be safe enough to at least try to have a private conversation with the man.

Valeria ducked into the house but she found the back hallway empty. Not knowing where Chris had gone, she walked further down the hall, a shriek dying in her throat when a hand snapped out to grab her at her elbow before someone yanked her into the downstairs bathroom.

"What—"

Valeria didn't even get to finish her sentence before he slammed the bathroom door shut, leaving her in darkness. A form pressed her against the counter. She knew it was Chris who pulled her inside by the *scent* of him.

Intoxicating, she thought, like his taste, too. Crisp and fresh like a freshly fallen snow.

"Turn the light on," Valeria said, air rushing with her words, trying to ignore the rushing desire in her bloodstream. "Please."

Chris did just that, the space lighting up although it took a second for her eyes to adjust to the brightness. He backed up a bit, giving her enough room to breathe, but that was all he afforded her in the small bathroom. It wasn't made for two people, and her body knew it given his proximity.

"We have, what, ten minutes before the fireworks stop?" he asked.

Valeria wet her lips. "About that. I have questions."

"About what?"

"Whatever you said to my daughter yesterday."

Chris blinked, the hard lines of his handsome face softening as a smile fettered over his lips. "*That's* what you want to ask?"

"Yes."

"Not about what I said to you in the stables? I figured that would be on your mind."

"It is," Valeria blurted, "but my daughter comes first for me ... *always*. No exceptions, and so if something about you might put her in danger, even unknowingly, then I have to handle that. Surely, you can understand."

Chris's throat jumped at her words, like maybe he swallowed something back before he muttered, "Hurting her— accidentally, or not—is the last thing on my mind, trust that."

"Still, what did you say to her?"

"Val—"

"I want you to tell me."

His gaze darted away, but his tone came out low when he said, "I asked her about Haven … and New York. I needed to give her something she *understood*. Something that would resonate with her, right, because she needs to believe I'm not like the rest of the people here. I'm *different*. She misses Haven and her school in New York. She doesn't like you crying a lot, or that her father hurts you."

That was not what Valeria expected. A mixture of things had a lump growing in her throat, the emotions lodging there to take her breath away, and make her want to sob at the same time. Her eyes stung with unshed tears, and she clenched her fists into tight balls at her sides.

The mention of Haven—her only friend they forced her to leave behind when Jorge found her—made her emotional, but the rest just drove the knife in deeper, and twisted until everything was *pain*.

"You're aware Haven got married," Chris added, "to Andino Marcello since you were there. That's who hired me. To come here, and figure out a way to get you the fuck out of here, in case you wondered. That's why I'm here."

God.

That wasn't possible.

She didn't dare say it though, because a brief flutter of hope danced through her heart, swelling to epic proportions, and threatened to drown her with the emotion. It had been so goddamn long since she felt anything akin to hope. How sad was that?

"She told me you're unhappy," Chris murmured. "Your daughter, I mean."

"Don't put her in danger by asking—"

"You don't give her enough credit, Val. She is young, but she is *not* stupid."

Valeria met his gaze, unsure and wary. "You made her a

promise. I heard you say that. What was it?"

His grin deepened. "I shouldn't tell. I made a pinky promise—"

"Stop it."

"Relax," he said, one of his hands coming up to stroke the line of her jaw with his thumb and forefinger. The soft touch made her sigh and tilt her head into his hand a little more, not that she had any business doing that at all. "I promised you would be happy soon, and no one would hurt you. All she wants is for her mom to be happy again, okay?"

Fuck him.

For doing that, and telling her, even if she asked. For giving her hope.

A tear fell from the corner of Valeria's eye, but Chris quickly wiped it away before it got very far. He did the same for the other side of her face when she blinked, and more tears threatened to fall.

"Why did you do that in the stables ... kiss me, I mean?"

"Not sure," Chris murmured, his thumb sweeping her cheekbone as he spoke. "It's not something I was *supposed* to do. I asked first, you nodded."

"I did," she agreed softly, "although I'm not sure why."

"Then, we're in the same position."

And what a position.

"Not part of the job, then?"

His stare snapped down to her mouth. "No. I just ..."

"What? Because I don't think you understand how dangerous this is for me."

"I do, Val. I promise I do, and if you don't—or didn't—want me to do that, all you have to do is say."

She sucked in a sharp breath, her back straightening at the directness of his tone. "I don't, no."

Chris frowned. "What?"

"Get a *say*. About sex. Or I never have, and I realized you're right, too."

His hands dropped to her thighs overtop the skirt of her dress, and his fingers flexed gently. As supportive as it seemed, his silent acknowledgement of her truth, it also reminded her all he had to do was push up her dress around her thighs, spread her wide, and he would have her.

She *wanted* it.

"Sex … anything like it," she whispered, "has always been used against me, and I've never wanted someone else before. Not *him*, not a stranger—no one."

"Except me," he murmured.

Valeria peeked up at him through her lashes, only then realizing she had been staring at the corded band of muscles lining his broad shoulders, and the way his throat jumped when his gaze dropped to her lips.

Desire.

Lust..

Always the possession; the *thing* Jorge won. Used because her husband wanted to. Coveted for his pride.

Men around her husband desired her for their own selfish reasons or gains. Because they saw her as the perfect *cartel* wife, their belief they too would be a king with a queen they handpicked and demanded. Or to others because they believed her unworthy of her status after running—a traitor to *break*.

And yet …

"No one has ever looked at me the way you are right now," she said, her voice almost unrecognizable to herself with the heat she found there. "I've never been wanted—not like this."

"And you never wanted—until now."

That's why this had seemed so confusing to her. From the

walk around the pool with an almost flirting, but very charming man, to the kiss in the stables had all seemed foreign to her in a way. She played a game she had never needed the rules to before now.

"Val," he said, tone thick.

"Yeah?"

Chris leaned in close enough so if she wanted—because he had made it clear this was on her terms, she had the *say*— moving forward would let her capture his kiss. His lips quirked up at the edges, sexy as ever, when he told her, "Has a man never loved your body the way it deserves to be, sweetheart?"

God.

If it were possible, she felt his voice everywhere. At the apex of her thighs, in between the beats of her heart, and straight to her mind. All the parts of her attention that a single man *never* caught of hers before.

Chris didn't give her the chance to respond before he added quieter, "Not with his cock—not while he's *fucking* you. Just him, Val, and his hands or his mouth. Touching you with parts of his body that makes it more intimate than just his cock. Has no one done that the way you want them to— the way they *should*?"

She swallowed hard.

Shook her head.

"No," she breathed.

"Fucking shame," he muttered, arching a brow. "Can I?"

Valeria blinked, the word slipping from her mouth before she even understood she had said it because staring at him was intoxicating. "Yes."

"Which do you want, then? My fingers, my mouth —*both*? Because we don't have a lot of time, and as much as I would like to spend hours showing how you should be fucked and adored, I only have a few minutes before someone realizes we're not out back where we should be."

He also had a way of reminding her about reality.

Damn.

"Just …"

He leaned an inch closer. "*Which one?*"

Valeria moved in, too, whispering against his lips as she kissed him, "*Both.*"

She kissed him hard, and fast, the sharp flavor on his tongue from the rum he'd been nursing earlier blooming across her palate. His fingers drifted between her thighs, his hard lines crowding her to the mirror when he came closer. He stroked her over the line of her lace panties first, making her hips rock into his touch with each soft swipe.

"*There*, yeah? You want me there?" he asked, his lips ghosting over her cheek. "That's what we need to do, Val. Wake up your pussy first, little by little, and then when you're nice and wet from this, I will treat you like a *feast*."

His words, and the way they sounded coming out of his mouth, lit up a fire inside Valeria like she had never felt before. His fingers flamed it as they worked between her thighs, now slipping under the gusset of her panties to stroke her bare flesh and the short-trimmed hair above the hood of her clit.

"Jesus," she breathed.

Chris chuckled. "Wait, it gets better."

She didn't doubt it.

Valeria couldn't imagine *how*.

This was already more than she understood—more than she experienced before. Overwhelmed. Sensitive. Her body became a live wire snapping with every encouraging, tanta-lizing touch.

"I bet you're pussy tastes as hot as you are on my fingers," he told her.

Valeria's head tipped back to the mirror as she dragged in a hard breath. "*Oh, my God*. Keep doing *that*."

He did; his two fingers stroking in and out of her sex before coming up to circle the tight bud of her clit. A rhythmic, perfect beat. Her legs trembled as she lifted them higher out of a deep need to spread herself wider for him.

She bet she was quite a sight.

Spread open.

A man between her thighs whom she had not spoken vows to … even if her husband had broken his vows to her more times than she was aware, and in more ways than she would ever care to count.

Begging like she did.

"*Please, please, please*," she heard herself say.

Although for what she asked for, Valeria didn't know. For the building need to continue, but for it to become *more*. For him to give her it because he *had* to see she needed relief. Or for things she didn't understand.

She would beg for it though.

All of it.

Chris pressed one quick kiss to her trembling lips, his own tugging into a sinfully wicked smirk that had her gulping, before he lowered between her thighs. The beat of his fingers thrusting into her wet pussy before coming back up to rub at her clit stopped.

Only for his tongue to take the place of his fingertips on her clit with a faster, harsher beat than before. Those two fingers in her sex became three, filling her deliciously as his tongue moved back and forth from licking at her clit to lapping at his fingers fucking her and covered in her cum.

She had to watch.

Chris looked like a man enthralled—eating her while he watched her, and his fingers worked her pussy until she teetered on an edge like never before. Valeria hadn't been ready to fall, then, hadn't known what it would be like when it wasn't forced, and she craved it—willing to let a man have her like this.

And then she fell.

Her bliss became a cliff.

She stifled the noises crawling from her throat as the orgasm tore through her core and rippled across all of her nerves. Shouting into the heel of her palm as she watched Chris replace his fingers inside her still-pulsing sex with his tongue to lick her essence right from the source.

Valeria never saw anything hotter.

Never been higher.

Chris caught her when the trembling started in her legs, his tongue drifting from her sex to lap at her inner thigh before he raised up. She didn't even think about it, just seeing his mouth wet with her arousal made her want to taste herself on his lips.

So, she did just that.

Valeria didn't know who this woman was—this person here, doing this with him. This *man* who came into her life without warning, saying things to give her hope, and terrified her to death at the same time.

She had no clue who she became around Christopher Guzzi, but she liked it.

That was a dangerous thing.

CHAPTER 10

"Where did you go off to?" Jorge asked.

Do not look that woman's way, Christopher.

He could feel Valeria's stare burning into his back from across the backyard. She exited through the rear of the home, but he decided it would be smarter if he didn't take the same way back to the party she did.

Better not to play with fire.

Hadn't they already risked a lot?

Chris thought so.

Stuffing his hands in his pockets, Chris came closer to Jorge, making sure his posture was light, and easy. "Fireworks always give me a headache, so I took a walk. Thought it might be nice."

"Ah, yes. They bother the horses, too. You'll make friends with those beasts."

Had he compared Chris to animals?

Well, whatever.

Chris took the clipped cigar Jorge offered him but used his own lighter to get it smoking. Jorge turned his back to Chris for the moment, watching the men who had gathered in a slight circle, and the two in the middle who were sharing punches. A bareknuckle match, it looked like.

Another time or place, and Chris might have joined in just because. Not here, though, and not with these men. These people weren't his family or friends, and he could not afford to forget that fact.

This job was already dangerous before he came here and got stuck in his head about a woman he needed to get the fuck out of this place. Now, he couldn't get her out of his head, and that made it worse.

Emotional attachments were bad.

Even if they felt good.

Speaking of which ...

Chris could still feel Valeria's stare on him, and with Jorge's back turned, it allowed him to check her way. Sure enough, she watched him from her position on the porch, looking no better or worse than she had before their little encounter in the house. Frankly, looking at her wasn't any good for his side of things, either.

The woman was a siren.

She called to him.

He didn't know what to do with that.

Knowing he should turn his stare away from her before someone noticed his attention, he gave Valeria a quick nod, and looked away. It was all he could do although he wished he didn't have to do that at all.

She needed someone to care. That much was painfully obvious with her. The woman was strong as hell, no doubt about it. Look at all she had gone through and was still dealing with regularly. No one could ever say she hadn't done all she could and still held her head high while she did it.

Simple as that.

Valeria was still human though. And very much a woman. Her mind, heart, and soul needed things, whether she craved it or it felt good. Affection, *touch* ... attention. All of it, those were basic human needs. He knew she wasn't getting those things from the man they forced her to marry, and he wasn't sure what to do with the fact he wanted to give it to her instead.

Yeah.

This was a mess.

A dangerous one.

"What's next, hmm?" Chris asked Jorge.

He needed to get his thoughts away from Valeria, what had happened in the house, and how he felt about her. If not, someone would notice his distraction, and he doubted it would take them long to put two and two together to make four.

No one needed that.

"For what?" Jorge replied over his shoulder.

"Me being here—what do I get to see next?"

Jorge turned, giving Chris a smile as he did so. "The tunnels, I think. There's a good chance part of your father's run will go through the tunnels, especially if ports of entry are too hot, or we can't take it across an unwatched part of the border for whatever reason. The easiest way for me to show you the tunnels is to take you to one we don't use a lot but was also one of the first ones my father ever had built."

Huh.

"And when are we doing that?"

"A few days, likely," Jorge replied, shrugging.

"Not sooner?"

"You forget that you are here on my time." Jorge turned back to the fighting men, the bonfire glowing bright with flickering flames a few feet away from their position. "Which means, I also have work to do, and so I will deal with you and what your father wants when I have time to do it, Christopher."

"I prefer Chris."

"I don't care."

Yeah, he was aware.

Clearly.

He left the conversation alone if only because he didn't think it would get him anywhere to keep needling Jorge about it. He lost any chance at civility with the man the first night they met when Jorge felt Chris had overstepped his bounds with his wife, anyway, and he doubted it would get better now.

Not that he gave a fuck.

He wasn't here to make friends with Jorge.

Chris was getting antsy even though this job could take a while to complete. He hadn't expected to be in Mexico for any more than two weeks, maybe three, at the most. Already, he had been here for two, and he didn't see an end in sight. He didn't have a way to get Valeria the hell out of here, but might those tunnels help his plan along?

Who knew?

His bigger problem was what would happen if the ruse ran its course, he had to leave, and he still didn't have a way out for Valeria? What the fuck was he going to do?

"I think you'll like the tunnels," Jorge said absently.

Chris looked Valeria's way again. Now, she wasn't looking at him. That was okay, he only needed to see her. If she was okay that's what he wanted to know. The rest, he would deal with as he could, or should.

What else could he do?

"I look forward to it," Chris replied.

The bay window of the small living room in the house Chris was using on the Lòpez ranch during his stay allowed him a good view of the rest of the houses on the property, and all the walkways connecting them. It was a nice, practical design, if someone admired that sort of thing, but mostly, he felt the need to imprint it to memory.

If something happened, he would need to know *all the* things about this place. Should something cause chaos, and it was his only chance to get Valeria and Maria out, then he wanted to walk it with his fucking eyes closed.

No questions asked.

That was why, every single morning, he took an hour-long jog around the property. He went out, took pathways, and sometimes didn't, and then came back to his house again. To the guards, or the family, it looked like nothing was amiss. He was focusing on his fitness, and little else.

That was fine.

It's what he wanted them to think.

The ring of a cell phone took Chris's attention away from the window, and the scenery outside. He didn't bother to check the caller ID when he reached for the phone on the coffee table behind him, simply picked it up and answered it, thinking it would be his father, or twin.

Although, Corrado had been careful not to call since Chris was here. So was his brother's way—always erring on the side of caution, rather than unpredictability. It was something he appreciated about his twin.

"Chris here," he murmured into the phone, going back to the window.

The voice on the other end of the call was not who he expected, and it put him on edge. "Chris, it's Andino."

"Why?"

"Excuse me?"

"Why are you calling me?"

Andino chuckled. "For an update to give to my wife, who

asks about her missing friend nonstop, that's why. Good enough answer for you, or no?"

Well …

Chris sighed. "You shouldn't be calling me, it's risky. You have no idea what I am doing here at any given time, and I usually have someone nearby. What if they saw the name on the phone, or heard me say your name? The Lòpez family are aware Valeria was with your new wife before they grabbed her again, and you want to play that kind of game?"

"I don't want to, no, but your father didn't have news. He thought a call to you—"

"Don't do this again."

Andino cleared his throat. "All right, noted. What can you tell me if you're able I mean? Do you have a plan to get the woman and her child out of there?"

"It's complicated."

"How so?"

"She's incredibly isolated away from the public," Chris said, "for fucking starters. Their compound in the middle of nowhere—yeah, that's where he keeps her. And when she may leave, he has a small army to keep her in line. She's not treated well here, but she keeps up a good façade. As of now, she knows why I am here, but I don't think she trusts me yet, which is a problem."

"Hmm."

"What was that noise for?"

"Sounds like you should figure out a way to make her trust you, doesn't it?"

"Thanks for the memo. Let me jot it down."

Andino grunted. "You and your twin … you are both a lot alike, yes?"

"We are *twins*. Identical in many ways."

In fact, he and his twin were different, too. The most

obvious being the way they lived their lives, things they enjoyed, and what they wanted for their future. On the surface, to people who didn't know them well—like Andino —the twins seemed more similar than opposite. All people saw first were the things that made Chris and Corrado the same, but they missed the more important bits.

The shit that made them unique.

"And what does my twin have to do with this?" Chris asked.

"I find him as equally bothersome as you."

"Sounds like an issue you should handle, no?"

Andino made another one of those annoyed noises. "Back to Valeria, and her daughter, if you wouldn't mind. I suspect you don't have all day to chat."

Right.

"The situation here is not as easy as I hoped it would be, and I don't have a clear path forward yet. When I do, however, you will be one of the first ones I tell. Also, have you considered what comes *after*?"

"I beg your pardon?"

"Jorge Lòpez came after her once when she ran, Andino," Chris intoned, wanting the man to hear every single word, "and chances are, when we get her out of here this time, he will hunt her down again. For as horribly as he seems to treat her, he's obsessed with keeping her at all costs. What then, huh?"

"We'll make sure he *can't* come after her."

"How?"

Because his focus was getting Valeria and Maria *out*. Nothing more, and nothing less. If he added the hit of a cartel leader onto this job, then they would have a hell of a lot more problems than they could handle.

Did he need to spell it out?

"We'll figure it out," Andino was quick to mutter.

Chris rolled his eyes. "Sure, sure."

He didn't like *what ifs*.

He hated unanswered questions.

Flying by the seat of his pants?

No fucking thanks.

He would have to roll with it whether he wanted to or not.
Great.

Out of the corner of his eye, he noticed a man stepping out of the house on the far left to his that the guards used. One of several. The man headed toward Chris's home, which meant his day was about to get started. For the last few days, the focus had been on transferring crates of product out of the barns, and onto trucks, all the while, they prepped for the trip to the tunnels this weekend.

It never stopped here, it seemed.

"I have to go," Chris told Andino, "and don't call again."

"I got it—get the job done, yeah?"

"Yeah."

That was the plan.

As unknown as it was.

"Right here, *amigo*," the Lòpez man said, pulling the back of a Jeep wide open for Chris. "Toss that bag in, we're just waiting on the boss, and his wife."

Chris nodded, pleased that Valeria was coming along for the weekend trip. He knew better than to show that on his face, however. "Thanks."

With his weekend bag thrown in the back of the Jeep on top of the other couple of bags piled there, the man closed the hatch with a slam. Chris settled on leaning against the back of the vehicle while the guard—or driver, whatever his desig-nated job was for the day—headed for the house closest to them.

It was funny in that the only vehicles Chris had seen come this far into the ranch were all ones the guards and Jorge used to come in and out. Even the man's siblings weren't allowed to take a vehicle in and out of the place.

He filed that information away for later.

Vehicles were a no-go.

The slam of a screen door had Chris pushing off the side of the Jeep to look around the side of the vehicle. Jorge stood on the porch with Valeria where the two talked fast. She tried to remain calm and pleasant. It didn't matter; her husband was animated and irritated enough for the both of them.

Chris's irritation picked up a notch.

The more he observed the two together, the clearer it became to him that Valeria was neither happy with Jorge, nor safe. She carefully measured her behavior, and words. Even if she hadn't told him the truth when he asked, it wouldn't take a genius to figure out that marriage was a steaming pile of shit.

It didn't help he had somehow got into his feelings about Valeria, and whenever he saw her being dismissed or mistreated by the bastard she called a husband ... it took everything in him not to kill Jorge right then and there with his bare hands.

Chris's gaze slipped past the two on the porch to the little girl peering out the screen door, watching her parents' quiet argument. Well, it was only quiet from Valeria's side of things. Jorge didn't seem to give a shit, to be honest.

Maria saw Chris looking her way, and the worry on her features morphed into a bright smile. She waved, and he returned the gesture with a wink. For whatever reason, the girl slipped out of the screen door, and headed past her parents. They didn't even note her leaving the house or coming down the stairs.

Maria came to stand in front of him. Chris kneeled to the ground to be closer to eye-level with her, uncaring that he was dirtying the knees of his slacks. He always thought it ignorant for adults to loom above kids when they talked to them. How would they like it to have someone much larger than them hanging overtop of them while they talked?

Not well, he bet.

"Hey," he said.

Maria beamed. "*Hey*. I made you something."

Chris blinked. "Did you?"

"Yes." Digging in the pocket of her dress, she added, "We're friends, right? Friends make promises, and you made me a promise."

Kids, man.

They had a way of simplifying everything. Of taking any kind of gesture and turning it into something *more*, innocent or otherwise. It reminded him of the good in the world when he was surrounded by things others might consider immoral, or even evil, sometimes.

"We are friends."

Maria glanced up at him, her hand stilling in its quest to find whatever item she wanted in her pocket. "*Best* friends? Like Mamá and me?"

Chris grinned. "We can be, Maria. But you didn't have to make me anything to be that, okay? Friends are just friends because they want to be—we don't have to give anything to our friends to keep them. Just our kindness, and the goodness in our hearts, huh? That's what counts."

She shrugged tiny shoulders. "But I *wanted* to. You'll wear it, won't you?"

"Wear what?"

She found the item she had been searching for. Pulling it from her pocket, she held it high for him to admire. A woven bracelet made from a dark, thin leather cord. She smiled, her eyes glimmering with pride as he stared at it.

"That's amazing," he said.

"Aunt Abril showed me how to braid it. Do you like it?"

Chris took the bracelet and held it flat in his palm. "So much, thank you."

"Put it on!"

He laughed but did as she said. It was a little too loose, but she showed him how to pull on one of the two end cords to tighten it firm to his wrist.

"It shouldn't get wet," she said.

"Okay, I'll make sure it doesn't."

"But you'll wear it always, anyway, right?"

Her genuine request had his chest tightening.

Chris nodded. "Absolutely. *Always*. I won't take it off."

"Good."

Maria darted forward, and gave him a tight hug, her little arms snaking around his neck so hard, he almost lost his breath. He didn't get the chance to hug her back before she stepped away from him and turned to dart back to the house.

She didn't get far.

Valeria stood two feet behind her daughter, now, surveying the scene with a soft gaze. She gave them a small smile, and then said to Maria, "Better get back in the house. Jorge forgot something and had to go back in to get it. We don't want him getting angry that you didn't listen when he told you to stay inside, right?"

Maria peeked over her shoulder at Chris, but turned back to her mother. "Okay, Mamá."

"I'll see you soon. Love you. *Behave*."

"I will."

Once Maria had disappeared back inside the house, Chris stood up straight again. Valeria climbed into the back of the Jeep without a word.

He followed her lead.

∼

Whenever he saw a Jeep in Toronto, Chris always wondered what in the fuck their purpose was for their owner. They almost always had mud on the tires, too. Where in the hell had they even found mud in a city?

Now, driving in a Jeep as Jorge's driver took a sharp turn onto a dirt road that took their vehicle down a winding path, deeper into a forested area with little population, Chris understood the appeal. The Jeep handled the terrain just fine, and with the doors and top pulled off, the wind kept them cool.

Beside him in the back, Valeria sat quiet and still, her gaze drawn to the blur of trees at their sides, instead of Chris. He would much rather have her gaze on him, but that was perilous territory that neither of them needed to play in at the moment.

Especially not with her husband sitting in the front.

"Have they caught up?" Jorge asked, his laughter disappearing into the wind.

Chris peered over his shoulder, seeing the front of another Jeep coming over the hill behind them as they reached the end. "Almost."

"Ah, have to make this fun for them. It's a long drive, *amigo*."

Apparently.

They had been driving for two hours now.

"You will enjoy this tunnel we'll show you," Jorge

explained, his attention going back to the dirt road ahead of them. "My father had the tunnel built in first, but when the authorities became suspicious over the activity out this way, he had a permit made for a house."

Chris blinked. "A house?"

Jorge smirked over his shoulder. "Yes."

Valeria sighed beside Chris, as though she had heard this story a million and one times before. If Jorge took note of her annoyance, he said nothing. The sunhat in her lap hid the clenching of her fists from her husband's view, but Chris saw the action given she had to hold on to the item to keep it from flying away.

Was there something else on her mind?

Something other than her husband's conversation?

"And so," Jorge continued, his voice bringing Chris back to the present, although he didn't think he had missed much from the conversation, "my father had the tunnels built into the basement. Or rather, he built the home *around* the tunnel with no one any wiser. They simply assumed the work we had been doing before was us digging the basement out of the rock and then pouring cement. Brilliant, hmm?"

"Smart, yes," Chris agreed. "And they have never found the tunnel."

"Once, almost. We had to dynamite a connecting tunnel when aerial surveillance found the entrance, and we didn't want it leading back to the house a few miles away. The vacation home tunnel is still the closest one we have to the border, and while we don't use it as much as we used to, well …"

"It's good to have."

"Just in case," Jorge said, nodding.

The man's attention went back to the road ahead of them, but he continued talking. Chris had no interest in a lot of things Jorge had to say, but he listened because the man gave details that sometimes helped him along here in this plan to get Valeria and her daughter out.

"I brought Val along for the weekend," Jorge said, even though no one had asked, "because it's good for her to get out of the house, and she needs a break occasionally. Isn't that right, *hermosa*?"

Valeria's jaw tensed, but she forced a smile—a fake one —on her face when she turned to nod at Chris. "*Sí*, that's what they told me."

Told, he noted.

Not *wanted*.

"And our daughter gets to stay at home with the nanny, to keep her out of trouble," Jorge added after a moment.

Chris kept an eye on Valeria out of the corner of his eye, and that's how he witnessed the flash of sadness and worry that passed over her features before she hid it by looking away. That was it, then. Not Jorge's story, or the fact Chris sat beside her in the backseat.

Had Jorge *made* Maria stay home?

Was this purposeful beyond what the man said?

Chris wouldn't put it past him.

"Almost there," Jorge said. "Another twenty minutes, or so. The men I sent ahead of us will already have the generators up and running. This will be a good weekend away for us all, even if you are here for the tunnels, Chris. We all need a break, no?"

"A break is good for the soul," Chris replied.

His attention was still on Valeria though.

Reaching over, he placed his hand on her jean-covered thigh. She tensed from the sudden touch and then relax. He swept his thumb over the denim, her shiver reverberating through her body, and into his palm.

Something else he shouldn't be doing.

Still, he wanted her to be aware.
It would be okay.
It would.
He would make sure.
Even if it killed him.

CHAPTER 11

The vacation home, as Jorge dubbed it, sat tucked away in isolation, as much as their ranch did. Perhaps, more so. Dry, desert land surrounded the ostentatious house from all directions, with no neighbor or civilization in sight.

Valeria had never understood the draw of the vacation home—could it really be that when it was in the same country as their usual home? It was the same size as her father-in-law's mansion, except out in the middle of nowhere, and without power unless all six generators were running, which caused a racket when one was trying to sleep.

Besides that, the house was just … *big*. Three levels, reaching toward the sky, a separate wing for whatever men Jorge brought along, and the servants that kept the house running when no one was around to live within its walls. There was no guest house like the ones at the ranch. That meant *everyone* would sleep in the same house, walking the same halls, and eating at the same table all weekend.

Didn't that sound fun?

Valeria thought not.

A large pool in the back stretched across dry land, and while landscapers had come out to decorate, Valeria still felt the place was ugly, and lonely. Or maybe that was the projection because of her own emotions, and current situation. She couldn't be sure, but she didn't like it here.

Valeria walked through the home—watching servants

scatter into the closest room whenever they heard Jorge's boots coming down the hallway—at her husband's side while he gave Chris a tour. She had other things to do, like hide away in her room, and go back to her daughter at the end of the weekend.

Jorge made it clear this weekend was nonnegotiable for her. Valeria was coming along whether she wanted to, and Maria wouldn't. Simple as that. It put her on edge to think of her daughter alone with that *nanny* all weekend.

Although, she knew Maria was also safe because nothing would save the woman from Jorge—certainly not his affection for her—if she thought to put her hands on their child. That didn't mean she liked her daughter spending more time with Carla than was necessary. Not that she cared to explain it to Jorge because this was just another way for the bastard to keep Valeria in line.

"And now," Jorge said, taking the stairs leading into the basement slowly as they sloped sharply, "the tunnel."

The keys in Jorge's hand jangled with every step he took. Valeria had to walk carefully in her heels, more so than the man in front of her. Jorge didn't notice, or if he did, then he didn't care. A hand came to rest on Valeria's back, and while it shocked her, her body only relaxed from the soft touch.

Chris.

His hand on her back let her know she was safe, and if she missed a step, then he would be right there to catch her. For whatever reason, and she blamed poor planning, they situated the light switch at the bottom of the stairs. She had seen the tunnel before, so there wasn't very much about this tour that was new or amazing to her.

Jorge flicked the light on, illuminating a stark, white hallway that led to a set of double steel doors at the end, a good twenty feet away.

"There's nothing else down here?" Chris asked.

Jorge waved a hand for them to stay where they were at the bottom of the stairs as he headed for the doors at the end. "Cement in this section. We filled the rest of the space in because we didn't need it. The basement is finished and furnished in other areas—bedrooms, and whatever else. Some storage, too."

Chris shot Valeria a look, but for what, she didn't know. So, she shrugged as a non-response. He didn't seem to mind.

Using the keys he'd brought along, Jorge unlocked the metal doors at the end of the corridor. It took an effort for him to pull the doors open to showcase what rested behind. Once he did, Jorge stepped back with a smile and a nod at the dank-smelling, dark tunnel the metal doors kept hidden.

Chris made a noise under his breath. "How is it ventilated?"

"A couple of different ways." Jorge shrugged. "A few pipes here and there that come out of the ground, and when someone is working in the tunnels, we force air through them."

"And this is the closest one to the American border?"

"We're still quite a ways away, but *sí*." Jorge gestured at the dark hole, asking, "Care to inspect?"

"Not particularly."

That earned a chuckle out of Jorge.

"Don't blame you, *amigo*. I won't go inside them, either."

"I take it this isn't where I will sleep for the weekend," Chris said, his attempt at a joke flying way over Jorge's head when the man gave him a pensive look at the other end of the hall. "I'd like to relax. It was a long drive."

Jorge nodded. "One of my men will show you which rooms you can use for the weekend. Find one and ask."

"Thank you."

Chris gave Valeria a quick smile, but didn't linger. If Jorge witnessed the exchange between the two, he didn't say. The receding footsteps echoed up the stairwell until a door opened and clicked shut. By the time she turned around to wait for Jorge to lock the doors back up, he was already down the hall and coming her way.

The doors at the end?

Closed.

That was how distracted Valeria became whenever Chris was in the picture. She knew, without a doubt, that wasn't a good thing for either of them. It would likely get them both in a world of trouble.

It scared her to death.

Jorge, though?

He terrified her more.

"I would like to call Maria," she told him, "once we're settled in."

Her husband chuckled, his arm coming to snake around her waist. To someone else, that hold might seem affectionate, but to her … it felt like another kind of prison. One she would never escape.

"No," he said.

"But—"

"Maria is fine where she is for the weekend, Val."

"I want to tell her goodnight, and to be a good girl while we're away."

When she couldn't get what she wanted from being honest, then she had to try another route. What she really wanted to do was make sure her daughter was being treated fairly by that bitch he forced her to leave Maria with.

"Come on," Jorge said, his arm tugging her up the stairs with him, "let's get settled in, and have something made to eat. I am starved."

"And then I can call Maria?"

"No."

"Jorge—"

In the stairwell, Valeria found herself slammed into the wall. Her spine ached from the force of her husband shoving her before he was quick to crowd her with his presence. She stared into his cold, dark eyes as his lips pulled down into a scowl that would rival the devil's. It frightened her, sure, but she refused to show it.

"You're too close to her, I think."

Valeria sucked in a sharp breath. "She's my child. I raised her."

"Yes, *without* me. Because what did you do, hmm?"

She refused to entertain *that* conversation. It always ended the same way, and that wasn't a game she wanted to play with this man today. One person lost every single time —*her*. That loss came in the form of a sore body, and bruises she needed to be creative to hide. She wasn't in the mood for it.

Her silence was not what he wanted though.

Jorge leaned in close, baring his teeth as he spoke in a hissed tone. "You spend *far* too much time filling that girl's head full of shit about me, Valeria."

"I do not."

On that, she wouldn't budge.

Valeria never told Maria anything bad about her father. Why would she when she didn't need to? Jorge poisoned his daughter against him all on his own, and with little to no effort on her part. If he couldn't see that, then how was that her problem?

"I think it would do her—and *you*—good to spend time apart."

"What does that mean?"

Jorge smiled. "Behave this weekend, Val, or she won't be there when you get home. The tutoring works well enough for her, doesn't it? I can't say how long that'll last, and there are quite a few private schools she can attend instead. Ones that will keep her away for weeks at a time. Do you hear me?"

Valeria swallowed the lump in her throat and nodded. "I hear you."

"Make sure."

The crack of a gunshot slicing through the air had Valeria jerking on the spot. She glanced upward in just enough time to see a skeet fly into the air by a mechanical arm before it exploded into shards of ruined ceramic. This little game of Jorge's and his men was now getting tiring, but she knew better than to go out there and tell him to knock it off.

Not that it mattered.

The sky was darkening as Valeria could see from her position on the bench seat at the large bay window in the sitting room. Soon, they would drink—let's be honest, they already had—and that would take importance over playing stupid shooting games with their rifles.

"You seem annoyed."

Valeria gave a look over her shoulder, and a small smile when her sister-in-law joined her at the window. "Decided to come along, did you?"

Abril waved a dainty hand. "Someone needs to keep you company, no?"

"Oh, was that it?"

"I had nothing better to do back at the ranch."

"Did you see Maria with—"

Abril's smile grew cold in an instant. "Carla knows what will happen to her should she step out of line with my niece."

Of course.

No question, Abril *was* just like her brothers. They didn't realize it, which was their mistake, Valeria supposed.

The raucous laughter from outside drew their attention to the window again. Valeria didn't wonder for long what had caused the men's uproar when she found her husband pawing at a woman while he stuck his tongue down her throat.

Valeria blinked.

The woman, wearing a gray dress with white buttons down the front, was a servant at the house. She couldn't be any older than twenty, if that, but she didn't seem to have a problem with the way Jorge groped her in front of a crowd of men while he licked the goddamn taste right out of her mouth.

She made a noise in the back of her throat, unsure of how she felt about the entire scene happening outside. Annoyed, maybe, but only because if the woman was bothered by the attention, she was far better at hiding it than Valeria.

"Better her than you tonight," Abril murmured beside her.

"That's cold, don't you think?"

Abril sighed. "I have learned that we all have to sacrifice to survive in this world, Val. And that means sometimes, thinking about yourself and what is best for you, even if that means someone else must hurt for it. You have too caring of a heart—you worry too much about people who wouldn't give a damn about you, and that's why you're an easy target for him, and whoever else wants to break your back on the way to the top."

Ouch.

That stung.

Abril wasn't wrong though.

"It's bad I care?" she asked quietly.

"It's bad you care so much, you would sacrifice yourself for someone else, yes. Women like us that's not how we make it in our life."

"Abril?"

"Hmm?"

Valeria glanced at her sister-in-law from the side, weighing her next words because she didn't want to offend the one person from her husband's family who gave a shit, and looked out for her. Then again, Abril had always appreciated Valeria's honesty, so she chose to say was on her mind.

"I don't want to be like you," Valeria whispered, "I'm *not* like you, or them. I never was."

Abril cleared her throat, her gaze drawing down to the ledge of the bench seat where Valeria sat, and she stood next to her. "I know, which is why I never understood his obsession with keeping you when you didn't fit him."

"I'm a trophy. Something he won. Nothing else."

"Shame, that."

Valeria let out a hard exhale and put her attention on the scene outside. "He told me earlier that if I didn't behave, Maria wouldn't be there when I returned home."

Abril made a dismissive noise. "He wouldn't bother. That's too much energy to spend for a *girl*, Val. And that's all she is to him, a girl. What he wants more is a boy, and so if he can keep you in your place long enough to get what he wants from you, then that's what he'll do. Even if it means using her, and your fears about her, to get it."

She swallowed hard.

Abril didn't miss it.

"What?"

"He will not get that boy," Valeria muttered.

"That's not how sex works, is it?"

"IUD, two years ago. A *just in case*. I have another four years before it must be replaced."

Abril whistled low. "Do *not* let him find out about that."

Yeah.

Valeria got it.

"But for her—Maria—he doesn't care," Abril said, "and if you were a smart woman, you would use that to your advantage more than you do."

"I don't understand."

"Because you're not like me, right?"

Valeria gave her a glance.

Abril cocked her brow. "Not a lie."

"Not a lie," she echoed. "What do you mean, though?"

"If he's willing to use her to manipulate you into *behaving*, then use her as a way to make him believe you're willing *to* behave."

Valeria blinked. "Do you mean—"

"He's a man, Val, and not a complex one to begin with. Should he think letting you have her and do what you want with her will make you react and behave better than his way, which do you think he'll use?"

Huh.

At the dawning realization in Valeria's eyes, Abril smirked.

"Keep it in mind." With that said, Abril turned to leave, but not before saying, "It's rude to spy. Or hasn't anyone told you that, yet?"

Valeria's head snapped sideways at Abril's chiding only to find the reason for it leaning in the sitting room's doorway room like he didn't have a care in the world. Chris shrugged when Abril strolled on past him, but his attention turned on her once Abril left.

Sadness.

That's what she found in his gaze.

How long had he been listening?

What did it matter?

Valeria avoided going to bed, but as the house grew quiet and the sky blackened but for the moon and stars, she no longer had a choice except to go to her room. It was always easier when she went willingly rather than Jorge needing to come and find her to drag her to bed.

The bedroom was empty and dark when she made her way upstairs, but she wasn't mad about it. At least, it gave her a few more minutes to be alone with her thoughts, and *without* her husband.

Everything was always easier without him.

Valeria also learned what she had to do to make her experience in bed with Jorge less traumatic and painful. As long as she seemed submissive, and unwilling to fight, even if every piece of her *wished* she didn't have to be there, doing what he forced her to do, then she walked away from nights with her husband in the morning less sore, and with fewer bruises.

Sad as that was.

So, Valeria readied for her night, sick to her stomach the entire time. Undressing from her day clothes, and slipping into something more appropriate for nighttime, and moved on to set out her clothes for the next day, the minutes ticked by.

Jorge still didn't come upstairs.

The longer she waited, the more nervous Valeria became sitting on the edge of the bed. There, she had a full view of the door, and what kind of monster might come through it.

Jorge had been in a mood all day, and that was going to

translate into the man who entered the bedroom. She much preferred to be ready to deal with it right away instead of being surprised by it.

Valeria had time to consider her life during moments like these, and everything that happened until this point. All the choices she made, and the things she might have done differently so that this wasn't where she ended up night after night.

She didn't want to blame herself.

Easier said than done.

Sighing at the sounds of footsteps in the hallway, approaching the bedroom, Valeria glanced down at the clenched hands in her lap. Her fingernails manicured to perfection because that's what her husband liked, but she was more concerned with the stiffness in her hands that reflected in the rest of her body.

She willed it to calm.

To relax.

It didn't work—it never did.

The doorknob jiggled, before it turned, and the door pushed open. For the split second she took to peek up, ready to deal with yet another nightmare in her daily life … only for her to freeze on the bed at the man who slipped into the room.

It wasn't Jorge at all.

"Chris."

CHAPTER 12

Valeria's shock at seeing Chris slip into her room only lasted long enough for him to close the door before she shot up off the bed like a bullet coming out of a gun. Her hands were already up, palms facing him as she came toward him, reading to push him back.

"You can't be in here," she hissed, "you *can't*—he'll be up any minute. You have to go!"

"Val—"

"Get out. This isn't funny anymore, Chris!"

"*Valeria.*"

She wasn't hearing him at all. Her hands hit his chest, and with all her might, she pushed him back toward the door. Or rather, she *tried*. Chris was a wall, tough as fucking brick, and unmovable. That didn't mean she wasn't willing to give her all, which he had to appreciate either way, as cute as it was.

Cute.

Yeah, that wasn't the right word.

Chris had seen Valeria go through a gamut of emotions and situations since his arrival in Mexico. He'd seen her sweet and loving with her child. Sad and scared with her husband. Indifferent when no one thought she was looking, and she was alone with her thoughts. The woman was a spectrum of feelings—never settling on one thing for too long before she had to put on yet another mask to satisfy her husband, and whatever he was demanding of her for the moment.

But anger?

He'd never seen her with that.

Until now.

Chris had to admit, she looked damn good angry. A red flush colored her golden-brown skin and brightened her eyes more than they already were. Sure, that beautiful smile he loved faded, but that didn't change his desire to kiss those full, sexy lips of hers at all.

Not in the slightest.

"Do you know what he'll do to me?" Valeria demanded.

Her hands came up to shove against him again, but Chris was quick to grab her wrists that time. Locking her in place with his fingers like bars around her wrists, he dragged her into his chest without warning, and tipped his head down to press a fast kiss to her lips.

He had control.

Always.

Chris was the one who, in the middle of chaos, would be as calm as the eye of a storm. No matter what, he took great pains to ensure that was the case.

Except with her, it seemed.

There was something about Valeria, something in her soul, he thought, that called out to him, and shredded any sense of self-preservation or restraint he had left. He swore that he could sense her sadness and loneliness from across a crowded room, and he hated that. This woman should never feel those things—*ever*.

The second his mouth touched to hers, Valeria answered him back. She kissed him hard, her lips moving against his in a way that seemed familiar although it couldn't be—he had barely touched this woman, and yet, a part of him felt like he had known her for his entire life.

How was that possible?

It was *crazy*.

Chris let Valeria's wrists go just so he could cup her jaw and draw her even closer to him as his tongue teased the seam of her lips. He wanted *in*—wanted to taste her, and if that meant handing over his soul to this woman to get what he wanted, then *fine*.

So fucking be it.

Their tongues clashed, a war in a kiss, if that were possible. Her fingers found the neckline of his shirt, curling tight, and holding close. She seemed determined to lick the taste of him right from his mouth with her kiss, and as much as he liked that, he still needed to talk to her.

As he was learning, there were few times when he could get Valeria alone like this—she was so protected, so *sheltered*. Someone was almost always around to keep an eye on her, and that put Chris in a bad position when he needed as much time with this woman as he could get.

And *not* just for this.

Not for moments like these, even though he needed them, too. No, because this plan—which he hadn't even figured out yet—would not work unless she trusted him. Inexplicably, and *completely*. This woman needed to trust him.

"Shhh," he whispered against the seam of Valeria's lips when he pulled away, and she opened her mouth to speak. "Just relax, yeah?"

Valeria let out a shaky breath, her dark eyes darting up to his. "Kind of hard, so excuse me."

He grinned crookedly, a thumb sweeping the line of her jaw. There was something silky about her skin—warm and *inviting*. She had to feel the hard ridge of his erection pressing against her body tucked into his, but she said nothing about it. That was the proof, though, about just how much this woman affected him, even if he didn't understand why.

All it took was kissing her.

Stroking her jaw.

And all of him wanted to discover as much as he could about the rest of her. Peel off these thin, soft bed clothes she had put on, lay her back, and *explore*. With his mouth, and his hands, and his cock. Learn how she enjoyed being loved, and the kinds of sounds she would make when he found what she liked the most.

"You shouldn't *be* here," she mumbled, her bottom lip trembling when he dropped a soft kiss to her mouth again. "What are you doing?"

"I shouldn't be, you're right."

He could do the job without *this*. God knew he had no business messing around with a married woman, even if said woman didn't want to be married, or in her current situation. There were vows in life a man didn't need to break, and this was one of those.

The problem for him was that it wasn't the forbidden that drew him back to Valeria, or even the thrill. No, it was simply *her*.

Something about her had him coming back, wanting more, and willing to risk it all.

Was it stupid?

Entirely.

It also might be worth it.

Chris would chance it.

"Jorge took off in one of the Jeeps with a woman," Chris said, still stroking the line of Valeria's jaw with his thumbs as he spoke to keep her calm, "and said he wouldn't be back until morning, likely."

Her gaze drifted away from his. "The servant?"

"Seemed so."

"Hmm."

"Sorry," he said quickly.

Valeria barked out a laugh, her dark stare coming back to his with a fire lingering there. "*Look at me*—in a bedroom with a man who isn't my husband, with his hands on me, and still able to taste him in my mouth. What are you apologizing for?"

"That look in your eyes," Chris responded, "that sadness I wish you didn't feel."

She stiffened, her chin quivered, but just as fast as that threat of her vulnerability came on, it left. Replaced instead by something colder, and stronger. Life had a funny way of doing that to people—of shaping them into a better version of themselves, even if it hurt a lot along the way to get to the end result.

Chris was proof of that.

"There are still people—*guards*—in this house that could get me in trouble for this," she said.

Chris shrugged. "They're busy."

"What does that mean?"

"Seems like when the king is away, the court will play."

Valeria's gaze burned. "He is no king."

"Agreed." Chris sighed, tipping Valeria's head back so he could stare down at her, and enjoy the sight of this woman in his hands for a moment. "You understand, don't you?"

"Understand what, Chris?"

Her words were a whisper.

A caress.

"That you're safe with me, Val—I'm not like him, and I

won't hurt you, or take from you when you don't want to give it to me. I'm not a perfect man, but I am a good one."

"I like to think I do understand that."

Chris smiled. "But?"

"Life has taught me to be wary."

Right.

He would be concerned otherwise.

"But I think I always knew anyway," Valeria said, her tongue snaking out to wet the seam of her lips as she spoke. "You were soft and sweet with my daughter, and I saw it in how you treated me. So, I *do* get it, but—"

"Life," he interjected.

"I have to be careful."

"I want you to be."

"Oh?"

He nodded. "And I also want you to trust me. This can't work otherwise, Val."

She let out a hard breath. "I'm not convinced it will work at all, if I'm being honest."

"Why?"

"You see my life, don't you?" A bitter laugh fell from her lips, and he instantly wanted to kiss it away. Somehow, he refrained, but it was *hard.* "Don't blame me for thinking freedom is a dream I'll never see come true, Chris."

"Except it will, and it starts with tonight."

"What does that mean?"

Chris chuckled. "Well, it means whatever you want. You run this show, sweetheart."

Valeria gave him a sly smile. "Does that mean you'll share all your secrets with me?"

"I don't have many of those, but what do you want to know?"

A quick shake of her head answered his question, and she looked away. "I was kidding, I didn't—"

"I have four siblings—*all* brothers," Chris said. "We're French-Italian Canadians, but only a couple of us can speak fluent French. All of us are fluent in Italian. My twin, well, this job was almost his, but he's ... married isn't the right word, but he needed time off, and so I took the job for him instead."

Valeria's brow lifted. "A *twin*?"

"Identical, too."

"Like ... the same?"

Chris made a noise under his breath. "On the outside, yeah. Corrado. He's always been my best friend, so I have to look out for him, that's all."

"Like taking this job?"

"Yeah, like this. We're one set of two twins, and we have an older brother who was the only singleton of our siblings. My mother was also an identical twin."

"It's a genetic thing, then?"

Chris laughed. "Seems so."

Valeria's smile softened. "And you love them. I can hear it in your voice."

"All of my family," he agreed, "to the ends of the earth and back. I would do anything for them, and they would do the same for me. That's how our parents raised us."

Chris shook his head, thinking about his family, but more specifically, his twin. "I joined The League—an organization that trains assassins—because I didn't want my twin to go it alone. I thought he needed me there to watch his back. That's what my family taught me; no matter what, we look out for each other."

"And did he need you?"

"Not for that, but it didn't change what I felt. It's like this, too, though. I need to *fix* things. It's what I do, it's who I am. All I want to do is fix this for you, to make it better, so you can be happy again. *Safe* again."

"I was happy once."

"When?"

"In New York."

"Not before?"

Valeria sighed. "When I was a girl, too, I guess."

"Were your parents good to you?"

That earned him another smile, but it faded fast. Chris hated that, and wanted to get her smiling again, but she was already talking.

"I was an only child, but my papa and mama spoiled me. We didn't have a lot when I was younger, and my father had grand ideas about all the changes he thought our country needed."

"That's why he went into politics?"

Valeria shrugged one shoulder, her gaze dimming. "I don't know if he thought he would be untouchable because he made it clear his loyalties didn't lie with those who could buy him, but it didn't matter, did it? The cartel got what they wanted when they went after the things that meant the most to him. And what good did it do to him—he's dead, too."

"I'm sorry."

"I ... don't want that to be the lesson my daughter learns."

"She won't because her mother is *better*."

Maybe it was the strength in his tone—the truth ringing out—but Valeria was quick to nod before meeting his gaze again. "I want to be, yeah. Know, no matter what happens here, or how this ends up ... if I am put in a position where I have to leave without my daughter, I won't go. I *can't*."

His hands that had slid down to her waist tightened. "I

would never put you in that position. If it can't be done my way, then we will figure out another way."

"And what is your way?"

Well, that, he hadn't figured out yet. Chris figured now was not the time to say that.

"And he'll kill Maria," Valeria added when Chris stayed silent, "if he even *thinks* I am planning to leave with her. It would mean hurting me, but also teaching me that if he cannot have me, no one can. She doesn't matter to him. She is a pawn for him to use."

"Not for much longer."

"You say that, but—"

"I get that, Val." Chris leaned in, and pressed a featherlight kiss to Valeria's lips as he murmured, "I made a promise to her—and to you, in a way—and I intend to *keep it*. But trust me. Just trust me."

With each graze of his lips against hers, her kisses answered him back. Soft, at first. Tentative, before each one of her kisses became more and more *hungry*. He hadn't intended to come to her room for this, but her demand was a loud echo—despite their silence—as her hands grabbed at his shirt with enough force to pull the buttons from the loops.

Chris didn't need to stop and ask Valeria if this was what she wanted with him, or if she was just reacting from her high emotions. This woman had been gaslighted and abused enough in her one relationship—he hadn't forgotten what she told him that first time she let him touch her, after all—that she didn't need another man to make her wonder if he was underhandedly second-guessing her.

She was a woman.

Capable of attraction, lust, and desire.

If she wanted to *fuck*, then that's what she would do. He

was more than happy to give her whatever she wanted because that meant he was fucking her.

It was a win-win, really.

"I … I want you," Valeria mumbled against his mouth, her voice a needy whine that had his cock hardening, "*please.*"

"Abso-fucking-lutely," he told her in a groan.

He pulled the six-pack of condoms he had bought for this trip to keep on him as a *just in case* from the back of his slacks, tossing them to the bed while kissing Valeria with enough force to have her walking backward. She only stopped when the backs of her knees hit the edge of the bed.

He'd never seen someone be as graceful or *sexy* as she was undressing him one piece of clothing at a time. Her intent, as heady as her determination, had Chris checking his more dominant nature to be the one to control during sex.

And then, as she pushed his boxer-briefs down his hips, the last stich of clothing on him, she stilled when his hard cock jerked out in her direction. Chris grinned at the color flooding her cheeks—a delicious red, innocent in some ways, and yet that want in her eyes made it seem so fucking sinful, too.

He thought, *a walking complex.*

That's what this woman was.

She was many things.

Alone, or together.

Sinful and innocent.

Harsh, and soft

It amazed him.

And turned him all the way *on.*

"What do you want, huh?" he asked. "You get whatever you want, Valeria, I need you to use your words, and tell me. I'll always give it, if you tell me. So, what is it, babe? I can lay you back on this bed, feast on your pussy, and then fuck you until you can't take it anymore … or I can let you climb on me, and ride until your heart is content. You can bend over this bed, and let me worship your pussy and your ass, or you can—"

"I want to touch you."

Chris audibly swallowed.

Damn.

He didn't mind making this all about her. Regardless of what other men liked to bullshit about when it meant busting a nut during sex, he got off on getting someone *else* off. And yet, to hear her ask to pleasure him almost had his fucking knees buckling.

What was she doing to him?

"Yeah, Val," he murmured, "fucking touch me. Get what you want, woman."

She did, deft fingers curling around his length after he'd stepped out of those boxer-briefs. Light tugs *really* stroked him awake, but it was the way she tightened and loosen her grip with a faster speed that had his head falling back for a moan to drag from his lips.

"You look so good like that."

Her whisper woke up his senses.

Every fucking one.

"All for you," he rumbled.

She did just that, taking her time to tease him into a tight ball of hot need with her hands while she watched him with hooded, lustful eyes. He about fucking died when she leaned in to press a featherlight kiss to the middle of his chest before subsequent touches of her lips lowered with each one.

"Fucking *hell*."

Valeria's light laughter lasted only long enough for her to get the head of his dick in her mouth. And if there was a heaven, it was Christopher watching this woman on her knees for him, learning the way he liked for her to suck his dick, while his hand tangled into her hair, and her gaze locked on him.

"Look at you, huh?" he uttered, jaw clenching from the way her lips kept tightening around the head of his cock when she came back up to the tip. "So fucking pretty on your knees for me. Do you like that, Val, do you want my load down your throat, babe?"

He swore her throat flexed at the head of his dick, an instinctual swallow, that about had him coming. He wasn't a fourteen-year-old boy getting his first pussy here—he would not bust a nut in two minutes—but she sure as fuck made him feel like it.

His hand left her hair long enough to snake in under her jaw. He held her still, his cock still stretching out those pretty lips of hers, as wide eyes looked up at him with the need to please, and *be* pleased.

"Let me fuck you," he whispered.

Valeria released his cock from her mouth, the heat of her breath a contrast to the sensitive skin of his length when she breathed, "Please do."

"God, yes."

It took Chris all of a minute to have her standing naked in front of him after he'd stood her up and pulled every piece of clothing keeping her from him off her body.

Had he mentioned how beautiful she was?

All her lines, and curves.

Hips that spoke of a woman who carried a child, shapely and *sinful*, and a round ass that made him want to take a bite. Golden skin with undertones of red and brown that made his fucking mouth water. That dark hair of hers fell over her shoulders in a wave, still a contrast to her skin, and shiny under the dim lights of the bedroom.

An angel.

Wicked as she was.

"You're beautiful," he told her, "it fucking *hurts*, Val. That's how beautiful you are."

She sucked in a jerky breath, breathing, "Show me. Show me how beautiful."

He said nothing, only moved forward to get Valeria to her back on the bed. His hands slid under her thighs, lifting her legs high and wide as his head dipped between her legs. Oh, he'd spend lots of time eating the juices from her slit later after he'd had her coming on his cock for a while, but right then he wanted her flavor on his tongue.

Chris licked her from her slit to her clit.

One tease.

Then, his lips worked up her body, past her navel, her stomach, and the valley of her breasts. He reached for the condoms he'd tossed aside earlier as he hovered above her, breaking open cardboard to get to the foil packets inside. Valeria panted beneath him, chest rising and falling while he sheathed his cock in latex.

Her hands found her knees, and she pulled her legs up, and open for him as he leaned back, and her head fell to the pillow to give him a beautiful view of her willingly spread out for him. He teased her with his fingers for a moment, enjoying the sight of her moaning into the pillow while her slick arousal coated his hand.

"Feel how fucking wet you are for me?" Chris asked. "I can't wait to get another taste of this after you've been praying to my name."

"*Please ...*"

This sweet woman.

He didn't deny himself, or her, longer.

The sound she made when he worked his cock into her tight pussy was *raw*. So hot, and needy all rolled into one sexy woman. When he seated himself deep inside her walls, Valeria let out a hard breath, those lips of hers a perfect *O* while she stared up at him.

His hand pressing into her lower stomach kept her trembling hips from being able to seek more of him as she tried to move against him. "You like that?"

"Oh, God, so much."

"You want more?"

"*Please*."

He loved how the word slipped from her lips. Airless, and yet so sure. Desperate in her want, but assured in her need.

Chris fucked her slow at first, his hands flattening to her sides to grab tight and pull her into every flex of his hips. And then when she whined, the broken cries she tried to hide muffled into the pillow, he fucked her faster.

A little harder.

Deeper.

Until she trembled, her skin flushed, and her lips a bitten-red from her teeth as she shook through her first orgasm from his dick. And just as fast, before she had even finished shaking through that orgasm, he moved them on the bed.

Him on his back.

Her on top.

"Ride me until you come again," he told her, thrusting his hips up, so she sat deeper onto his cock while her breaths burst out of her chest, "use me like you want to Val, and I'll get what I need, too. Fuck me, woman."

She did.

So damn good, too.

~

As much as Chris didn't want to leave that bedroom, or Valeria's side, he still pushed out of the bed slowly. Once the two had cleaned up, redressed, and he tucked her into his side in the bed, she fell into a deep sleep.

Small blessings, he supposed.

A quick look out the window told him the sky was still dark, and would be for a while. If all went well, the house would be quiet, and the rest of the people would be asleep, or damn close to it. No one would look sideways at him coming down the hallway in the middle of the night, not if they were already drunk, or sleepy.

An easy excuse—he had to use the bathroom.

Who would question it?

Still, Chris didn't want to risk running into anyone at all. One or two incidents he might be able to brush off, but if caught in a compromising position with Valeria, then this whole thing would be over.

That was not a risk he wanted to take.

A check of the clock on the bedside table told him it was three in the morning—lucky he hadn't fallen asleep, too. It would be a long day for him tomorrow with only a couple of hours of sleep, but with Valeria still pressed against him, her taste lingering on his tongue, and the sounds of her bliss echoing in his mind …

Worth it.

This had been worth it.

Leaning over the bed, he tangled his fingers in the stray waves of Valeria's black hair that had fallen over her shoulder. Tucking the strands back, he let his fingertips glide over her delicate shoulder, and down her arm. She slept on, unbothered by his attention, lost in her dreams.

Like this, she was peaceful.

He wanted her to have more of that.

Peace.

Someone who gave a fuck.

He wanted to be that person.

Carefully, he dropped a soft kiss to her shoulder, and the corner of her mouth. He swore he saw her lips quirk into a smile in her dreams, but he couldn't linger any longer than he already had.

"See you soon, sweetheart," he murmured.

Before he found another reason to stay—wasn't the woman sleeping in the bed reason enough?—Chris headed out of the bedroom, checking the hallway first. An empty hall stared back at him, thankfully. He closed the bedroom door behind him without making a sound.

Down the hall though?

Another door *clicked*.

Chris looked that way, but saw nothing.

Someone going back to bed?

God.

He fucking hoped so.

CHAPTER 13

The next morning, Valeria stepped into the large dining room, surprised at how quiet it was considering how many people were staying at the home with them for the weekend. She didn't have to wonder for long what caused the stillness when her gaze landed on the man sitting at the head of the table.

Jorge scowled at the older man who brought his breakfast to him. "Took long enough, don't you think?"

"Sorry, sir. Would you like your coffee—"

"*Now.*"

His voice, slurred and harsh, told the truth. Jorge was hung over, and that *rarely* spelled good things for anyone else in his direct vicinity. The man loved to drink, but hated to deal with the morning after because of it, too.

The only good thing about his hangover?

Jorge barely paid Valeria any mind.

She joined them at the table, willing to ignore she hadn't seen her husband at all the night before, and had no idea when he returned to the home. It meant she spent her entire evening and morning without him, and that wasn't a bad thing.

Not that she had been lonely.

Across the table, Chris worked on buttering a bagel as one servant poured him a cup of coffee. He smiled up at the woman pouring his coffee, nodding. "That's good, thank you. I'll prepare it the way I like it."

"If you're sure ..."

"No worries, I have it."

"Where is my *cream*?"

Jorge's bellow echoed down the table and silenced the rest of the people trying to enjoy their breakfast. A lot of them weren't any better or worse than Jorge if Valeria was to believe what Chris had told her the night before.

He had no reason to lie.

She might have been sorry for them and the headaches they had, but she didn't give a shit. And given her husband was busy snapping at anyone who didn't move fast enough for his liking, or dared to breathe in his direction, she also had better things to do.

Like stare at Chris.

He looked back.

It was insane.

Foolish.

His wink from across the table was enough to make her crazy, and hot all at the same time. God knew she had spent more than enough hours the night before beneath this man, letting him learn all the parts of her body he wanted, and still ... somehow, she wanted more.

Definitely insane.

There was no other explanation for why Valeria seemed willing and ready to get Chris between her thighs as soon as she could. Not when she knew each time was yet one step closer to being caught, which meant the end of her life.

Not that it mattered.

No one noticed her staring.

Or his.

Chris's lips quirked up at the edges, and Valeria had to glance down at the empty plate in front of her because of it. The flood of heat that traveled straight down to her pussy, making her thighs clench under the table as she tried to soothe that sudden ache, was dangerous.

And *addicting*.

She had forgotten what sex should be until Chris. A part of her thought it would never be good again—that she wouldn't *want* for it, or a man, again because of the hell Jorge put her through. She had forgotten about the things she wanted, and *deserved*, because she was too busy trying to survive. Or even, taking care of someone else's needs, like her child. Although, she didn't regret that. Ever.

With little effort at all, Chris reminded her that she was very much a woman with needs, and one who wanted them fulfilled. She should be grateful for that, and she *was* ... but it also scared her.

Everything about this terrified her.

Trust me.

His words rang in her mind.

Valeria wouldn't soon forget them.

She couldn't.

Glancing across the table again, she found Chris tipping his coffee up for a drink. Over the rim of the mug, while everyone else around them was trying to avoid Jorge's morning wrath, Chris watched her with a knowing glint in his eye.

That look said *soon*.

It murmured beautiful things.

It promised, too.

Hope, Valeria realized.

That's what she was feeling in those moments—*hope*. As traitorous as it was, and as destructive as it might be. Because what might happen, she wondered, if she did get that freedom Chris promised her.

What would happen with him?

With her?

For her child?

She had never dared to hope before.

Now, it was all she felt.

Because of him.

"But have you explained to Papá what you're planning yet?"

"Why, so he can ruin the Canadian deal?"

"Jorge—"

"Samuel, I told you how this will work. Didn't I?"

The Spanish between the Lòpez brothers flowed fast, and while Valeria was fluent, her years away from Mexico and not needing to speak her mother tongue sometimes made it difficult for her to follow along when two or more people spoke quickly. Her steps slowed coming down the stairs of their ranch home, so she could focus on *just* the conversation happening between Jorge and his brother in the kitchen.

"He's already planned Abril's wedding to Roberto García," Samuel said, a sigh following his words. "If you think by ruining this arrangement, he's made with our rivals will only piss them off, then you are mistaken, brother."

"Have you considered that's what I want?"

"Excuse me?"

Jorge let out a bitter laugh. Valeria shivered. Her husband was a lot of things, and a bastard was at the top of the list. He didn't care who he had to hurt on his way to the top as long as that's where he landed at the end of it all.

His family?

People he should care for?

Those he proclaimed to love?

Fodder.

That's all they were to him.

Things to use.

"That's what I want, Samuel," Jorge said, his tone thick with pleasure at his plan coming together. "*Finally*, this will be the message I need to send for it to be clear where Papá and I stand—he is no longer running this organization. *I am.*"

"You're looking for a problem, then."

Valeria knew better than to spy, and yet, she stayed right where she was. Sometimes, eavesdropping was the only way she got any information. No one ever thought to inform her because what did it matter? She was a woman, nothing more. Jorge's wife—his *thing* to do with what he wanted, whether anyone cared what happened to her.

A part of her figured she needed to listen to Abril more and take the woman's advice. If she planned to make it out of here alive, then she would use everything to her advantage.

"He's old, and his ways show it," Jorge snapped. "What is he going to do at his age? Step back—that is his only option, now. To step back and see my way is the better way. And if we have to tear apart the García cartel when this is all said and done to finish it, then so be it."

"You don't understand the issue with that at all, do you?"

"No, I don't understand *your* issues."

"They are the same things!"

Jorge's annoyance came out in a dark grunt. The sound told Valeria that Samuel was walking a thin line with Jorge's patience. A dangerous thing, no matter which way someone tried to spin it.

Mostly, she tried to stay out of her husband's way when he was in this kind of mood. Come to think of it, he had been like this for the last week. Ever since they returned to the ranch from the vacation home. She had seen little of Chris throughout the week, other than his occasional walk around the property.

Here, Jorge sheltered her.

It made things hard.

"This is *done*," Jorge hissed to his brother, "and nothing you say to sway my decisions will work, so quit before it becomes an annoyance I will have to deal with, Samuel. Do you hear me? *Stop*."

"I'm only trying to make you look at the bigger picture. All you see is what you *want*, but not what will happen because of it, or who will suffer *for* it, Jorge."

"I'm done discussing this. The deal with the Canadians will be completed soon. Once it is, and we have the full supply control or all of Canada, we won't need Papá, or his fucking deal with the Garcías to merge our organizations. And with that much territory behind our name, it won't matter what the García cartel tries to do to us—it won't leave a dent."

"How soon until it's finalized?"

"Chris will leave by mid-week, or that's what he explained," Jorge replied, "so I assume before then."

What?

Valeria's heart stopped.

Chris was leaving?

That soon?

Within a couple of days?

Maybe less?

What did that mean for her? Or … for Maria?

She didn't give a single shit about the rest of Jorge's plans —nothing he planned against his own father, or the rival cartel, helped her. It would not get her out of here, and would only force him to seclude her and his child further away from the public while his manufactured wars raged on.

That's how this life worked.

The conversation continued in the kitchen with her husband and his brother unaware that the fluttering hope she had allowed herself to feel now seemed like shards of glass inside her chest. Her legs became weak, and she slipped down to sit on the step, drawing her knees to her chest as she realized this was over.

They would never get free.

How could they if he left?

Her last hope.

What was hope good for, anyway?

Nothing.

That's what.

Hope is for the fucking weak. It's why she had never bothered before now because it all ended the same. So, why did this hurt so much?

"What are you do—"

Valeria scooped her daughter up from the ground where she had been playing with the kitten that her father still threatened to take from her. She ignored the nanny's shout at her back as she turned and headed toward the stables while Maria's wild black curls flew in every direction.

"Careful, my kitty!"

"Hold him tight," Valeria told her girl.

Maria did just that, tucking the squirming kitten into her arms, cradling it like a baby doll. Behind them, Carla shouted louder.

"You can't just *take* her, Valeria!"

"She is my child. I can do whatever I want."

"I'll tell Jorge you said that."

Fuck it.

"Do so," Valeria snapped over her shoulder.

Carla's fish-mouthed stare almost made her laugh. The bitch also wasn't as important as she tried to seem to be, so Valeria didn't give her another thought.

Oh, sure, she would pay for this.

Jorge would make her aware.

Valeria didn't give a shit.

Not right now.

"Where are we going?" Maria asked.

"For a horse ride."

Away, she wanted to say,

Just … God, away from here, and this place, and these people. Away from pain, and fear, and the hell that would someday catch up with her. Not that it mattered. Eventually, she would have to come back, and if she didn't, then someone would come find her.

For right now, though, she was going.

She needed to.

Once she had calmed down earlier after overhearing Jorge's conversation with his brother, Valeria's only wanted to *get away*. It screamed in her heart—to *go*.

Somehow.

Knowing she didn't have much time, Valeria took the one horse that someone already tacked up. That way, she didn't have to waste time getting their favorite riding horses ready.

She put Maria on the horse first, tucking the kitten into a rucksack for her daughter to carry close to her chest, before heaving herself onto the animal, too. They came out of the stables in a slow trot.

"Don't look back at the house," she told her daughter.

Maria frowned, tipping her head back to peeked up at her mom. "Why?"

"Because if they know we see them, then we can't lie later when we come back."

"Not supposed to lie, Mamá."

Valeria struggled the most with these moments. She wanted her child to be a *good* human being—a person with values, and morals. And with one white lie came more white lies, right?

Still …

"Sometimes, we have to lie, Maria."

Her daughter blinked. "To Jorge?"

She didn't miss how it wasn't *Papá* when someone couldn't hear Maria. That just proved to Valeria that her daughter understood what she said even if she wanted her mother to explain it better.

"To him, and people that help him," she agreed.

Maria nodded. "Okay, Mamá."

Valeria checked behind them, though she told Maria not to. No one watched them leave, and even Carla had disappeared. No one saw them take the horse out.

It didn't matter.

Valeria pressed her heels into the sides of the horse and clicked her tongue. That slow trot became a gallop, and she continued looking over her shoulder until the ranch disappeared. Still, no one saw them go.

The ride to the cliffs went by quickly. She should have planned the ride better—attempted to grab food to take with them so that Maria could have a supper.

Her daughter didn't seem to mind.

Maria busied herself with wildflowers and her kitten. She didn't notice her mother sitting along the edges of the cliffs. Valeria watched the horizon, and the choppy waters down below. They stayed like that, Valeria staring, and Maria playing, and before long, she heard hooves hitting the ground in a gallop.

Approaching.

She just knew.

It wasn't someone coming after her.

Not to take her back.

It wasn't Jorge, or his men.

Valeria peeked over her shoulder. She could tell who it was by the way he sat atop the animal, both comfortable and confident.

She also sensed him.

Chris.

Apparently, her heart hadn't finished breaking.

CHAPTER 14

The risk of following Valeria on horseback to the cliffs was high, but Chris weighed it before he left. Given he was already out on a horse, one he took out around noon when the guards were doing their shift change, nobody saw him leave, and so they wouldn't expect him to be returning soon, either.

Chris often came and went on the property. After a spread of time on the ranch, it almost seemed like the guards and the family had become accustomed to Chris doing his own thing, and as he didn't interrupt their business, they didn't bother his.

That worked in his favor.

Like now.

It wasn't seeing Valeria on a horse that concerned Chris, as she often took the animals out to ride, but rather, the look on her face. If sadness had a picture in the dictionary next to the word, it would have been of Valeria. A deep ache settled in his heart at the sight, and before he knew what was happening, he had turned his horse around in the field as he had been approaching the ranch, and followed behind.

He'd noticed Maria, too, but the girl didn't seem to be in the same state her mother was, and she rode on her own horse whenever she took one out. Not today, though. This time, she was riding with her mother.

Chris's anxiety spiked when he realized Valeria was heading for the cliffs. Since his arrival, he had only visited the cliffs once on a ride. Their proximity to the water, and the obvious danger, kept him from taking the horses out that way. He didn't need to be urging his fears on more than he already did whenever he felt the need to test himself.

He did his best to ignore that Valeria was sitting on the edge, overlooking the water, when he approached. She glanced back at him, dark eyes filled with a line of water that had his chest clenching.

Something was wrong.

But what?

"Chris!"

"Hey, *bambina*," he said to Maria, slowing the horse to a stop before jumping down to the ground. The animals were well-trained and didn't wander off as he learned, so he dropped the horse's reins and didn't give it a second thought. Maria peered up at him from her spot in a patch of wildflowers where her kitten napped in her lap. "Out for a ride?"

The girl shrugged. "Mamá wanted to."

Chris nodded. "Stay away from the edge of the cliffs, okay?"

"I will." Then, Maria held up a white wildflower, offering it to him with a brilliant smile. "Here, a gift."

How could he refuse that?

Chris took the flower from the girl, twirling the fragile stem between his fingers as he looked it over before putting it in the breast pocket of his jacket for safekeeping. "It's beautiful—like you, hmm? Thank you."

Maria's cheeks pinked, but when she looked back at her mother who stared out across the cliffs and not paying them attention, her happiness faded. "Mamá is sad."

He was quick to bend down, reaching out to soothe the girl because he wondered how many people thought to stop and do that for her. She was still a *child*—small, and young. He bet she faced adult issues far more than she should.

Next to her mother, Maria was one of the few people on the ranch that Chris found himself drawn to, and she was *just* a child. Her smile lit up a room, and the way she cared about things—from her mother to the kitten in her lap—was as sweet as could be.

This job had turned out to be far more than what he expected, but Chris would not complain about it. How could he when he met these two wonderful souls because of it? He no longer wondered why Valeria's friend was so willing to approach an organization like The League to get her home where she belonged.

He wanted them home, too.

Chris wondered if home might be with him.

"Let's see if I can make your ma happy, okay?" he told the girl.

Maria grinned. "Okay."

He gave her a quick pat on the top of her black curls before standing. Valeria said nothing as Chris came to sit next to her on the edge of the cliffs. He swallowed back the discomfort the position caused and kept his gaze on her instead of the water down below. She spoke before he did, giving him the exact reason for her sadness.

It was not what he expected.

"You're leaving," she whispered.

Yeah.

He didn't bother to ask how she knew that. It didn't matter.

"The business side of things have run their course here," he explained, although it wouldn't help her feelings on the matter. "I can't stay just because I want to. Jorge has wanted me gone since I arrived."

"Right."

"Val."

She refused to look at him.

Chris tried not to let that hurt.

"*Val*.

"What?" she asked.

"Hey," he murmured, reaching for her.

The second his palm came in contact with her cheek, Valeria blinked, and the tears she had been holding back tracked lines down from the corners of her eyes. He could handle a lot of things from this woman, but crying did not seem to be one. When the tears started, all he wanted to do was make them stop.

Now.

"Don't cry, don't cry," he said, his arm snaking around her waist to pull her into his lap. He wiped the tears from her face, and met her gaze. Although, when that didn't work to make her stop crying, he did the next best thing. *Kissed her*. His lips touched to hers, he tasted the salt from her tears, and the rest of the world faded away. Still, he breathed against her mouth, "Please, don't cry. It's not over, I promise."

Somewhere behind him, he heard Maria's little gasp.

Then, her *giggle*.

Kids.

Valeria pushed away from him, but not very far. She couldn't get away when he was holding her locked in his arms. "Maria might tell—"

"She won't."

That, he was most sure of.

All little Maria wanted was for her mother to be happy. She was tired of seeing her mother sad and hurting. That's all Valeria ever was here.

Chris used the pad of his thumb to wipe away the last bit of wetness from under Valeria's eye. "Hey, look at me."

Valeria did, but he wasn't sure he liked what he found staring back. "I was *never* going to be free. I never will be. Hope was a lie."

"What?"

"I can't even protect my daughter because she is the sacrifice he's willing to use to punish me. And now you're *leaving*. What am I going to do?"

Those tears had started again.

Her voice climbed higher.

Chris kissed her quiet. Her fingers tightened into the collar of his jacket as their lips moved in a familiar rhythm. Soft, and sweet. A heat spreading between the two of them he had never known existed before this woman.

Against her lips, he said, "I didn't want to leave until I had a clear way out for you—that won't happen with the way he has this place run, but I know that now. Which means as soon as I am out of here, I will gather a team, and they'll come in to get you out. Do you understand?"

"That's not poss—"

"It is, and that's what will happen. I don't want you to stay here a second longer than you need to, but this is my only way to make it work."

Unless something else came up.

As of now, nothing had.

Chris grabbed Valeria's chin and tipped her head back so she was staring at him again. "Don't you want a chance?"

"W-what?"

"A chance to do whatever you want—to live, or to *love*? To be whoever you want to be, and not who someone else demands from you?"

Fire rushed her stare. "Of course, I do."

"Then, don't give up. You can't." Chris sighed, glancing over his shoulder to scan the land in case someone was coming. Although, they would have heard the horses approaching. "Did anyone see you leave?"

"Carla—the nanny—knew I was going, but she didn't see us leave the stables."

"No one else? Jorge?"

Valeria shook her head.

Chris nodded. "Okay, go back before he sends someone out after you and her. Don't make him angry—keep the peace, however you can."

"I can't do this anymore. I can't keep letting him use me and hurt me."

He didn't have the right words for that.

Nothing to make it better.

"I'm sorry," he whispered.

Valeria's shoulders lifted and sank with her heavy breaths. "I just … I want that chance, Chris."

"You'll get it," he promised. "I'll make sure."

"I don't want to go back."

"Yeah."

The unspoken words hung between them—*but you have to*.

Valeria climbed out of his lap with help, and then Chris stood too after brushing off his clothes. Silently, his hand found hers, their fingers wove together, and he squeezed before letting go.

"Jorge said you would leave mid-week."

"Probably tomorrow."

He got a flight.

Valeria made a heartbroken noise.

"Shh," Chris hushed, tugging her close to his side to press

a kiss to the top of her head, and hide her away from the rest of the world while he was able. "It will be *fine*."

"It won't."

"Let me show you."

Then, another thought popped into his mind.

"The stables," he said, "at midnight. That's when the second shift change happens for the guards—every twelve hours. They meet at the gate for an hour before heading back to their posts. If you're there, that's where I'll be tonight. Okay?"

She nodded.

Chris gestured at the horse she brought along. "Go ahead. Get back before he sends someone out for you."

Maria glanced up from the kitten in her lap. "You have Butter."

He smiled at the girl and passed a glance at the horse he brought along. Butter, that was. "Butter is a great horse."

"My *favorite*."

Oh?

"You can take him back for me," Chris said, knowing it would be a five-mile walk back to the ranch, "as long as you promise to keep this a secret."

Maria stood up from the ground, packing her kitten away in the rucksack hanging across her small body. "Deal."

He helped Valeria to get the horses ready for the ride back, but before she left him behind at the cliffs, he grabbed her wrist. Her gaze met his, and he tugged to make her lean down. One more kiss between them, and he held her gaze.

"I always keep my promises, Val."

That fire was back in her stare.

He liked it better, now.

"You better," she said.

He *would*.

Chris watched the girls and the horses fade in the distance. Pulling that flower Maria had given him from his breast pocket, he fished out his wallet, too. He flipped the wallet open to a spot in the back, and laid the flower on the leather before closing it up, pressing firmly to keep it in place. Once he had the chance, he would take it out and press it safely between the pages of a book he kept on his desk at home.

Someday, he wanted to show Maria that he kept it, and her mother, too. Because this day? It felt like it changed everything.

The sky had blackened by the time Chris walked those five miles back to the ranch. Not that he minded—walking hurt nobody, and he used the time to clear his head. The weather had stayed decent during his stay in Mexico, so he wouldn't say anything bad about that, either.

He wasn't at all surprised to find the ranch quiet when he returned. The one guard walking the pathways between the houses gave him a nod as he passed, but the man didn't even realize Chris wasn't out for one of his normal strolls. That had become normal to them, and so they didn't even question it, now.

A blessing, really.

Chris intended on heading to the house he was using on the ranch, having a quick shower, and then making his way to Jorge's home to sign off on the deal for his father, even if was still a ruse. A throat clearing to his left stopped his walk up short.

Sitting on the porch of the small bungalow she and her

brother used, Abril Lòpez raised an eyebrow when Chris's gaze landed on her.

"Good walk?" she asked.

Chris nodded, careful with his words because he wasn't sure what to make of this woman. She went along with her brothers, and their plans more often than she didn't. After watching her for a while, he found that she followed the rules, even if she seemed to enjoy pushing the boundaries around her.

A complex.

Nothing like Valeria.

She had been easy to figure out.

Abril … not so much.

"It was nice," he said.

Abril leaned forward on the steps, a sly smile curving her lips as a glint twinkled in her russet gaze. "I thought you took out a horse earlier? I was in the stables, remember? Butter."

Shit.

Chris forgot about that.

A mistake he couldn't afford.

"You didn't see me come back?"

He hoped to distract the woman with a lie, but perhaps he should have known better than to even try. There was something about Abril that was not the same as her brothers although *what* it was, he wasn't sure. She was quiet, always sticking to the shadows, but never inserting herself into conversations.

However, Chris understood it was the silent ones someone had to watch more than the others. They were the people who saw things, but never said a word. They heard conversations and filed them away in their minds for a later date.

He doubted Abril was different.

"No, I didn't see you come back," Abril said, resting her arms over her jean-covered knees, and tipping her head to the side. "But I saw Val leave with one horse, and her daughter, and then come back with two horses. Maria was riding Butter."

Chris cleared his throat.

Abril smiled.

"You're playing a dangerous game, Christopher Guzzi, and I want you to tell me exactly what kind it is."

"I'm not sure what you're talking—"

"Cut the shit. I've seen you dancing around her since you arrived. Last weekend? You got out of her room just in time because Jorge got home an hour later and passed out in the hallway before his men came up and put him in a spare bedroom."

Fuck.

"The door closing," Chris murmured.

Abril shrugged one bare shoulder where her flimsy blouse had fallen down. "I don't trust new people, and I had every reason to wonder about you."

"Why?"

"I'm aware of *just enough* about the cocaine trade in Canada to say your father has a good supplier, and he didn't need to come here. Jorge and my father? They think I'm a pretty face to give to whoever the fuck they want, but that's their mistake."

He didn't miss how she didn't say her other brother. The one that stayed in this house with her.

Chris didn't point it out.

"I like Val," Abril said, "and I don't like very many people, so that says a lot. And my niece? She didn't ask to be here, either."

"What do you want?" he asked outright.

Abril smirked. "Not much … just a guarantee. Tell me what you want, and then we'll see what I can do for you."

"I'm not sure you can help me."

"Don't make the same mistakes they do. Those who underestimate me tend to get what they deserve. Do you want to fall into that category, too?"

Well, all right, then.

"Valeria, and her daughter."

Abril's expression didn't change, and she gave nothing away when she replied, "What about them?"

"What do you think?"

"I think if you came here to remove them from my brother, then you will have an uphill battle to make it happen."

Chris laughed darkly. "That's not news."

"What if I help with it?"

"How so?"

Abril glanced up at the stars overhead. "I love this place. It's *mine*. Always has been, always will be, but they've changed it over the years. And now, they want to give me to someone who will take me away from it."

"Your arranged marriage to the García man?"

"Mmm."

Her hum was the only agreement to his question.

Chris didn't mind.

"Do you have the capability to take the two out of here?" Abril asked.

"Within reason."

"What *reason*?"

"Time to get it done."

"I need the night to do what I have to," Abril said, "and I'm sure it'll then give you some *time*, as you say you need."

"How?"

The woman smiled at him.

Coldly.

"How about you follow along, Christopher? Things always go better when someone just does what I tell them to."

"You haven't told me anything yet."

Abril nodded. "By the morning, you'll have everything you need to do what you have to." The woman picked up the wine glass at her side and winked as she tipped it up for a drink. After, she let the stem dangle from the tips of her fingers as she asked, "Do you know in English my name means April?"

"I didn't."

"Have you heard the saying—about the showers, and the flowers?"

Chris's brow furrowed. "What does that have to do with anything?"

"Do you know it?"

"Sure. April showers bring May flowers."

Abril grinned wickedly. "I think it's about time for some rain."

What did that mean?

He still wasn't even sure he should trust this woman, but what choice did he have?

CHAPTER 15

"Mamá?"

Valeria looked up from the book she had been reading to her daughter to find Maria peering over at her from just under the edge of her comforter. "Yeah, *niña*?"

"Jorge was angry we took the horse today."

Well, *sort of.*

Mostly, Jorge got pissed that Valeria took her daughter away from the nanny and did so without telling him. Which meant she had to listen to him rant and rage for a good hour after she arrived back at the ranch.

The good thing?

He didn't realize what happened out on the cliffs. No one picked up on the fact Valeria had taken out one horse but came back with two. They didn't seem to notice Chris wasn't around, either. Then again, Jorge had a one-track mind, and since Valeria took his focus when she stepped out of line, that's all he cared about.

He calmed down.

After a while.

"Don't worry about Papá and what he says," Valeria told her daughter, lowering her tone even as her gaze drifted to the open doorway of the bedroom. She could take care of Maria without someone looking over her shoulder in the evenings. Meaning, the *nanny*. Or Jorge. Even still, she had to leave the bedroom door open, and she didn't trust that someone wouldn't listen down the hall. "He was angry with me, not you, Maria."

"But—"

"But *nothing*," she assured, leaning over in the bed to kiss her sweet girl in the middle of her forehead. "You don't have to worry about that stuff, okay? All you have to worry about is you and being happy."

Maria glanced down at her comforter. "But I don't like it here, Mamá. I am *not* happy."

God, yeah.

Didn't she know it?

Rolling over in the bed, Valeria tossed the book aside— she'd almost finished it, anyway—and slipped under the blankets with her daughter. Jorge would ready for bed soon, and expect her in their room, but she took five extra minutes with her child. She didn't get enough time with Maria now.

She hated that.

Once she had her arms locked around her child, Maria settled, closing her eyes as her mother kissed her temple, and sung a sweet lullaby she remembered her own mama singing to her long ago. As she finished the song, Maria sighed.

"Do you remember the promise you made to Chris today?" she whispered to her daughter.

Maria nodded. "I will not tell."

"That's a good girl."

She didn't want to put her daughter in that position, but she also didn't think she gave Maria enough credit, either. Maria was smart—quick as a whip. She recognized when something didn't seem right, or rather, when something *was*.

Chris was right.

Just in different ways.

"Do you like Chris?" Maria asked.

Valeria blinked. "I ... that's not an easy question."

"Why not?"

Because it was complex.

Difficult.

Dangerous.

Yes, she liked that man. She more than liked him. With nothing more than his presence, and attention, he showed her good men existed. He reminded her she deserved care, and adoration by someone like him. He made her *want* him more than anything … she wanted happiness, and if possible, she wanted to find it with him. She knew happiness because he had given her glimpses. And at night, when it was just the two of them away from the rest of the world, he'd given her back the ability to be her own woman, too, although she didn't think he understood that.

She loved seeing him with her daughter because he never dismissed her child. He didn't walk past Maria without at the least, stopping to speak to her. He handled Maria with kindness, grace, and a tender heart, as a good man should.

She cared for Chris because of many reasons, and wanted him.

And she had more reasons why she couldn't have him. At least, not right now. Valeria wasn't the type to punish herself. So, she forced herself not to think about him at all because that was easier.

For now.

"It just isn't," she told her daughter.

Maria shrugged in her mother's hold. "I like him."

Valeria smiled. "Oh?"

"Yep."

"Why is that?"

"Because he doesn't hurt you," Maria said, "and he likes you. That's why I like him."

"That's all?"

Maria nodded. "That's all, Mamá."

Huh.

Children were still children. The only people on the earth who looked past the surface to see what was underneath. Children saw bad things, and yet, still found the good, too.

That was their innocence.

The beauty of kids.

They found hope.

Possibility.

Even when no one else did.

"I like him," Valeria murmured into her daughter's hair.

Although, if Maria heard it, she didn't acknowledge it. Valeria was fine with that because she wasn't sure how to deal with this herself. Away from this place, at a different time, had she met Chris … it would have been amazing.

They could be wonderful.

And maybe—*God*, maybe—if she had the chance he promised her to get away from here, and live her life the way she wanted, then she might let herself feel all those things she kept holding at bay. For now, though, she didn't dare.

Heartache was one thing.

Heartbreak was quite another.

Valeria was not ready for that. Giving her heart to a man she couldn't be with would only bring her pain.

Someday, that might change.

Her thoughts were a whisper.

They reminded her hope wasn't dead.

Not yet.

Valeria had closed the door to her daughter's bedroom when Jorge came stumbling *drunk* down the hall. His drinking had become more regular, and that concerned her if only because he was a mean drunk, and she always seemed to be right in his fucking line of fire.

"*Hermosa*," Jorge slurred, coming closer to her. "We need to celebrate, woman."

Valeria took a careful step backward. "Why?"

She ignored the red lipstick stain on the collar of his shirt, and the undone buttons because she didn't give a fuck who put it there as long as it wasn't her. The strands of his hair stuck up everywhere. Sweat dotted his forehead and wrinkles covered his slacks.

It wasn't like Jorge to be messy.

Except lately, he was more often than not.

He reached out for her when she was close enough and grabbed onto her. Valeria didn't have the chance to react before his disgusting mouth came down on hers. The taste of the rum he had been drinking flooded her tongue, making her want to gag. Her hands hit his chest, ready to push him away even though that would cause her more trouble.

She didn't get the chance.

In a flash, the two of them stumbled into their bedroom. Jorge stepped back from her, realizing where they were, and grinned. He pointed a finger at her while pulling his shirt down his arms, and nodding.

"Ah, now get undressed for me, *si*?" He winked, as stupid as that looked. "*Slowly*, Val. I like that, don't you?"

God.

"You're too drunk," she told him.

Jorge rolled his eyes and fell back to the foot of the bed to get his shoes off. "I am *not*. Get undressed, or I will cut the fucking clothes off you."

She didn't doubt it.

She also didn't lie.

He struggled to pull the leather loafers from his feet, almost falling face first to the floor. Another night, and she might have laughed at him. Except, the time closed in on eleven-thirty, and in a half an hour, she needed to meet Chris in the stables. She hadn't forgotten about that.

If she could help it, she would not let her husband touch her one more fucking time. She searched for a way out of this situation while Jorge continued to struggle with his shoes, and his socks, too, when he finally removed the loafers.

"What are you standing there for?" he snapped up at her.

Jesus Christ.

The last thing she wanted was this drunk pig hauling his body on top of hers to get himself off—whiskey dick was a real thing, and not specific to only whiskey, either. Sex with Jorge was bad enough when he stayed sober although she didn't think of him raping her as *sex*. When he was drunk, though, it became a whole different horror.

"Did you remember to let the kitten in?" she asked, hoping for a distraction.

Jorge's brow furrowed, and sleepy eyes stared up at her.

Hazy eyes, too, she noticed. Drunk as fuck. She might have asked him how much he drank downstairs before coming up to bed if she cared. Except she didn't, and really, if he gave himself alcohol poisoning, she would not cry about it.

Damn.

Might he fall asleep if she gave him the chance?

Pass right out?

"What kitten?" he slurred again.

"Never mind," she blurted, "I will use the bathroom— freshen up, okay? I'll be right back out. Lay back and take a break. You deserve it."

Right.

That's what he deserved.

Jorge sighed, pleased with her submissiveness. That's all this bastard ever wanted. To *believe* Valeria was willing and capable of going along with whatever he needed and demanded. He was easier to handle but shit … it killed her to do it.

No point in lying.

"All right," he mumbled, folding his arms behind his head, "but don't be too long. I need a good sleep. Big things happening tomorrow."

"Oh, like what?"

She asked the question over her shoulder as she headed for the bathroom. Moving around inside the space, turning on the taps and lifting the toilet seat to make it seem like she was doing something, he wouldn't know the difference if he stayed resting on the bed. Knowing Jorge like she did, when he was drunk, if he stayed on his back for long enough, he would fall asleep.

A win-win for her.

Stupid, yes.

Risky, absolutely.

Valeria didn't care. Not right now. Not knowing soon, Chris would leave, and tonight was the last chance she would have to be with him. She would do what she needed to do.

"Business, Val," he muttered, "with the Canadian."

"Chris?"

"Mmm, I don't like him."

"Why?"

"He looks at you too much."

Valeria stiffened near the sink.

How often did Jorge watch when she didn't pay attention?

"Does he? I never noticed."

"They all look at you, woman … but they're smart about it. He doesn't care, and I don't … like that."

His words came slower, now, so Valeria kept talking as she pretended to wash her hands.

"I don't notice," she admitted. "What are you celebrating?"

"The deal is …"

"Hmm?"

"Completed," Jorge mumbled. A beat of silence passed before he asked almost unintelligibly, "Are you finished?"

"Just about."

She took a minute to dry her hands, and brushed her teeth, a familiar sound echoed into the bathroom.

Snoring.

Valeria smiled at her reflection.

It worked.

She came out of the bathroom, and sure enough, Jorge had passed out on the bed with his arms still acting as a pillow beneath his head. Using the blanket that acted as a decoration on the chair in the corner, she covered him. Not because she cared should he become cold, but because he slept better when he was warm, and she needed him to stay asleep for as long as possible.

Should he wake up, and realize she wasn't in the room, that wouldn't be good for her. She also turned on the small radio … just in case someone came to knock on the door, it was unlikely the noise would even disturb him.

Valeria glanced over her shoulder as she closed the bedroom door behind her when she left, only to see Jorge snoring away.

Alcohol was good for that.

She used it enough to sleep next to that man.

≈

Valeria tiptoed through the stables, her heart in her throat as she passed stall after stall, realizing Chris wasn't there at all. She'd not expected him to be out in the open but it seemed like he hadn't been here.

She almost passed the final stall, resolving herself to sneak back to the house—their chance at a stolen moment gone, when someone yanked her into that last stall of the stables on the right. They used it to store care items, feed, and other things for the horses. Including *blankets*, if a terrible night or a storm came through unexpectedly.

Valeria barely had the chance to catch her breath before Chris's lips found the back of her neck as her chest met the stall wall. *God*, she didn't even care that the rough wood might leave a splinter in her palms when his hands fisted into the skirt of the wrap dress she had thrown on to leave the house.

"Val," he started.

"Just fuck me," she breathed, "and we'll talk later."

If they had the chance.

That's what made desperate sex the best kind of sex. She was sure.

Chris never made her feel even the smallest bit unsafe. Not when his touches came rougher, and her cheek pressed to the wood. Not when his teeth dragged across the racing pulse in her throat while his hands shoved her dress high before slipping between her thighs to cup her sex. He *squeezed* her pussy, fingers sliding through her wetness to prove how fucking much she wanted his.

Valeria drowned out the sounds of her pleasure into her palm as Chris worked her pussy open with his fingers first. Wet sounds filled the stall as his fingers pushed and pulled, twisting into her G-spot with every curl of the tips. Her hips jerked, a sensation like she had never experienced before spiraling through her gut when his lips danced across her ear lobe.

His words?

A dark *promise*.

"Feel that?" he asked, "You're about to rain all over my hand, Val. You'll leave a fucking puddle in this stall. I bet you haven't done that before, huh?"

"No, never."

It almost embarrassed her. The very idea.

Yet, she didn't have time to think about it before she came. And not *just* an orgasm that seemed so fucking good, but one that almost brought her to her knees from the intensity. It started deep within her womb and flared outward with violent intent. The rush of wetness between her legs, hot and *slick*, came fast. It ruined her panties, but that didn't seem to matter to Chris as he pulled his hands free from her pussy only to yank the soaked undies down her legs.

He was back on her, fast with those same dirty words promising she would *see stars* and *gonna be so fucking good when I'm done, babe* while his hands went back to working on getting her dress off entirely. Valeria only had time to catch her breath while Chris stepped back from her to take care of himself, shedding his clothes, and sheathing his cock in latex before he was back behind her.

One hand slid under her right thigh, lifting it high and the head of his dick slid through her sensitive slit. That wet sound came back, a reminder of her own arousal and how hot she was for him.

"*Breath*," he demanded.

She did, sucking in a hard breath. He thrust in, seating himself all the way inside her pussy with one flex of his hips.

She'd been so ready to take him, her need indescribable, until he was filling her full and stretching her open.

"Oh, my *God*," Valeria whimpered.

"Hold on," Chris murmured along the column of her throat.

She did, finding purchase with one hand on the wall, and the other reaching back to grasp onto his hips as he pounded into her from behind. His lips found her neck, kissing and tasting and biting her into bliss while his cock drove her crazy with every fast, deep stroke.

It was too much, and not enough.

"I c-can't—I can't …"

Valeria couldn't form words, or explain that she hovered right on the precipice of an orgasm that would leave her in shattered pieces on the ground, if only he gave her a bit more. The words wouldn't come, and yet it didn't even matter.

Chris knew.

How to work her …

How to play her body …

All of it.

His hand on her hip slid around to the front of her body, drifting between her thighs, so his fingertips rubbed tight circles into her clit while his other arm wrapped tight around her chest. The air exploded out of her chest in a high cry. Probably *too loud* for their current circumstances as the orgasm tore through her body with devastating intent.

It was heaven.

And she would die happily like that.

"Fuck, yeah," Chris said, his words a hoarse murmur along her throat, "that's what I wanted, babe. Come all over that cock—fucking now. Take it all, Valeria."

Each thrust that followed his words came deeper and

harder inside her pussy, accompanied by the jerking of his hands against her body with his own orgasm.

Her air wouldn't come, or her thoughts.

And that was okay.

It meant, for that moment with him, she didn't have to feel anything at all.

But especially not the pain.

CHAPTER
16

"What do I do now?"

Valeria's voice was a whisper, her gaze locked on the stall instead of him where he wanted it. Chris didn't mind because he figured everyone had to protect themselves, and Valeria's way was like this. He didn't take offense, even if he wished this woman knew he was doing everything in his power to get her away from this place, and happy again.

"You give me time, and before you know it, I'll be back to—"

"No, *me*, I mean. What am I supposed to do now?"

Chris tipped his head down and pressed a kiss to the line of Valeria's naked shoulder. He couldn't resist her on his lips —her scent had mixed with his, and it reminded him of woman, sex, and *heaven*. "I don't understand, love."

Two blankets he grabbed from the stable shelves kept the hay-covered floor of the stall soft enough for them to rest comfortably on. The other, he'd used to wrap around his shoulders before he tightened the ends around them both. The high stall door allowed them to remain unseen from the stables, and other than the six-inch space at the bottom where he saw out into the main corridor, no one had a view of them unless they opened the door.

No one came into the stables this late though.

He knew because he watched.

"*You*," she whispered.

Chris made a noise under his breath, thick and unsure. "Val—"

She sighed. "You know, before when I was on the run, I went years without being in a relationship—but is that what we can call this? *Should* we call it that?"

Huh.

"I don't know," he admitted, "but we can call it whatever you want to call it. I want what you want that's all."

Hadn't she figured that out yet?

Chris didn't think it needed to make sense, but frankly, why should it? They hadn't met under normal circumstances. She wasn't the average woman, and he wasn't every other man, either. They couldn't simplify anything they did together down to one label, but he didn't care. As long as he still had moments like this with her, rather it be now or when she was away from here, then that was all that mattered to him at the end.

Valeria tipped her head back and rested it against the crook in his shoulder. It gave Chris the perfect chance to kiss her cheek, and then the corner of her mouth. So, he did just that. He thought about this woman, and all the things he wanted to do with her—*to her*—far more often than he should.

This job turned out to be more than he expected, but he wouldn't complain. How could he when, he'd found an angel?

Someone was looking out for him.

"I meant ..." Valeria gave him a sweet smile when he used the pad of his thumb to trace the line of her cheekbone while he watched her. She didn't possibly know it, but he found her most fascinating like this. She didn't have to pretend to be someone else. Happy, pleased, and content. All his. As she should be, he decided. "I tried to date, but I didn't. I didn't want to."

"Nothing wrong with that," he rumbled.

Not that he would tell her, but Chris was a jealous mother-fucker. Even the thought of Valeria spending time with another man—before him, it didn't matter—had his green monster beating at the bars of its cage. He kept the bastard in place if only because he didn't think she would appreciate it. Hadn't she put up with enough bullshit from a man who thought he owned her?

Chris would not be another.

Valeria peered up at him, her pink lips curving into a soft smile as he stroked two fingers up and down her arm under the blanket. "I was young when they forced me to marry Jorge, but you know that, don't you?"

"I do, yes."

"He was the first man ..." She flinched, but added, "He was the first for me. And then I ran, stayed running for years, and kept busy raising my daughter because she was always most important."

Ah.

Chris thought he might understand what Valeria had been trying to tell him, but he remained quiet, and allowed her the chance to say it without his input. This woman didn't use her voice enough, and when she did, God knew she watched every single word that came out of her mouth.

Shame, that.

She said beautiful things.

People were missing out.

Their loss, he supposed.

His gain.

"I never learned what it meant to enjoy being with someone emotionally, or physically. Love was always abusive. Sex only hurt. I never had the chance to figure out what I wanted and what was good for me until you, and this isn't even a *thing*. It's not right, we shouldn't have done this, but I'm not sure what I'm supposed to do when you go. I can't let him *touch* me, anymore. I can't—"

"Shhh," Chris murmured, leaning down just enough to press a kiss to her forehead. Valeria's eyes fluttered closed, and her frown melted away. That was better. "Val, listen—"

"I don't want you to leave."

Yeah.

There it was.

"I don't want to go, either," he muttered.

He needed to be here. Someone had to keep an eye on this woman because no one else was doing it. Undoubtedly, leaving would kill him inside when it meant she would face hell alone. Yes, she had been doing it for years before him, but that didn't matter to him at all.

She shouldn't *have* to.

"What do you want?" he asked.

Valeria looked away from him. "I don't understand."

"When this is over, and you can do whatever you want to do, what is it you want?"

"Still not sure when that'll happen, Chris."

Right.

"Part of hope is having something to hope *for*," he murmured against her cheek, letting his nose nuzzle her soft, warm skin. "So, what are you hoping for, Val?"

She stayed quiet.

He waited her out.

"You," she said. "I'm hoping for you, and what you gave me here. I don't want to forget it when you're gone, I don't think I can because I'm hoping for something better, and that's you."

Chris tightened his arms around her trembling form because, all too soon, he would let her go again. "You'll have that. I promise."

He didn't break those.

He wouldn't.

"Will I? *How*?"

Asking her to trust him again—how many times had he said that now?—didn't seem like it was what she wanted, and so Chris said nothing at all. Actions were still louder than words, and he was working on making this a reality one fucking step at a time. It was the best he could do right now.

His silence wasn't the response she wanted either. Valeria turned in his lap, the blanket around them falling to the stall floor before she was straddling him. Her hands found his face, and those sharp fingernails of her dragged teasingly against his skin as she pulled him in for a hard kiss. There was no *give* to it—only her taking.

He didn't care.

She wanted it?

Have it.

In the back of his mind, Chris recognized they were running out of time here. She needed to head back to the house before someone noticed she left. Or even, before a guard made a trip through the stables just because.

And yet, all those thoughts faded away when her hands fell between them. Her palms found his cock, grabbing tight and stroking him alive in a few firm pulls. He didn't speak the truth—that she needed to *go*—when her lips still crushed against his, and her tongue seemed intent to lick his flavor straight from his fucking mouth.

God.

It was so damn good though.

He swore, over the notes of the hay and the horses, of old

wood and dirt floor, he still smelled the lingering whiff of their sex in the air. Of her fresh, yet warm perfume that reminded him of a summer rain in the dead heat.

"Again, once more before you go," she whispered. "*Please*."

Her words danced along his lips, sinful and tantalizing. Who could say no to that? It's what he wanted, too. If he could keep this woman with him forever, he would do exactly that.

Chris reached for his discarded pants, digging through the pocket to find the last fucking condom he had. She took the foil packet from his fingertips, ripping it open before making quick work of sheathing his hard length in latex. Air hissed between his teeth when she settled on top of him, hovering with the head of his cock sliding between the fleshy lips of her sex while she watched him.

Perfect.

She was so fucking perfect.

When she came down on his length, he swore he found heaven. Even if it was his personal brand of hell, too. After all, it only reminded him that she wasn't entirely his.

Not yet.

"You made me trust you," she breathed against his mouth, but it almost seemed like something else. It almost sounded like *you made me love you*, and fuck, he felt that inside his bones. He heard that louder, echoing in his heart with the beats it pumped, and spreading like a wildfire ready to devastate his soul. Not that he had a soul anymore because he gave it to this fucking woman, and he had no idea when that happened. "And now you're *leaving*."

"Not for long. I swear, not for long."

That hurt.

It hurt him, too.

~

The day Chris would leave the ranch came far too soon for his liking. Despite having a ticket bought, and a time he had to be at the airport to make his flight, he still took his time packing up his bag in the guest house he used during his stay. One thing at a time—*slowly*.

Soon, he'd packed his bags, and set them on the front porch of the small house. Crossing his arms over his chest, he stared out over the property and the houses connected by small pathways.

Time to say goodbye.

Even if wasn't a goodbye.

It still seemed like it.

Chris picked up the bag at his feet, settling his raging heart to finish this. The quicker he left, the faster this plan —even if he didn't understand everything, and still had more yet to figure out on his end—would get started. And that's what he wanted and needed more than anything, right?

To get Val, and Maria, away from here.

It sucked he had to leave first.

Chris hadn't expected Jorge to be waiting in front of his house, a handful of men loitering within shouting distance, as he came down the pathway. While the man had been mostly respectful during his stay here, Chris understood it wasn't because Jorge wanted to be. Rather, it was because he *had* to be.

He wanted that deal.

Now, he had it.

He thought.

"Ready to head out?" Jorge asked, his foot kicking out at Maria's striped gray and white kitten that jumped over his boot. "Damn *cat*. Maria! Get out here and put this goddamn thing somewhere before I throw it off the cliffs!"

Chris tried not to show his annoyance at hearing the little girl he cared a great deal for be yelled at in that way. And by her own father, no less. She was such a sweet child, but her father didn't seem to care.

"I am heading out," Chris said as the screen door on the porch pushed open. Little Maria came out, but wouldn't meet anyone's gaze as she came down the steps. Not too far behind her was her mother. Valeria stayed in the doorway, arms folded over her chest, and watched Chris from a safe distance. "Have to catch that flight, or I will never hear the end from my mother when I don't show up for her dinner tomorrow."

Jorge made a noise under his breath. "*Women*. They're all the fucking same. More trouble than they're worth." Then, to his daughter who picked up the kitten, he snapped, "And keep the fucking thing out of my sight, got it?"

Maria looked over her shoulder and nodded. Still, her gaze drifted to Chris for a moment, meeting his. He swore, in the depths of her irises, he saw the little girl's secrets, all the things she had seen and known, staring back at him.

"Remember," she said to him, "you promised."

His heart ached.

All over, so painful, and unrelenting.

It hurt.

Chris nodded. "I did, Maria, and I'll keep it."

In the doorway, Valeria called for her daughter, the flash of worry on her face disappearing when Jorge looked her way. "Come on, Maria, and we'll get the kitty milk in a bowl, so she'll be sleepy."

"Okay, Mamá."

Maria darted up the stairs, and into her mother's waiting

arms. It killed Chris to look away from them, but he did it. He was not good at hiding his affections. One of his only flaws, but he couldn't afford for it to be on display.

Jorge shifted on his feet, shoving his hands into his pockets as his attention came back to Chris. "And what did you promise my daughter?"

He chuckled.

Dry and tense as it was.

"Just that I would come back and say hello someday," Chris murmured. "She's a sweet child. You should be proud of her—fathers and their daughters, hmm?"

Jorge arched a brow. "Proud, *sure*."

Fuck him.

He didn't deserve that child, or her mother. Jorge might have helped to create Maria's life, but he had nothing more to do with it than that. He provided the sperm, but Maria didn't reflect the man.

She deserved a good man in her life—a father who would show her what real love and care was between a daughter, and her dad. She needed someone to show her how she deserved to be treated by the men in her life, so she didn't go looking for it somewhere else.

Jorge understood nothing about that; his reaction wasn't shocking. It still annoyed Chris to no fucking end, and only strengthened his resolve to make sure Maria, and her mother, found the happiness they deserved far away from this place, and the people here.

Including Jorge.

Any man could be a father.

All it took was the spunk from his balls.

Being a *dad* was not the same.

"A car will meet you at the gate," Jorge said, nodding toward the dirt road, "like when you arrived."

Right.

Because the only vehicles allowed this far into the ranch brought the family back to their homes, or ones carrying drugs. Jorge's rules never changed, not even for a guest who had promised to make him billions on a smuggling deal.

Whatever.

Chris didn't mind the walk.

"Pleasure doing business with you and your father," Jorge said. "Have a good flight, Chris."

He smiled. "Oh, I don't think it's finished yet."

Chris didn't allow Jorge the chance to question him on what he meant because he had already spun on his heels and headed for the road. He figured … *let him wonder*. It would be good for him even if he wouldn't see what came next.

Chris took in the darkening sky as the town car crawled through a busy section of the city. His driver, one of the Lòpez grunts, kept quiet throughout the drive. The man in the passenger seat, only there for decoration because he did nothing else, also remained silent throughout the drive.

Not that Chris cared.

He had other things on his mind.

A few miles from the airport, the two men in the front conversed back and forth in Spanish. It still left Chris out of the conversation, mostly. He had picked up a few words and phrases since his time here, and some language was close to Italian—or rather, close enough he made do.

"Happy … gone," he caught from one.

"It is who Jorge is," he understood better from the other.

Chris almost chuckled, understanding they were talking about him, and that Jorge wanted to see him go. He was fine with that, too, but he would be a hell of a lot better once he took Valeria and Maria from the man's clutches.

Soon, he told himself.

It would happen soon.

"What time is the flight again?"

The quick switch to English had Chris looking forward to meet the driver's stare in the rear-view mirror. A brow raised in question to his silence, but Chris said, "Five-twenty."

"Ah, we're making good time, then."

Chris checked his Rolex, saying as he tilted his head down, "Looks like it."

"*What the fuck*—Juan!"

He didn't get the chance to find out *what* the other man in the passenger seat shouted about because the impact of something hitting their car sent Chris flying across the back of the vehicle. He hadn't buckled in. A mistake. His head cracked against the glass of the rear passenger window, but that was the least of his worries.

Tires screeched and crunched.

Metal *crashed*.

One man cursed, another yelled.

Chris's ears rang as he flipped over in the backseat again, unable to stop his body from rolling all the way to the other side of the car. This time, his shoulder snapped hard against the plastic of the door, an ache spreading.

He didn't focus on the pain.

Not when adrenaline coursed through his system, making him hyper aware of the bits of debris flying all around his head, and the force of the rolling car sending him flying to the roof on his back. *Holy shit.*

He should have buckled up.

The car came to a stop, but on its *top*. Chris rolled over to his knees, the pressure in his ears making the men's voices from the front sound like they mumbled under water. His hands scraped against the shards of glass that had littered the roof of the car, but he barely even felt the sting when it cut his palms.

"*Fuck,*" he mumbled, still trying to figure out what happened.

What had happened?

That hit he took to the head made his vision cloudy, and his mind slow. *Too slow.* He lifted his head, nausea filling him as his hearing came back with an almost painful clarity. Outside of the car, an alarm sounded.

Their vehicle?

Maybe.

The alarm didn't concern him.

The three men coming for the car did.

Shit.

The men said nothing, and the fools in the front of their overturned vehicle didn't even have time to react before they had leaned in the car with guns aimed. Guns with silencers already attached.

Pop.

Pop.

Two shots.

Two men dead.

The three men didn't even speak together as they worked. This had been planned, obviously, and they understood what they had to do. Simple as that.

Chris blinked, seeing the blood that sprayed against the side of the windshield that hadn't broken into little pieces like the rest. The rusty tang of the blood filled the car, and gunpowder, freshly fired, mixed with it. He'd smelled that before. It still made his stomach roll into knots all the same.

The third man, the one who hadn't fired his gun, kneeled

to stare in the back seat where Chris remained on all fours, trying to figure out his next move. Any other time, and he would have already been dead.

"April showers bring May flowers," the man murmured, his English decent, but his accent still thick, and clear. Chris heard the words, and understood what they meant, but his shock still hadn't died yet. "Tell the Lòpez family the Garcías aren't going anywhere, *Canadian*, and because of their deal with you, the war is on."

CHAPTER
17

"Val, come in here, *now*."

Maria peered up at her mother from the pile of wooden blocks they had used to build a *school* for her three Barbie dolls. Valeria was quick to give her daughter a smile, not wanting the girl to worry herself over Jorge, and whatever he wanted. His sharp tone had likely caused Maria's concern, but then again, the man was always harsh.

He didn't have a concept of kindness.

"I'll be right back," Valeria said, "and by then, you can decide what we will build next, okay?"

Maria nodded. "Okay, Mamá."

Valeria wouldn't waste time, so she headed to the rear of the house where Jorge worked in his office. Although working on what, she didn't know, and she didn't care to ask. Coming to stand in the doorway, she didn't walk inside the office because that was yet another one of his rules.

This space was his.

Not hers.

"Yes?" she asked.

Behind the desk, Jorge kept his head down on the paper-work in front of him that he shuffled into a folder. He didn't bother to glance up at her entrance, nor to greet her before he said, "I am heading out for a week—I need a break after these last few."

Great.

She didn't want to be here, but she also didn't want to be elsewhere with her husband, either. That sounded like a problem waiting to happen, and not at all one she wanted to deal with, all things considered.

Still, Valeria kept her attitude in check. That way, Jorge would keep his fucking moods, and his hands, to himself.

"What will we need?"

He chuckled. "No, *me*, Val. I am going away for the week. You will be fine here with the guards, Maria, and Abril to keep you company, I am sure."

Well, *yes*.

She didn't show her happiness at his news. That wouldn't do her any good.

"Where are you going?"

Jorge glanced up, dark eyes nailing her to the floor with his displeasure. "Does it matter?"

"No, of course, not. I wonder—"

"Don't bother."

Valeria nodded. "When are you coming back, then?"

"When I feel like it, *hermosa*."

Fine with her.

"Okay," she said quietly, "I hope it's a good trip."

And that you never come back.

Valeria forced a smile on her face when Jorge looked her way again. He arched a brow, lifted a finger, and pointed at the doorway, saying, "Leave now."

She didn't need to told again.

Spinning on her heel, mind reeling over the fact she would have at least an entire week without this man looking over her shoulder, Valeria moved to leave Jorge's sight.

"Well, wait a second," he said behind her.

Valeria's shoulders dropped.

She knew it was too good to be true.

All day, she had focused on keeping her emotions under control. From the moment Chris had disappeared down the road leading out of the ranch, she had all she could do to keep from having a mental breakdown. She distracted herself with her child, and work around the house. Not to mention, staying the hell out of Jorge's way.

What could he want now?

Turning around, she asked, "What else can I do for you?"

He tipped his head to the side, his gaze roving over her slowly like he was drinking her up. Had that been another man looking at her that way—*Chris*—she would have shivered, filled with anticipation about what might come next. Not this man though.

It made her shiver, sure.

But in *disgust*.

"Maria," Jorge said.

"What about her?"

"That private school I had mentioned. I think it's time we—"

Valeria opened her mouth, ready to plead if that's what this asshole wanted, to keep her daughter with her, but the ringing phone on the desk saved her the trouble. For now, anyway. There was no way in hell she was allowing him to send Maria away.

"A moment," Jorge muttered, giving her a glare as he reached for the landline. He didn't even bother to pick the phone up, instead hitting a button that put the call on speaker phone as he answered with, "*Hola, casa de Lòpez.*"

The man on the other end of the line spoke fast, his Spanish coming out jumbled, making it hard for Valeria to follow along. Although, she managed to catch a few bits and pieces. Not that she needed to.

The expression on Jorge's face told it all.

He'd moved from annoyed with her to *stunned* in a blink. And then, just as fast, his gaze darkened as his lips pulled into a sneer when he snarled, "*What*?"

"Attacked, they attacked the car," the man muttered.

"*How*?"

"I don't know … I—"

"You better figure it out!"

"Sorry, sorry," the man rushed to say, stumbling over his Spanish yet again when he added, "T-the one, boss, they left him alive. The Canadian."

"Christopher?"

"Yes, him. That one. He asked for a hospital, they told me. After the police arrived, and had called for an ambulance, he asked—"

"*Which hospital*?"

Valeria's heart thundered in her chest. Her fingernails bit into the palms of her hands when she squeezed her fists into tight balls. All that relief she had over Jorge leaving fled in an instant. Instead, a fear replaced it—a fear like never before.

Chris, her heart whispered.

Chris, Chris … Chris.

It had become a mantra.

Repeating with the beats of her heart.

God.

What happened?

She didn't dare ask.

Really, she shouldn't be standing there at all. The second Jorge realized she was still there listening to his conversation, he would snap at her to leave. Until then, however, she planned to stay right where she fucking was because she couldn't move.

Her feet had become cemented to the floor with panic.

"Which hospital?" Jorge demanded again.

"Hospital de Jesús Nazareno," the man said, "but I sent a man over, and they checked him out."

"Where the fuck is he?"

"I'm not sure."

"You're *not sure*?"

Jorge's voice slithered across the room to Valeria's spot in the doorway. Deathly calm, and a little too quiet. That tone meant violence was about to happen.

"Someone attacked the Canadian on the way to the airport, with my men inside the car, and now he is missing, but you don't know where he is?"

"It was the Garcías, boss. They did it."

Jorge stiffened behind his large desk. "Why—"

"The deal with the Canadians, I heard. Word is going around. They're letting it be known they are aware you planned to use that deal to ruin the merger."

"*Fuck.* Who let that information out?"

"I don't—"

"*I don't care what you don't know!*"

Another day, and the sound of Jorge's growing rage would have sent Valeria running. A part of her wasn't as scared of it as she had used to be. Oh, she needed to be careful, and to watch her step when he was in a mood, but it didn't leave her paralyzed with fear anymore.

"You best find out where the Canadian is, because if that man dies before we can get him the fuck out of Mexico, his father will *never* go through with the deal. As for the fucking Garcías, fuck the bastards. The deal is done, we don't need the merger now. Let them have their tantrums."

"It's more than that … they said something else, boss. The officials at the scene—one of them is on our payroll, and he said the Canadian told him the war with the Garcías is on. They're coming for us. We have to get ready."

Jorge noticed Valeria in the doorway, or rather, that she was still standing there. His glowering scowl landed on her before he snapped, "What are you still there for? Don't you have a child to take care of? Get the fuck out of my face!"

She didn't want to move.

She wanted to ask about Chris.

Jorge cocked an eyebrow at her, his stupid mouth already opening to bark at her again like she was a dog who couldn't be trained. Valeria didn't bother to give him that satisfaction before she turned on her heels and headed down the hallway. And even still, his rage continued to flow out of the office, chasing her even after she sat with Maria in the living room again to play.

Her daughter looked to her for an explanation to the man's rage. Valeria said nothing. She couldn't; her heart was still breaking.

She didn't have answers, either.

Jorge said they would handle the Garcías.

He could *not*.

That had never been more apparent to Valeria as she watched the chaos between brothers unfurl in a mess of shoves and shouts between Jorge and Samuel.

"I told you—*I fucking told you*!" Samuel pointed a finger in his brother's face, for once refusing to back down when he had always been willing to do it for Jorge before. "We lost *two* storage facilities the night after they attacked the Canadian on the way to the airport, and—"

"They attacked our father's home," Abril whispered, coming to stand beside Valeria on the porch. She tried to follow along with the newest fight between Jorge, and

Samuel, but her curiosity peaked about what Abril had just told her. At her raised brow, the woman nodded. "This morning—he's in bad shape, unlikely to come out of it."

"No one told me."

"Jorge doesn't care," Abril murmured, "that's what he planned to do when all this was said and done, anyway. Kill our father and take over. Samuel tried to go along with other parts of the plan, but it didn't work out."

She sounded so cold.

So ... *unbothered*.

As though Abril expected this to happen.

It had only been a couple of days, but already, the García cartel was hitting them in every single place where it would hurt the most. Valeria had woken up the night before only to hear Jorge raging down the hall about the fact police raided one of the Lòpez businesses they used as a front to smuggle, but also to launder dirty money. According to what she understood, those weren't things the Garcías should be aware of without someone on the inside helping them.

So, who was it?

And what did it mean for her?

Or for *Maria*?

"Mamá?"

Valeria turned to find her daughter stood on the threshold of the front door. Her wide, tearful eyes stared up at her mother. She rushed to soothe her girl, not wanting her to see the mess happening outside.

Not that it mattered.

Maria was not stupid.

Something was happening. Things weren't right. Jorge didn't care who listened to his fits, or his phone calls.

"It's all right," Valeria told her daughter, kneeling to open her arms so she could bring her child in for a hug. Once

Maria was in her arms, she felt like she might hide her from the rest of the word, and the unknowns. It was a wish, though, and not at all real. "It'll be okay. Aren't you supposed to be in bed?"

It was a little early for bedtime, but it kept Maria out of trouble.

Her daughter shrugged. "I heard yelling."

Valeria plastered on a smile. "They're just having a disagreement, that's all. Nothing to worry—"

"Open the gates! Open the fucking gates!"

At Jorge's shouts, Valeria was quick to scoop her daughter up from the porch when she stood. Turning fast, she watched the whole group of gathered men head for the dirt road. Except Jorge, and his brother.

Abril, however, stayed on the porch.

"What's happening?" she asked.

Her sister-in-law smiled. "Good things."

"*What*?"

Abril glanced sideways, anticipation lighting up her gaze. "I said, *good things* are happening, Val."

It terrified her to ask if Abril said that because she might have had her hand in causing this chaos. Had she? Was that even possible?

"Who is at the gates?"

Abril shrugged. "Chris, they said. Your Canadian."

Valeria would have noted the *your Canadian* comment, but she was a little busy with the fact Abril said it was Chris.

"Are you sure?" she demanded.

"That's what they said before they took off."

Valeria stared out into the distance, watching the men disappear down the darkening dirt road. Jorge and Samuel stared in the same direction; their fight forgotten for the moment.

Was it him?

Was it Chris?

God.

She hoped so.

She needed it to be so.

Maria's arms tightened around her mother's neck. "Mamá?"

She couldn't speak or smile for her child.

Valeria looked to Abril who was far calmer, and ready. Although, for what, she didn't have a clue. "What do we do now?"

"We get a bag ready for you and her."

"A bag—"

Abril nodded. "Quickly, before they get back or Jorge notices something is up. Wouldn't want to ruin his part of the plan when mine went off without a hitch, no?"

What was happening?

Valeria didn't dare ask.

Right now, it was just better to do what she was told.

Valeria came back out of the house, although she had to make Maria stay tucked away in her bedroom with the little pink book bag hidden under her bed, as the men appeared on the darkened road. They walked in a line, with one moving slower than the rest in front.

Her heart ached.

"Is that him?" Jorge asked. "Is it?"

Samuel grunted under his breath the closer the men came. "It looks like it."

Abril, who had now taken a seat on the wicker chairs on the porch, stood and gave Valeria a quick nod. "You good?"

"Yeah, Abril."

"Good. Keep up, okay?"

What?

Valeria didn't get the chance to ask, her attention going back to the men as their boots crunched against the gravel road. One guard picked up his pace, jogging past the slower man heading the group to dart in Jorge and Samuel's direction. Overhead, the blackened sky twinkled with stars, but for whatever reason, it seemed foreboding to Valeria.

Night always held secrets.

Didn't it?

"Chris says they're coming, boss," the man told Jorge. "*Here*—the Garcías got a hold of him and then let him go to send us a message. They will storm the ranch."

Valeria went cold all over.

They were secluded.

It was a strength as much as it was a weakness out here. There was no way out of this fucking ranch except the road. The miles and miles of desolate land surrounding them only led to the cliffs, or more fucking *land*.

How were they supposed to get out?

Or ... was that the point?

Jorge stared over his shoulder to the women on the porch. "So, we fight back. We've got the artillery, and—"

"The girls need to go," Samuel muttered. "They can't be here for a fucking *gun fight*, Jorge. You were the one who demanded we stay on the ranch while the Garcías were tearing us apart outside of here because it would be *safer*. That's what you said, but it's not fucking safe anymore. They need to go if the Garcías are coming here. Don't be stupid."

"I'm *not*, I'm—"

"You won't have time," came a quiet, yet still strong, voice.

Valeria's gaze drifted to the bruised, sore-looking man approaching the group with the rest of the guards at his back. He looked like Chris, sure. From the browns of his eyes, to the shape of his face. He wore the same clothes, although now they were dirty, tattered, and bloodied, that he had when he left. Everything about him reflected a man she fell in love with through stolen moments and heated stares. With only a passing glance, one wouldn't be able to see he *wasn't* Chris.

She sensed it in her *heart*.

His raising hand, empty of a familiar woven leather band, only confirmed what her heart and soul already recognized. He swore to Maria he wouldn't take that band off his wrist, and he didn't break his promises. *Ever.* The man standing in front, the one who sounded and looked just like Chris, was not Chris at all.

His twin, she realized.

Valeria was looking at Corrado Guzzi.

She had another striking understanding. She was the only one who saw the difference. He had never mentioned his twin to anyone else there—never spoke about his life, family, or siblings.

The man—*Corrado*—passed her a glance, but didn't linger. There was no familiarity in his stare beyond recognizing her face, perhaps because someone had told him who she was. She wasn't sure, but he didn't stare at her the way Christopher did.

His eyes didn't hold love for her.

Because this man didn't love her.

"What does that mean?" Jorge snapped.

"They dropped me off just far enough away to walk in," Corrado said, wiping at the blood on the corner of his mouth with the sleeve of his jacket, "but they weren't waiting. If they're not already coming in on the ranch, they will be soon.

You won't have time to get out of here. And not the women, or your daughter."

Abril stepped forward, taking the front stairs on the porch two at a time until she reached the ground, interjecting herself into the conversation with, "The horses. We can take the horses out with a couple of men, yes? We'll be safe as long as we're away—they won't think to search for us out there, Jorge."

"I don't kn—"

"Let them take the fucking horses," Samuel snarled. "We don't have time for this shit!"

The roar of an engine punctuated Samuel's statement in the distance. Following that came the sound of rapid fire shattering the silent night.

Pat, pat, pat, pat.

Jorge was already turning to head for one guard homes where they kept the guns, and whatever else they needed to defend the land. "Take the horses, then. And a man for Val, and one for Abril. *Go.*"

He didn't glance back as he left.

Because he didn't care, Valeria realized.

Jorge never had.

It didn't even sting.

Abril wasted no time looking Valeria's way. "Get Maria … the horses are already tacked up."

Right.

Because anyone who had been to this place would understand that there was no way out … without a horse, and a fucking boat. Someone like *Abril*.

That should have been another clue.

Nothing here was as it seemed.

~

"What's happening, Mamá? Why is it so loud?"

Valeria hushed her daughter as she shoved the girl up into the saddle. "Just hold tight, okay. We're going to go on a little —" Gunfire cut through the air, far enough away from the stables, sure, but loud enough to take her breath away. Maria's eyes widened further, but she was determined to get on these horses, and leave, *now*. "Come on, move up for me."

Maria did.

Valeria mounted the horse, too.

"Abril—"

"Let's go! We don't have time to fuck around in here!"

One of the two guards that had been waiting out by the stable doors came around the corner just as Valeria turned to tell her sister-in-law to hurry. She saw the way Abril bent down, her fingers sliding into the leg of her riding boot—she had already been dressed to ride, although Valeria only noticed it now—before standing straight with a knife in her hands.

That blade swung around and embedded deep into the neck of the guard. Valeria sucked in a sharp breath, her arm swinging around to cover Maria's eyes as the man dropped to the ground, and Abril yanked the blade out.

Blood *sprayed*.

The man choked.

Abril looked her way. "*Go*."

"Not without you," she said just as fast.

"What the fuck was that back there?"

Abril's attention flew around the corner of the stable, the knife in her hand flipping around so she had a good grasp on the hilt. "Valeria, *go*."

"But—"

They already had the two horses ready for her, and Abril to ride. Standing in the stable's middle floor, the horses tacked up, and edgy because of the noise of gunfire and shouting men outside the building, but ready to go.

Ready to run.

Abril reached out and slapped the thigh of Valeria's horse with a loud *crack*. "Heeyah!"

She had time to grab hold of her daughter, and the reins before the horse reared back from the slap, and jerked forward. They came out of the stable doors in a full gallop, the man coming back toward them barely got out of the way.

Valeria looked back in just enough time to see Abril kill that man, too. Which meant no guards would follow them off the ranch, she realized. It was just them, and the horses, now. Abril was quick to jump on the horse waiting for her, wasting no time coming out of the stables at full speed.

Her horse was fast, but skittish from the noise. She managed well enough to get the animal steered toward the fields behind the house that would take them further away from the chaos behind them. It took Abril no time at all to catch up with Valeria, her horse coming alongside hers as she glanced over.

"We're going to the cliffs," Abril said, her voice faint, the words almost disappearing in the wind. "We don't have a lot of time."

"Why is that where we have to go ... or how do you kn—"

Abril smiled. "Who do you think helped to start this war, Val?"

"But why?"

She was *so* grateful.

So much.

Was this her freedom?

It seemed like it.

Tasted like it.

"Why?" Valeria asked again.

Abril would have sacrificed so much for what she did here tonight. Most certainly.

"I needed to be free, too," Abril said. "Just differently than you."

What could she say to that?

"Mamá," Maria whispered before the girl peered up at her mother. "I smell *fire*."

She did, too.

Whispering in the wind.

What was burning?

Her arm tightened around Maria's waist, and her heels pressed hard into the horse's hind end. "Keep looking forward, *niña*."

Because they weren't ever going back.

Not now.

CHAPTER
18

Someone slammed a Kevlar vest into Chris's chest, and he barely caught the item before it fell to the ground. His mouth opened to thank the man who had given him the protective item, but Alessio Sorrento had already turned to move onto the next waterproof storage crate they had brought along for this assault.

The tension in Alessio's back—his twin's lover, one of two people that Corrado spent his life with—said the man wasn't in the mood to talk. On a good day, Alessio's moods regularly swung one way or another. Today, however, he was swinging toward the bad side of things, and it all had to do with Chris.

Or rather, the plan Chris and Corrado came up with over the phone during a late night call after the morning Abril told him what she would do to help. Chris had to figure out the rest, how to *get in* the ranch without coming in through the front—the cliffs would be the only way, he knew. Then, he needed people. He couldn't do this alone, and so he called his twin, who made more phone calls. Amid all that, Corrado thought switching out the two of them—because his twin was far better in an assault-type situation one-on-one than he was —would be a good idea.

Alessio did not agree.

"Les," Chris said.

"Just get fucking dressed. We don't have time."

The man's sharp order wasn't just for Chris, and it slithered through the small crowd that had gathered on the edge of the cliffs. It was a handful of men—the three that The League spared for this mission, a couple from his father's organization that had skills in retrievals or assaults, and the handful Andino Marcello gave to them to use.

It wasn't much.

Still a team though.

Dressed in tactical gear, with assault weapons that would mow down a crowd, if needed, this job should be easy. Get in once the girls were out, clear the ranch, and hightail it back to the cliffs where they would all leave like this had never even happened.

Simple, right?

Yeah, Chris hoped so.

This all came down to a prayer.

Down below, three boats waited. Speed boats that one of their guys had got a hold of when he called through to a contact he had in Mexico. Alessio scaled the wall, his years of rock climbing coming in handy when they needed to secure a rope ladder with metal steps down the cliffs.

There should be only one way into the ranch.

Just one.

They were wrong.

Someone just needed the means and the mode.

His means were Valeria and Maria.

His mode was The League.

Two days.

That was all he had to put this plan together, get these eight men into the country and *here*, and make this fucking shit work. It had been a toss-up whether they pulled it off. No one would say it might work, and but for the grace of God, they were here.

Now, it was Abril's turn.

Half of this plan had been Chris's. The other side of things belonged to her. None of it would work if she didn't get her part of the plan in order, and so now he waited beside cliffs and water that made his heart race. He'd just come up from there, and one way or the other, he was going back down those cliffs to get in a boat before the night was over. That fear of water would never leave him.

Of that, he was most sure.

Chris had never been more grateful for his father forcing him to get in water after the almost drowning incident, and making him learn to swim because *you have to learn, Chris, you have to*. Never had he thought he hated his father more than he did when Gian dunked his head under water at only aged seven, apologizing because he knew it scared his son, but still determined to make him work through the terror.

He had.

It still made him fucking edgy.

Chris turned to the readying men, wanting to go over the plan just one more time—everyone needed to be on the same page, and while The League members likely already were, it was the men who came from outside of their organization that concerned Chris. No one needed to be a fucking hero here. It wouldn't help.

His speech stopped at the galloping in the distance. The unmistakable *clip-clop* of hooves hitting soil hard. With the sky a blank canvas of black, it was hard to see into the dense stretch of forest that separated a small portion of the desolate land before one came out to the cliffs.

His gaze strained.

Heart *thundering*.

Chris forgot everything he would say, everything he wanted, as his world came to a standstill. *Now or never*.

Either those horses would carry a woman he had somehow fallen hopelessly in love with during the process of trying to save her life, and her child, or all of this had been for nothing.

He didn't think that way though.

Those thoughts were *poison*.

Time slowed when the horses broke through the tree line, and even in the darkness, he recognized how she rode the animal. As the animals came closer, he distinguished little Maria in front of her mother with Valeria's arm keeping her safe, and her pink book bag tight in her small hands.

Chris rushed forward before the horses had even come to a stop. The clock in his mind ticked down again. They were running out of time, surely. How long would it be before someone realized the fight between the rival cartels had been a manufactured war, only meant to distract just long enough for them to finish all of this?

They needed to get out of here.

"Come on, let me help you down," Chris said, coming alongside the horse to reach for Maria first. Unsurprisingly, she reached back, and he almost laughed when a little gray head with two pointed ears peeked out of her backpack. *That kitten of hers.* "Snuck her out, did you?"

Maria grinned in Chris's arms. "She's my kitty, I *had* to."

Right.

Goddammit.

He would get her a million kittens if that's what she wanted.

Just not tonight.

Chris kneeled down when he had Maria's feet on the ground, and Valeria hauled herself off the horse, too. Turning, he pointed at Alessio who was tying safety lines to the stakes he had beat into the ground for when they took the girls down the cliffs to return to the boats. The ladders were fine, and they would use them, too, but the lines were just for added protection.

His demand.

"See that man right there?"

Maria nodded.

Chris smiled her way. "He's my brother's ..." Okay, that was a difficult one to explain, but he managed with, "My brother's spouse, yeah? He will take you down the cliffs, and you hold on tight, okay? Listen to everything he says, make sure you keep a tight hold on your kitten, and—"

"We're going down the cliffs?"

He glanced up at Valeria, seeing the worry in her eyes. "It's the safest way out of here without drawing attention. It's how we came in, and it's how we planned to leave, too."

He didn't miss the way her throat jumped at that statement.

"What?" he asked.

"You came up from the water?"

Oh.

It wasn't her that she worried about, he realized. It was *him*.

"You do what you gotta do, sweetheart." Chris went back to Maria, giving her a playful wink, so she didn't feel as scared. "Think you can handle it?"

Maria shrugged. "It's very dark."

"The boats will shine lights up."

"There're boats?"

Her surprise made him laugh.

"They go *really* fast, too."

"*Wow.*"

"Les?" Chris called.

Alessio didn't waste time coming over with harnesses ready in his hands—three. One for Maria, Valeria, and Abril who still hadn't gotten down from her horse. Chris figured he would deal with that one after he handled Valeria.

Maria went to Alessio with no arguments.

Chris turned to Valeria as he stood.

It took their gazes meeting in the darkness for his world to slow again. Two days he had been in pain because he had left her, punishing himself second by second for the suffering she endured behind closed doors with no one to help. And yet, here she was, as beautiful and perfect and *strong* as ever.

While people moved all around them, unpacking AKs from waterproof cases, and getting the finishing touches ready for their oncoming assault on the ranch—Corrado needed to make it out alive, after all—Chris took a moment to step forward. His arm linked around Valeria's neck, tightening to pull her close to him until he hid her away from the rest as she folded into his chest.

Closer was better.

He needed her closer *always*.

Chris tipped his head down and pressed a kiss to the top of her head. Her fingers curled around the edge of the Kevlar vest he'd thrown on, and he breathed her life in.

Because she was ...

Alive.

"He'll take you down the cliffs, too," he whispered.

Valeria looked up, eyes dimmed with confusion. "Aren't you coming?"

"Later. We have to get my brother out first."

"But that means you're not coming with—"

"Soon, okay? I will follow you soon."

"*Chris*."

"Don't make this hard, Val. Argue with me another day. Tell me this was crazy some night when you're next to me in bed. Give me the silent treatment over dinner because I didn't follow you like you wanted me to. Right now, though, let Alessio put the harness on you, and take you down the cliffs to the boats. Because that means you can do all those things someday. And that's what you wanted, right?"

She nodded, bottom lip trembling. "A chance, yeah."

"Here's your chance, babe."

Her grip on his vest flexed tighter. "But you're coming *right after*?"

"As soon as I can."

Valeria made a soft noise in the back of her throat before standing on her tiptoes to press a fast, burning kiss to Chris's lips. She didn't linger, not nearly as long as he wanted her to, but it was enough to remind him why he was here doing this.

And that was worth *everything*.

Her hand patted his chest over the Kevlar vest. "I'll … see you soon, then?"

Chris grinned. "Absolutely."

"Okay," she said in a breath.

He didn't watch her walk to the cliffs because that was easier, and while he wasn't at all scared to run into a gunfight between rival cartels for his twin … watching that woman walk away was the hardest thing he would ever have to do in his life.

He wasn't ready for it.

Instead, he looked to Abril still on the horse.

"You're next," he told her.

Abril arched a brow. "I'm not leaving."

"I beg your pardon?"

"This is my home—*my family*. I have a place here, a purpose here. I can do what they can't, and I can do it better."

The cartel, he knew.

"Abril—"

"Do you have an extra gun for me?" she asked.

There would be no argument. Her tone made it clear.

"Pink?" he called to the Marcello enforcer handling the guns.

The man's attention flew his way. "Yeah?"

"Toss me a gun that's ready."

An AK was in his hands in ten seconds, and he handed it up to Abril on the horse. She used the strap to secure the weapon at her back before nodding at the horse Valeria had brought along.

"That's Butter—it's a good horse. I want to keep it. You'll ride it back."

Well, all right, then.

"I take it, the plan has changed?" he asked.

Abril laughed airily. "For the cartel, plans *always* change."

"And the new plan is …?"

"I walk out of here on top. The rest of you have to follow along."

Chris nodded.

Seemed simple enough.

Truth was, some women didn't need to be saved. They didn't *want* to be saved. Not when they would do it themselves and do it better. Abril was one of those women.

Chris was fine with that—she wasn't *his* woman. She could do whatever she wanted as long as he got what he needed.

He had that now.

On horseback, Chris and Abril arrived back at the ranch first. The group, in their tactical gear and with guns ready, wouldn't be too far behind them, though. That was the least of his concerns when the property line of the infamous Lòpez compound came into view.

Flames licked at the sky.

Smoke clung to the air.

"Oh, my God," Abril whispered.

The ranch was burning. From what he saw, a barn, three of the houses, part of the stables, and a good portion of the land. The Garcías came in hard, and they weren't fucking around here. The whines of the horses echoed from where they were stuck in the stables, and unable to get out of their stalls. The loud smack of their hooves crashing against the wood walls told him the animals were panicking, and right-fully so.

Around the corner of one building, Chris caught sight of a man peeking around the side with a gun aimed across the property at one house that wasn't burning. Gunfire lit up the sky, from several directions, although it all seemed aimed right at that house. With the windows blown out, he figured they'd been shooting at it for a while, now.

That's where he needed to go.

"My horses," Abril said, her tone growing frantic when she added, "*they will die!*"

Chris pulled his shirt high to cover his mouth and give him the ability to breathe cleaner air. Abril did the same when he nodded over at her. "Head for the stables, and get the animals out," he said, "be fucking *careful*, and quick. That house they're shooting at, I bet it's where Jorge is, and the rest."

His brother, too?

Maybe.

"How long?" she asked.

"Ten minutes," Chris said, "because that's how long the

team estimated it would take for them to run in—what's your plan *now*?"

"White flag it."

He raised a brow. "Really?"

Abril shrugged. "I have to make it look good, don't I?"

"You play a dangerous game."

"I intend to *win*."

Chris tipped his chin down, a silent agreement to her statement. "Ready, then?"

"So ready."

She pressed her heels into the horse and took off. He did the same to Butter although he felt the animal's hesitance to approach the chaos in front. No animal—none with any instinct—wanted to walk into a smoky blaze with this much noise. Still, the horse went as it'd been trained, it's trot turning into a gallop with Chris's encouragement.

He swung that gun at his back around to his hands, a tight grip on the reins with his other as his finger wrapped the trigger. All he needed to do was keep pulling back that trigger, fast and repeated, and a bullet would come out each time. It was his aim while on a horse that concerned him.

Apparently, for no reason.

Coming around the side of the building that one man was using as a shield, he caught the fucker in the side of his face when he turned to look at the approaching horse. Blood and matter sprayed the wood of the wall before the body hit the ground.

Chris snapped his heels into the horse, a *heeyah* coming through his clenched teeth to urge the animal closer to the gunfire around the west side of the property. Aiming that gun as the horse jumped over a six inch line of fire snaking along the dried grass on the pathway between the houses, his distraction stopped the sounds of whizzing bullets just long enough for attention to turn on him.

His finger pulled back on the trigger fast—*pat, pat, pat, pat*. Rapid fire, or rather, as fast as his finger pulled on the fucking trigger. He knew how many bullets were in his clip, and until the rest of the team came onto the property, he needed to be conservative with his ammo.

Although, by the time the men from the García cartel realized what was happening, Chris had already gotten his horse around the side of the house under attack. He rolled off the animal, hitting the ground with his feet, as bullets sprayed the corner of the home, sending wood splintering and flying past the horse's hind end.

Abril would find the horse.

They wouldn't go far.

Chris let his hand drift over the shuddering coat of the animal before he patted it. "*Merci,*" he told the horse. A quick slap and a shout to *go* from him, and the horse took off, hooves beating against the ground fast to get far away from the noise.

More bullets hit the side of the house.

Fuck.

Chris darted for the back porch, flinging himself over the railing and rolling to the back door that looked like someone kicked it open. The dead body in the hallway—a Lòpez guard he recognized—was a grisly sight he stepped over as he headed deeper into the back of the house. His gun was already back in his hands and aimed in front of him. He didn't put on as much tactical gear as the rest of the team, like covering his face, because he had plans here.

He wanted Jorge to *understand.*

He never said whether he would kill the man to Abril—it felt more like an unspoken agreement between the two. Jorge needed to go. Not only for what he did to his wife and child, but because Abril needed *no question* to her place here once it was all said and done.

A man popped his head around the corner, down the hall. Near the staircase that led into the upstairs of the home. They used this house for the guards, and servants on the property. He didn't recognize the man's face, although even if he had, he still would have fired.

The more gone, the better.

Less work when the team got here.

Chris pulled back the trigger before the man even realized what was happening and stepped over the corpse when the noise started upstairs. The shouts in Spanish, orders, he thought, although he wasn't sure.

Didn't matter.

He recognized that voice.

Jorge.

A spray of bullets came in through a broken window five feet to his left, peppering the wall with *more* bullet holes. It looked like swiss cheese.

Damn.

Chris took the stairs two at a time, keeping that gun in front of him and ready for whatever was coming next. He took no time at all to find where the group upstairs hid themselves in a back bedroom with three large windows. With the glass gone, they were using the windows to rest their own assault weapons.

Four, he counted.

One glanced over his shoulder.

Chris grinned.

It was like staring into a fucking mirror.

Corrado.

"Brother," he murmured.

Corrado returned his smile. "Chris."

Their quiet exchange drew the attention of the other three men. Two, guards for the family that Chris recognized, and the other … *Jorge*. Corrado was quick to lean back along the windowsill, readjusting the aim of his gun before he pulled back the trigger twice in quick succession. Just like that, the two guards were *done*.

Jorge turned with his gun already aimed for Christopher. His eyes widened, shifting between Chris in the doorway, and Corrado on the other side of the room.

"Figured it out yet?" Chris asked, his own gun ready, blinking red light from the sights nailed to the spot between Jorge's eyes. "Meet my *twin*. The Marcellos say hello, but me? I only want to say fuck you."

He pulled back the trigger.

He didn't care to let the man talk.

Jorge just needed to *die*.

Chris watched the bullet rip through the man's head, sending him flying back into the windowsill where he'd been standing to shoot. His body damn near flipped out the window, but instead, hung there.

"How far are they away?" he heard his twin ask.

"Not far now, I imagine. And thanks."

Chris looked Corrado's way.

His twin shrugged.

"Wasn't a big thing," Corrado murmured.

That was a lie.

This was a *huge* thing.

"Sometimes, let me watch your back," Corrado said. "It can't always be you looking out for me, man. That's all."

Chris nodded. "Sometimes. We have to wait, now."

"For what?"

"The white flag."

A false surrender.

~

"*Alto—para!*"

The command cut through the air when a figure, womanly in her shape with a white rag held high, emerged through the smoke in the middle of the dirt road. With her head tilted down, the darkness behind her form made her quite a sight with the gray cloud lingering in the air.

The shouts for the firing to stop came again, louder the second time. Through the broken windows of the house, the men of the García cartel passed verbal orders between them, one at a time.

Stop.

Stop the firing.

Halt.

Repeatedly until the bullets stopped flying, and a silence settled over the ranch. Oh, there was still noise, sure. Hooves clattering in the distance, and the crackle of flames from buildings that were still burning to the ground.

The war, though?

All at once, it stopped.

"Where is Samuel?" Chris asked.

Corrado glanced his way. "What?"

"The other brother—*Samuel* Lòpez."

"Never saw him."

Chris wasn't even sure his brother knew what the man looked like, but perhaps Jorge had been so distracted in the gunfight he'd forgotten about his other sibling. It didn't matter as he had other things to focus on right now.

Like the woman outside.

Abril kept her head tilted down low as she walked the

road, one slow step at a time. Still, she kept her hand and that white rag high, a clear signal that the Lòpezs were giving up. During his time in the house, he pinned down where the leader of the other side had been hiding out—in a barn that didn't burn—because the García men flanked the structure from all directions, never turning back to retreat, but only facing forward to keep anyone from getting too close.

Chris hadn't been wrong.

The man that emerged from the barn, hands free of a weapon, dressed differently than the rest. He carried himself differently even in his steps—confident and sure. A war had been raging all around him, and yet the man's suit looked tailored to his form and without even a speck of dust on the dark fabric.

He tipped his head back as he came closer to Abril, a pleased smirk curving his lips as though he just caught his prey.

"Abril," the man—Roberto García, the man Abril would have to marry through an arrangement made by her father—called about thirty feet away from the approaching woman, "Thank you for helping me."

Abril said nothing.

She kept walking.

"What's happening?" Corrado asked.

Chris made a noise under his breath. "With her, you never know."

It wasn't a lie.

The García men gathered behind their leader, allowing Chris a quick count of the remaining men on their side of things. About twenty, he thought. How many were here before?

Twenty wasn't a large number though.

Easily handled.

Twenty also wasn't the *entire* cartel, but Chris bet Roberto had been smart enough to bring what would be more than he needed to strong-arm the ranch under his control. His mistake to assume, however.

He'd learn soon enough.

Abril and Roberto stood face to face before they spoke again. Abril stared up at him, her face a mask of nothingness. She gave nothing away—the calm in the eye of a hurricane.

Chris thought … *God help the souls who come up against her.*

She would be a force.

"You've given me all I wanted, *princesa*," Roberto said clearly, his voice traveling over the silent ranch to reach even Chris's spot in the window, "I have the cartels, and I have *you*."

Abril laughed light and sweet, her lips curving salaciously at what he implied. "Is that really what you think?"

Roberto stiffened. "I don't—"

"I only needed to make this easy," Abril interjected, her gaze burning as she dropped that white rag to the ground, "and round you up like *dogs*."

Roberto took a step back.

Abril dropped to the ground, body flat on the dirt as a line of figures came out of the smoky darkness where she first emerged. The team arrived, it seemed, and Chris finally figured out where Samuel Lòpez had gone.

It looked like he'd been waiting on his sister. Everyone had loyalties. Rarely did others know what they were though.

The Garcías made it easy on the team by gathering behind their leader. Samuel fired his AK first, peppering Roberto García with at least fifteen bullets before the man's bloodied body fell back to the ground.

Abril covered her head.

The team moved in.

Chris looked to Corrado. "Time to go."

"We should stay out of Mexico for a while, huh?"

"Oh, yeah."

Most certainly.

CHAPTER 19

Valeria thought she knew what exhaustion was, but she had no idea until she was in the backseat of a town car, driving through dark streets, and feeling like if she closed her eyes, she would instantly fall asleep. She didn't know where Alessio was driving to, and he didn't answer many questions once he had guided their boat to a port where he paid a waiting man a bribe to look the other way.

Still, Valeria forced her eyes to stay peeled open even as her daughter had fallen asleep with her head in her mother's lap. The kitten—she still wasn't sure how Maria snuck the cat into her bag—slept happily on the floor of the car near her feet, unbothered by the occasional swaying of the vehicle.

"Not long now," she heard Alessio say from the front.

"Oh?"

"We'll be staying at a hotel for just long enough to get the jet in the air."

Valeria glanced up, confused. "The jet?"

"Compliments of your friend. They also brought papers along—forged, mind you—that will get the two of you through customs without problems when the time comes. We need to keep moving. The others will follow, but through their own plans."

She still didn't understand.

Her tired brain again.

"They will be okay, right?" she asked.

Alessio's gaze darted to the rear-view mirror, meeting hers for a moment before he put his attention back on the road ahead of them where it needed to be. "They better be."

His underlying threat couldn't be missed.

It reminded Valeria of what she had heard Chris say about Alessio to her daughter. *Spouse* was the word he used, but to her, he had also told her that *married* was not the right way to describe his twin's relationship.

"How long have you been with Corrado?"

Alessio's stare darted back to the mirror. "Straight to the point, aren't you?"

"I need to talk or I will fall over."

"It's okay to sleep."

"It's okay to talk, too."

The man chuckled. "Many years—we have been together many years. However, we have only been with Ginevra for a little over a half a year."

Valeria blinked.

He *laughed*.

"Wait, it's *three* of you? Together? *All of you*?"

A part of her had thought Chris's twin was gay. This man suggested something else, with an extra twist, and she had to process that to respond appropriately.

Alessio nodded. "Poly. New concept?"

She thought about that for a moment.

"Well, if it works for you."

"It does," he murmured. "For us, it is perfect."

"That's what counts."

Silence drifted through the car for the rest of the drive. She was grateful that Alessio had been telling the truth, and the hotel wasn't far away. Another ten minutes of driving, and he pulled the vehicle into the underground garage.

She would have carried Maria inside, but Alessio stepped

forward to take the girl before she could even try to get her out of the car.

Valeria wouldn't say it out loud, but she doubted she had the strength or energy to carry her daughter inside the building. She was happy to follow behind Alessio as he strolled through the main lobby of the hotel as though he knew where he was going, and he had been here before.

Maybe he had.

How long were they planning this?

Valeria knew better than to ask.

It didn't matter.

She was *free*.

"We should get a call soon," he said as they stepped into an elevator.

"From who?"

"Whoever is still alive at the ranch."

Valeria stiffened.

A cold dread slipped down her spine.

Alessio chuckled, passing her a look. "Mmm, and now you know what I have been thinking for the last several hours. It was me, or Corrado, though, and since he is the only one who looks like Christopher, it made sense for him to go in. Which meant, no matter what, I had to stay behind … our —*Ginevra*, well, at least one of us has to go home. That's what we promised her. This time, it's me."

Valeria smiled, as faint as it was. "Him, too, I'm sure."

"He better."

She heard it loud and clear in his tone—that threat *again*. Only this time, she realized he wasn't only making it for the woman in his life, but because he loved someone back at the ranch, too. She understood that feeling all too well.

It ached in her chest, too.

Soon, the elevator reached the floor that Alessio had

chosen, the structure jumping before the doors slid open to expose a hallway that led to only one door at the end. At her questioning glance, he shrugged.

"Marcellos have expensive taste," he said. "And he wanted the best for his wife while she waited. I guess she didn't want to stay in New York ... she wanted to see you as soon as she could."

Valeria froze. "Do you mean—"

"Val? *Oh, my God, Val!*"

Haven.

Valeria found her best friend coming out of the door down the hall. The person who had helped to protect her for years when she was hiding from Jorge, who helped to raise her daughter ... the woman who helped to teach Maria how to speak English, who read her daughter nighttime stories when Valeria had to work late nights, and couldn't be there to put her child to bed.

Haven.

She hadn't been able to think much about her friend after Jorge caught and took her back if only because she didn't want to draw attention to Haven. God forbid the cartel go after Haven when all she had done was *help*.

"Haven," Valeria said, her voice faint, locking gazes with the blonde-headed woman down the hall. "Why did you do all of this for me?"

Haven, in her skinny jeans and silk blouse, tall and confident, head high because she had always been proud, came forward with arms already opened. "It was nothing ... nothing you wouldn't have done for me. I'm sorry it took so long."

She shook her head.

"Don't be sorry for that ... *don't be.*"

It was all she said before her beautiful friend came all the way down the hall to wrap her in a hug that reminded her of home. That was the thing—Valeria never had a home for so many years, and then she stumbled upon this woman. Who gave her a place to live, fed her, taught her how to survive, and helped her raise her child.

She *adored* Haven.

Loved her so fucking much.

Valeria let out a hard breath when her friend's arms tightened harder around her frame, but it was so fucking good, too. Down the hall, a man came to stand in the hotel's doorway room. His familiar face, still stone cold, and his frame, filling up the doorway as though he should be on a defensive line for a football team and not the head of a major crime family, watched them from a distance without intruding.

Andino.

Haven's new husband.

Valeria just kept hugging her friend.

"Come on," Haven murmured in her ear, "we'll get food into you. We have enough time for that before the jet will be ready for us to leave. It's not safe to stay here—it won't be long before people find out where we are. Apparently, bribes only last so long in this country before someone else's bribe becomes more interesting. Maybe we can wake Maria up so she can eat, too? I miss her so much."

She nodded, but Haven still hadn't let go.

That was okay.

Home almost seemed like home again.

Except it was missing one person, now.

Chris.

∾

The plan to remove Valeria and Maria from Mexico was in motion long before Chris came on the scene, she came to learn on the long flight back to New York. It was *how* they would retrieve the two from the clutches of Jorge and the rest of the cartel they needed help with.

Removing them from the country?

Protecting them after?

Easy, Andino explained.

Valeria had no reason not to believe them, although she didn't think it was as easy as the man said in his dismissive way, but it still stunned her. They only stayed at the hotel long enough to get food in their stomachs before they were on the road again. A Marcello-owned jet waited at a private gate for them to board at an international airport with agents that barely glanced at the fake passports Andino gave her.

Although, they looked kindly upon the envelop of cash Andino passed to them when he walked through first. It worked the same way when they entered the states after landing in New York at a small airport outside of the city where apparently, the Marcellos had connections and didn't mind pulling them to get their business handled.

It all happened so fast.

Simple.

Valeria still felt like she was floating.

Once in New York, they moved to a hall of suites in the Manhattan Waldorf where she found more people waiting. She tried to keep track of her daughter, but let Maria run freely amongst the rooms with Haven when she figured out that the woman looking her in the face was Chris's mother.

How did she know that?

Alessio.

"Cara," Alessio said, smiling as he leaned in to kiss the pretty, red-headed woman with lines around her eyes that appeared whenever she grinned. "No phone calls from your boys yet, but they told me some phones ended up in the water on the way down the ladder."

Cara frowned. "As long as *they* didn't end up in the water."

"Chris can swim."

The statement came from the man who approached behind Cara, making Valeria's eyes widen in familiarity when he smiled her way. "Been a minute since the two of us had the chance to speak, *oui*?"

"Gian," Valeria said, taking the hand he offered when he came to stand beside his wife. "had I known that first day your intentions for being there were to help me—"

Gian shook his head. "No need to say anything or wish for different things. We're here, now, all of us."

"Most of us," Alessio corrected.

Cara gave him a smile. "Still in that mood, hmm?"

"I didn't like the *plan*."

"He's headstrong."

Alessio made a noise under his breath but said nothing.

Cara's gaze turned back on Valeria in an instant. "You must be exhausted."

"Very. And ... still in shock."

"I bet."

"I want Chris, and the rest, to get back safely."

At that statement, all eyes turned back on her. It was only them in the small sitting room at the Waldorf that connected to a larger bedroom, sure, but it still seemed like she suddenly had a huge audience that became enraptured with whatever she might say or do next.

Gian gave Alessio a glance. "Something we should be told ... on *that*?"

Alessio arched a brow. "I'd say so, but we'll wait for him to say it."

"What did I miss?" Valeria asked.

Cara reached out, taking her hands with a warm smile that reminded her of the mother she lost years ago. "*Nothing*—it means nothing. We're so *thrilled* to meet you, Valeria. I would love to spend time with your daughter if that's okay with you?"

Valeria was quick to nod. "Sure, she loves people. Always wants to make them smile."

"I bet she's an angel."

"She's certainly been mine."

One of *several*, Valeria realized.

Her daughter was one of many angels in her life.

"Thank you."

Haven smiled as Valeria took the mug of tea. "You really should try for more than an hour-long nap, Val. Being tired will not make him get here any fast—"

"*There they are! There's the cars! Mamá, look!*"

Valeria peered around Haven's side to see Maria standing on the edge of a chaise at the window, her hands gesturing at whatever was down below. "Maria, it could just be guests coming to the hotel."

"No, it's *Chris*. It is!"

Maria hopped down from the window, the dress Valeria packed for her daughter flying wide around her legs as she darted for the doorway.

At the window, Andino who entertained Maria, smirked back at them. "She's not wrong—they're coming in now."

What?

Valeria no longer cared about her tea, or the fact she was exhausted. She didn't bother to glance at the people milling between the rooms as she followed her shouting, excited daughter as the girl headed out of their room, and down the hall of the hotel. She caught up with Maria before she pressed the button on the elevator for it to open.

She grabbed Maria around her waist, pulling her back as she kneeled to say, "Just wait ... let them come up, okay?"

Sure, she said that.

Didn't mean she meant it.

Valeria's heart thundered as she watched the elevator, and the little sign above it that said the doors opened on the ground floor. The Marcellos closed down the corridor of the hotel, renting every single room for the night to make sure they had all the privacy they needed for whatever might happen.

Footsteps approached behind them.

Their *voices*.

Valeria continued watching the elevator.

"I *saw* him, I did," Maria whispered.

"I bet," she said, believing her daughter. "Just a minute, okay?"

Still, the girl practically vibrated in her mother's arms. It was only in that moment that Valeria realized ... she was not the only person caught in Chris's snare. His caring nature, sweet and yet still firm, caught her daughter's heart, too.

Maria looked up at her mom by tilting her head. "We never have to go back, right?"

Valeria met her daughter's stare, so the girl understood she was telling the truth. "Never. *Ever*."

"Good."

The elevator dinged as the two of them broke their staring contest. The first men out of the elevator weren't faces that

Valeria recognized, but she was still quick to stand, and keep her daughter out of the way so they were able to come through.

And then there Chris was.

At the back with his twin.

"*Chris!*"

Maria's squeal, punctuated by her jumping in place, had him turning with a wide smile in their direction. Valeria let her girl go, and Maria wasted no time darting forward. Corrado slipped out of the elevator first, but her daughter didn't seem to have an issue differentiating who was who between the identical twins. She gave him a smile, sure, but the man Maria wanted was the only one she reached for.

Chris came out of the elevator with arms open, already kneeling to hug Maria. The girl's arms locked around his neck, and he stood, holding her tight all the while. He pressed a kiss to her temple, murmuring something to Maria.

"You still have it?" Maria asked.

Chris grinned and flashed his wrist with the woven leather bracelet. "Of course, *bambina*. Never take it off if I can help it."

"Better not."

"Be nice," she told her smartass child.

At her quiet admonishment, Chris's gaze came her way, and she swore the world stopped. Like her ability to breathe, and the beats of her heart.

It all just … *stopped.*

For him.

"I love you," she whispered.

Chris's features softened. "Do you?"

She was very aware of the people behind her. Of the family that gathered, and the others saying hello to men who arrived back. None of that mattered to her though. Better people be aware now.

Was it crazy?

Yes.

Was it true?

More than anyone understood.

"I do," Valeria said quickly, "I love you."

Chris came forward, still holding Maria—although he shifted her to one arm instead of two—and reached for Valeria. Once his arm locked around her neck, he pulled her in close, his mouth finding hers for a soft, long kiss that made her heart restart all over again.

Damn.

She would have preferred he kept kissing her, but she didn't mind when he pulled away just long enough to touch their noses together, his eyes locking onto hers. Softly, he said, "*Ti amo—sempre.* I love you *always.* As long as you want me."

That was perfect.

Because she wanted him forever.

CHAPTER
20

"You went to Mexico for a *job*."

Chris chuckled as he poured a small glass of whiskey at the wet bar. "I did."

His father came to stand next to him with a knowing smile. "Seems you came back with more than you intended to, Christopher."

"And?"

Gian sighed, his gaze drifting across the room to where Cara was helping Valeria settle Maria for the evening. Once she was in bed, his parents had promised they would leave them be to relax for the night, or as much as they could.

"Bit … rushed," Gian murmured. "What is it about you boys of mine *rushing* into love, hmm?"

"Don't you know?"

Gian shook his head. "I don't, so tell me."

Chris thought it was simple.

Obvious.

"You taught us not to be afraid of love, Papa. You and Ma —watching the two of you growing up showed us what love is supposed to be. Not perfect. Not always easy, or *given* to us. We earn it, we nurture it, and we do that so we can keep it. That's the wonderful part, or I thought so, anyway."

Gian made a soft noise in the back of his throat, turning so that his back was to the wet bar, and he could watch the women across the room as he spoke. "So, what you're telling me is not to worry, yes?"

Chris smiled. "Not about this. I have it handled."

"You always have everything handled. You were not the one of my five boys I had to worry about *that*. Trust me."

He did.

"And I am proud of you," Gian added after a moment.

Chris tipped his glass up for a drink, letting the spices of the heady liquor rove over his tongue before he swallowed it back. Setting the lowball down, he asked, "For what?"

"Doing the impossible. And finding something you wanted, I suppose." Gian glanced his way, that soft expression of his father's turning into something else. The Don was in the room—just like that. All it took was his father flipping a switch, and his mood changed. "As for the cartel ..."

"What about it?"

"I would appreciate knowing what we're looking at now where they are concerned." Gian shrugged his broad shoulders under his tailored, black blazer. "I let you go into Mexico with little plans, or even understanding how all of this would play out."

"To be fair," Chris replied, amused, "even my plans got fucked up. Someone else had her own plans, and she did what she wanted do whether anyone else cared."

"And who is this *someone*?"

"Abril Lòpez. The youngest daughter—same age as Val, but nothing like her, if we're being honest here. And that's not a bad thing, let me say."

"She helped?"

"Helped ... caused a war." Chris made a dismissive noise and waved a hand in the air. "What do the details matter if it's all the same, yeah?"

Gian grunted under his breath. "And what, I assume a

surviving male will now take over the cartel? Will we have to be concerned about retribution for our part we played down there, or not?"

"Oh, no. I assume nothing. Abril is now a new queen on a very broken throne, and that's fine, she likes it there."

His father blinked.

Chris nodded.

What else could he do?

He had not planned for Abril, and when he *decided* to use her help ... the woman had her own schemes running. She was dangerous, a lot like the rest of her family, but a hell of a lot less obvious about it, too.

"We should stay out of Mexico as much as possible," Chris said. "Entirely. I suspect she will be busy tearing down what remains of her father's cartel to rebuild it in the image she prefers, while—"

"Warring with her rivals."

"Mmm."

Gian folded his arms over his chest, considering those words. "You think she would ... use us to her advantage, if we were to return, even for vacation?"

"I think anyone—man or woman—who thinks to assume to underestimate Abril Lòpez will deserve everything they get, and our family should not be the ones who she makes an example out of."

That seemed to be enough for his father.

"I will pass the information along to Andino, then. I am sure the Marcellos won't be welcome down that way, either."

"To be safe," he agreed, "yeah."

Gian glanced his way again, the kinder smile replacing his stony expression. "As for *you* ..."

"What about me?"

"I hope you will settle down, now. I've never said one

way or the other, Chris, on *famiglia* or The League because I thought you had decided long ago."

He cleared his throat. "I thought I did, too."

"And now?"

A laugh burst from his chest.

"This was enough for me. I am a made man, and nothing more. That's where I need to be, and where I want to be. Corrado and I, well, we're old enough now we don't need to be looking over each other's backs all the time, I think."

"You're not wrong." Gian nodded, reaching over to clap his son on the shoulder. "And on the made bit, *good*."

"What would you have said, if I chose the other option?"

"The same thing, son."

Right.

Because that was his father in a nutshell.

And his mother, too.

Speaking of which …

Across the room, Cara took a hug from Maria before the girl darted to take her mother's outstretched hand. Valeria shot Chris a smile over her shoulder before the two disappeared into the connected bedroom of the hotel room. Once the door was shut behind them, Cara looked her son's way with a familiar smile that had his chest growing tight.

He loved his ma.

All the Guzzi boys did.

"She is a sweet child," Cara said, crossing the room to stand in front of Chris. She patted his cheek with a soft palm, pride and support shining through in her actions, and in her eyes. "I was worried about you."

"Sorry, Ma."

"You didn't call enough."

"It wasn't safe, really."

Cara's thumb stroked his unshaven cheek. "And just what do you plan to do with the two of them now, hmm?"

Chris smiled. "We have all the time in the world to figure it out."

Inside, though?

He already knew.

Keep them forever.

~

"That's *three* books," Valeria said, laughing.

Chris grinned to himself in the doorway when Maria gave her mother a dramatic sigh. The girl wasn't at all spoiled, but she still had her mom wrapped right around her pinky finger, as cute as that was.

"But—"

"And we had to get the concierge of the hotel to find the books, Maria."

"Just one more?"

Valeria was trying to get her daughter to fall asleep, but Chris figured the events of the past couple of days had been a bit much. They all needed time to absorb what happened, calm down, and get back to a normal routine. Maria included.

Behind him, the echo of water running into a tub reminded him of what Valeria had been trying to do before Maria crawled out of the bed meant for her, and found them in the bedroom as they talked.

"I'll read her another book," he said, "and you can go have your bath."

Valeria gave him a look. "I don't mind—"

"Neither do I."

"Yes, Chris can read," Maria said. "I want *him* to read me a book now."

He hid his chuckles when Valeria shook her head and tossed the handful of children's books to the bed.

"Anything to get out of bedtime," she teased, strolling past him in the doorway.

He caught her with his hand to her wrist before she could leave. Dropping a quick kiss to her mouth, he murmured, "Enjoy your bath, okay? She's fine with me."

"She is."

That was all she said before leaving him alone in the bedroom with Maria. Chris gave the little girl dwarfed by the big bed and huge blankets a look.

"One book," he said.

"Three," she shot back.

Oh, now they were bartering.

Kids were great.

"Two," he countered.

Maria considered that before nodding once. "Fine, two. Chris?"

"Hmm?" he asked as he crossed the room. "What, *bambina*?"

"Do we get to stay with you now?"

He hesitated as he sat on the edge of the bed, already reaching for the books. "Do you want to stay with me?"

"You kept your promise."

"I did, yes."

"No one except Mamá keeps her promises."

Chris shrugged. "I always will."

"Can we make a new promise?"

"What is that?"

"That you won't leave."

"I don't need to make that promise." He smiled, leaning back on the bed with the book already opened in his hands. "I can't leave, *bambina*."

"Why not?"

"People don't leave things they love, Maria. That's all."

"Oh."

Her soft exclamation echoed in the quiet bedroom.

"Promise to be ours, then?"

Chris nodded as he flipped the page to the beginning in the book. "I can definitely promise that."

She suckered him into *four* reads of two books, but he didn't mind. And by the time he finished, Maria snored away in the bed's middle, unaware when he slipped out of the bedroom to find her mother.

Valeria made it easy for him, considering she left the bathroom door wide open.

"You know," Chris murmured, leaning in the doorway to enjoy the sight of Valeria's tanned legs spattered with bubbles and hanging over the ledge of the tub, "my mother asked me a question earlier."

"Oh?"

"Yes, about you and Maria."

A sly, yet still sweet, smile curved her pouty lips when her gaze darted up to his. It was taking every ounce of his willpower to stay where he was, and not slam the door shut, go to her, and take what he wanted.

Somehow, this woman who had once been so confused about her lust and need for sex because of the constant abuse she suffered, could now look like his personal minx ready to torture him with seduction. Chris was more than willing to let her do that, too.

"And what was that question she asked?"

Chris cleared his throat, refusing to let thoughts of his mother into his mind when this beautiful woman was just across the room, naked but for the water and bubbles hiding her curves from his view. "What I planned to do with the two of you, actually."

Valeria arched a perfect brow. "What does that mean?"

"Better question," he returned, "what do you plan to do?"

"You."

"Pardon?"

Her tongue peeked out to wet the seam of her lips as her hand came up from the water, covered in bubbles and dribbling water down her throat as she pointed a delicate finger at him. "*You*, Chris. I plan to be with you as long as you want me. That's what you told me on the cliffs, right?"

"It was."

"And that still stands?"

"Absolutely, Val."

She grinned. "Then, that's all I care about. Although, I would like to hear your plans."

"With you?"

"Anything. I enjoy hearing you talk. Do you know how long it has been since I wanted to sit and have a conversation with a man? A man that *wanted* to hear me talk, too?"

He blinked.

Swallowed thickly, too.

"You can do anything, and I will be here to help you do that," he said, shrugging. "If you want to put Maria back in her old school, let's do it. Come to Canada with me, or travel back and forth—all right. Maybe I can take you out on a proper date, too."

Valeria winked. "*Maybe*?"

His gaze lifted to meet hers when he murmured, "Yeah, and someday, you might let me marry you. Because that's the thing about this. I don't care what we do as long as you let me love you while we do it."

She sucked in a quick breath.

Chris smiled.

"I see you, and her, and it's all possibilities now. Unending possibilities, sweetheart. We can do anything— everything. You're both looking for something, but I'm right here. You can stop looking now, Val, you found me."

"Yeah, we did, huh?"

"I just wanna learn."

"Learn what?"

He came further into the bathroom, closing the door behind him to quiet the noise so it didn't wake up Maria in the next room. Crossing the space between him and Valeria, he kneeled beside the tub, resting his arms along the ledge so that the two of them were eye-level.

"This," he said, tipping his head to the side when she leaned a little closer to him. Almost close enough that her lips pressed to his if she wanted that. "*Us*. Love, but without everything else, too. That's what I want to do now."

Her dark eyes drifted over his face, pleasure and happiness curving her lips as her wet fingers came to draw a line along the edge of his jaw. "That sounds like the best plan."

"You think?"

"Perfect."

"Like you, then."

She dragged in a quick breath, her top teeth catching her bottom lip as she mumbled, "You always say the right things, you know?"

"Honest things, babe."

"*Still*."

"And only for you," he promised.

Valeria nodded. "Just me."

She closed the distance between them, her soft lips moving against his in a slow, tantalizing kiss that had his cock hardening under his slacks, and his chest pounding in his chest. Her tongue teased at the seam of his lips, ready and willing to take more of what she wanted from him. Chris wanted to give it, too.

Just kissing this woman was intoxicating.

A *privilege*.

It's what he wanted to spend the rest of his life doing, too. Kissing her first thing in the morning, and right before he fell asleep. Love was strange like that, but he didn't mind. He would happily spend the rest of his days at the mercy and whims of this woman if that's what God had planned for him.

She reached for him, soaking wet and dampening his already ruined dress shirt. He hadn't even changed his clothes after arriving back. Which was fine, because she was in a perfect position—wet, in a warm bubble bath—to help fix that little problem of his.

Chris stood, stripping out of his dirty clothes faster than he thought possible. All the while, Valeria's sexy laughter colored up the bathroom, fading once he stepped into that large bathtub, already reaching for her to get what they both wanted the most.

For the first time, he didn't think about needing a condom to be with this woman. He didn't *care*—he fucking wanted her. All of her, and to have her be his. To mingle with her in a way only he would for the rest of their lives.

Nothing was better than that.

As soon as he was sitting in the tub, Valeria climbed into his lap. Her hands found his semi-hard cock—a permanent state for him now whenever he was near her—to stroke him alive until his chest burned with every breath while her hips and ass did this slow, grinding dance, making the water slosh along the tub.

"Did you know," she whispered to him, a sinful grin curving her sexy lips, "that I used to dance?"

Chris blinked. "What?"

Her body kept moving, a sensual beat that had his gaze following all her lines and curves as she moved to a beat he couldn't hear, but swore he sensed it in his bones. Her hands jerking him off was enough to drive him insane, but the memorizing sway of her body had his attention split between the two things.

"What do you mean, *dance*?"

"Stripped," she said simply, "for Haven's club. I used to dance a lot when I first started, but then I moved into helping her more with the business, and only danced occasionally after. It was what taught me I *could* be sexy, and desired, but it was just a *thing*. You made it real for me ... tangible."

"Fuck."

He was still trying to picture the image of her dancing on a stage, a thrill shooting through him, but Valeria gave him a good, real life view right there in the large tub. She let him go, turning around in his lap so that her ass rested halfway above the water, her hands steady on the edge of the tub, keeping her up. She shook her ass beautifully, and there was something primal curling through him as he reached out to grab her while she danced for him, the sliver of her wet pussy peeking out from the water when she lifted high enough.

Her dancing turned into something more erotic—if that were possible—when his hand slipped between her thighs to rub against her pussy. Her hips ground into his palm and fingers. A tremor worked its way through her body because of it.

"Get off," he murmured. "Get off for me and then let me fuck you."

His words only urged her on to grind harder against his hand, letting him feel the pulsing of her pussy when her orgasm approached. Her soft, desperate cries climbed higher until shudders raced through her body all at once, and a gasp rushed from her.

Chris was already pulling Valeria back into his lap before she had even finished shaking from the force of her orgasm. He spread her thighs wide, tucking her back into his chest as he slid his cock into her flexing pussy.

Damn.

"So fucking *tight*," he rumbled against her throat. "Got you milking me, Val, *God.*"

His hand slid along the side of her neck, tipping her head to the side to suck and bite at her racing pulse while she rode his cock like that. He was sure they were making a mess, the sounds of the sloshing water hitting the side of the tub mingling with their hard breaths and his groans.

This right here.

Always.

That's what he wanted.

"Make me come again," she whined, the demand clear even in her neediness. "Please, Chris ... *please*, I want to come."

There was something about his name in her mouth.

It always fucking did it for him.

Jesus.

His arms locked around her like bars as her hips kept that fast tempo. Sliding a hand between her thighs, he worked her clit while she moved her body against him to get what she wanted. His fucking balls ached with a base need to just *empty* into her.

It was only when she was breathing his name like a prayer when she came again that he finally let go, holding her tight to his cock as he released deep inside her shuddering pussy.

"Holy fuck, I love you," he mumbled against her damp skin.

Valeria's breathless laugh filled him with satisfaction because that's what it sounded like, too. "You *better*."

He shifted her in the tub, allowing her to turn around and curl up into his lap as his raging heart settled.

Pleased there, Valeria's breathing came out slow, and steady. His fingers traced lazy, wet circles across her shoulders, and down her back. Each swipe of his fingertips had her shivering and sighing. Minutes passed—too many to count. Long enough for the steam to leave the bathroom, and the hot water to turn only *warm*.

They were content to stay like that, together, still humming from sex, and almost ready to fall asleep, but a quiet call from outside the bathroom had Chris perking up. Little Maria's cry for her mom came again, and Valeria stiffened before she pushed up from his arms.

"Stay in the bath, enjoy it," she said, "she's probably just scared because she woke up in a new place, and—"

Chris leaned in, quieting her words with a kiss. "I'll come, too. You don't have to do anything alone anymore. You know that, right?"

Valeria pulled him in for another burning kiss, whispering, "Yeah, I do."

CHAPTER

21

THREE MONTHS LATER

"Is it weird to have two homes?"

Valeria tipped her head sideways, careful not to interrupt the kind woman who was removing the curling rollers from her hair. "You're asking me that?"

Haven's brow dipped. "Well, yeah. Why not?"

"*You*, Haven."

"What?"

"Doesn't Andino have two vacation homes on the west coast?"

Soft laughter floated throughout the hotel room, reminding Valeria that they weren't alone. It was easy to get lost in the pampering she was experiencing, considering it had started the moment she opened her eyes that day.

It was, after all, her wedding day.

"I think," Ginevra said, the roundness of her twenty-week pregnancy swell coming into view of Valeria's gaze as she stepped between the two women's chairs, "what Val means, is that Andino still has the brownstone, doesn't he? Oh, and the vacation homes. The mansion in the—"

"I don't *use* those," Haven said.

Ginevra winked at Valeria, and she grinned back. This was nice. The easy banter between friends, no topic off-limits, and no worries. She couldn't remember a time in her life when she had more than one friend to count on, and now it felt like she had a small army around her at all times.

Between the people Haven brought into her life from the Marcello side of the things, and with Chris's family ... Sure, her circle was still small in a lot of ways, but it was wider than it had ever been.

That's what counted.

"And you actually live between your two homes," Haven continued. "Weekends in New York, and the week in Toronto. I wondered if that gets tiring."

The travel could be annoying.

Also, very much worth it.

"You let Maria choose, didn't you?" Ginevra asked.

Valeria nodded. "I did. I knew she missed her school in New York, but she also liked Chris's home in Toronto, and the private school she would attend there. As long as I promised she could visit Haven every weekend, she decided Toronto was where she wanted to stay."

Chris, bless his heart, hadn't said a thing. Oh, Valeria knew he wanted to ... more than anything, that man wanted her and Maria with him as much as possible. Yet, he kept quiet for those two weeks it took Maria to decide what she wanted to do.

Really, Valeria had always known what her daughter's decision would be. Chris didn't realize it, but Maria loved him *inexplicably*. He was the exact opposite of the men that had been forced upon her as male influences, including her—may he enjoy his place in hell—dead father.

And to give credit where it was due, Chris loved her little girl. He would spend hours with Maria doing whatever she wanted just because. Bedtimes were spent reading a dozen books because he couldn't seem to tell her no. He learned how to manage her thick, unruly hair because Maria liked their conversations in the mornings while Valeria cooked, and Chris styled it for school.

It was painfully sweet.

Everything she thought they wouldn't have.

Some people didn't understand how, in just a few months, Valeria went from not knowing a man, to living with him and marrying him, but it was an easy choice for her. The *right* one. Because that's what Chris was.

The right man.

The perfect one.

Hers.

And her child's.

"I thought, after a couple of months, you might have felt differently about weekends in New York, and the rest of the time spent there," Haven said, bringing Valeria back to the conversation. "That's all."

"Or are you slyly asking me to spend more time in New York with you?"

Before Haven responded, the stylist pulled the final curler from Valeria's hair, and urged her to tip her head over. A brush was dragged through her thick strands, leaving it wild, and wavy. Once she was sitting straight again, the woman nodded.

"Let me get the hair piece, and I'll work on the style you wanted, Valeria."

"Thank you," she told the stylist.

"And I am *loving* this," the woman added, pointing a finger at the gold lettering on her silk robe.

Mrs. Guzzi, it read.

She wasn't a Guzzi yet. A few more hours had to pass before she would walk down the aisle to meet Christopher waiting at the end, but still ... she loved the robe, too.

"It's great, isn't it?"

"I'll let Corrado know his gift is appreciated," Ginevra

said, sneaking a piece of cheese from the tray next to Valeria's chair. "This is good, I need more."

The stylist went off to do her own thing.

Valeria went back to the conversation with Haven. "Well, which is it?"

Haven laughed. "Neither. I *would* like to see you more, but we're both busy, and it's not like we can't make time, right?"

"Right."

"Oh," Ginevra whispered.

Valeria shot her a look, but the young woman's hand drifted down to rest atop her swell covered by a pale pink, silk robe. "You okay?"

A wedding day was stressful. Her future in-laws did every single thing to make today easy for her, not to mention wonderful and beautiful. Valeria barely needed to lift a finger to plan this wedding from the moment she said yes when Chris asked her at his father's birthday celebration.

The most she had to do was sit down with an event coordinator and pick out things she liked. They delivered everything else for her approval.

The most difficult decision she had to make was picking her wedding dress, and deciding whether she should choose her girls' dresses, or if they should. Haven picked her own dress. Ginevra ended up bringing Corrado and Alessio along last minute for her final fitting because she didn't like the way hers looked with her pregnancy starting to show … and those men calmed her about the dress, *and* the way she wore it.

Valeria smiled at the memory.

Yet another reminder she wasn't alone anymore. She had a whole family, now, spread out amongst many people. Three months ago, she had not realized how much her entire life would change when she rested in a bathtub with Chris, and told him, yes, she wanted to be with him.

It moved fast.

Kind of like them.

Valeria didn't mind.

A wedding day was still … stressful.

She didn't want Ginevra to experience any stress today. Not when she was carrying her niece, halfway through her pregnancy, and should only be glowing.

Which she was.

Mostly.

"It's good," Ginevra said at Valeria's worried expression. "Here …"

Ginevra took Valeria's hand and pressed her palm into the side of her stomach. The soft movement of the baby girl turned into a hard jab. She remembered those hard movements from her long-passed pregnancy with Maria.

"Ouch," Valeria said to Ginevra.

"Right?" She sighed. "I like the cheese—baby girl doesn't."

"Well, she doesn't know what she's missing out on," Haven said, laughing as she grabbed a piece of cheese from the tray before popping it into her mouth. "Just saying."

They were still laughing when the stylist came back into the room, followed by Cara, and little Maria who was already dressed up to the nines in her pretty flower girl gown. She danced over to her mother, doing a little twirl at Cara's urging who beamed.

Already a proud grandmother. Or, that's what Cara said when Maria asked if she could call her *Nonny*.

"She wanted to show you her dress," Cara explained.

"Little early to put that on."

Cara shrugged. "I'll bribe it off her with something."

Valeria shook her head. "Well, if it works."

"Do you like my dress, Mamá?" Maria asked.

Valeria leaned down to kiss her smiling princess. "*Love it.*"

"Come on, now," Ginevra muttered, rubbing circles into the side of her swell. Cara didn't miss it, a concerned frown growing when her attention turned on the woman. Ginevra was quick to explain, "The baby won't relax—the cheese didn't agree with her, I guess. I think I'll find Corrado and let him calm her down."

"Not Alessio?"

Ginevra laughed. "*No*, he makes her dance."

"Ah," Valeria replied, "well, we're okay. We've got lots of time."

"Thanks."

Ginevra was quick to slip out of the hotel room. Valeria didn't worry because Ginny would find Corrado soon enough, undoubtedly. Their entire wedding party had the whole room block booked for the weekend at the tucked away, private villa-styled bed-and-breakfast. It was one of the few things she wanted. A small wedding. The people she cared about the most.

And the man of her dreams.

Valeria had him.

"Mamá, it's not raining," Maria said, climbing up in her mother's lap to sit. "I *checked*."

Valeria laughed.

Yes.

Her *one* worry for today.

Canadian weather was tricky.

"That's great," she said, kissing Maria's cheek. "It's a beautiful day to get married."

Cara nodded.

Haven, too.

"It is," they echoed.

Haven made quick work of smoothing out the lace train of Valeria's wedding gown. She held tight to the bouquet of white roses in her hands, staring at the double doors still closed in front. *Almost time.*

"Now?" Maria asked, bouncing on the spot.

Ginevra laughed. "Not yet."

Haven came to stand in front of Valeria, and for a moment, the rest of the surrounding distractions seemed to disappear. "You okay?"

"So good."

"That's what matters. This dress … *wow*, babe. Banging, huh?"

Valeria grinned. "You think?"

The form-fitted, sleeveless, heavy lace gown wasn't what she had envisioned when she first thought about her wedding dress. She found the gown hanging on a back rack in a dress shop. It fit almost perfectly although they had needed to take the fabric in at her sides to make it tight to her curves. The ivory lace, decorated with pearls, covered the gown from top to bottom where the skirt flared out. The three-foot train was just enough, but not too much.

Regal.

Beautiful.

Like Valeria wearing it.

"It's perfect, Val," Haven said.

"It's not at all like my first."

Haven's smile slipped. "No?"

She hadn't talked a lot about her first—*forced*—marriage,

but especially not to Haven. Not even when she was on the run and had lived with Haven for years. It was something she didn't bring up because she figured … then she wasn't putting Haven in danger unwittingly.

"No, that was some stupid princess … God, it was an ugly thing."

Haven grinned. "Yeah?"

"Not what I wanted."

"And this is?"

That's what she was trying to say.

The emotions made it difficult.

"All of this is exactly what I want," Valeria whispered. "I'm still trying to convince myself that it's real, you know?"

"This is so fucking real, Val. That man loves you. His family *loves you*. Your kid? She's theirs, now. You did *good*, okay? You will not wake up tomorrow and find out this was all a lie, I promise. This is real life—your life as long as you want it. Got it?"

Valeria nodded, dragging in a shaky breath to keep the tears lining her eyes at bay, lest she ruin her makeup. What a mess that would be, and they couldn't fix it when she was a couple minutes away from walking to her future.

"Yeah, I understand," Valeria whispered.

"Good. Sometimes, we need to hear it, right?"

"Right, Haven."

Her best friend winked. "You are worthy of this, never forget that. Him? These people? *Me*? They *deserve* you. We are lucky to have you, and we are better because we know you."

"I think it's the other way around, too."

"Maybe," Haven agreed, "but today isn't their day, either. It's yours."

"Yeah."

"Ready to get married?"

"More than ready."

"Then, let's get you married."

Haven's pep talk came at the right time because beyond the double oak doors lined with waves of white and red tulle, the music changed to a familiar tune. Ginevra shot a wide smile over her shoulder and lifted her bouquet of red roses high.

"That's me," she said.

The doors opened a little. Not enough to show the rest, but it allowed Ginevra to walk through first. Haven gave Valeria a wink.

"Me next. You're not sad, right?"

"For what?"

"Well, I'm not sure. Maybe because your side of the aisle might be a little … empty."

Valeria shook her head. "Not at all. The people who count are already here, and the only other person I might like to see … well, my parents are dead, and Abril called to congratulate before she asked after Maria. I'm not sad."

"Good. I love you, huh?"

Valeria nodded. "I love you, too. Thank you … for everything."

When she had nothing, Haven was there. Against all odds, Haven had been the one who never gave up on Valeria. Now she had everything, and she was so glad she could share this with her best friend. That was the beauty of life.

"We're just getting started, Val."

"Absolutely."

A minute later, Haven slipped through the doors when they opened for her. That left Valeria and Maria waiting in the corridor. Gian, Chris's father, had offered to walk her down the aisle, and while it meant the world to her … she still asked to do this alone.

So much of her life was forced upon her. She wasn't given any choice, and she had never been free to do something *willingly*.

More than anything, she wanted to do this.

Gian understood.

"Almost time, Mamá," Maria whispered, smiling.

She looked so beautiful in her red and white gown.

"Almost," she echoed.

Maria would walk first, spreading her rose petals down the aisle. When the song changed to the one she chose for her walk, then she would go, too.

"And then we get to keep Chris forever, right?"

"Yeah, baby, we get to keep him forever."

Maria turned with her basket ready when the doors opened for her. Instead of walking in, she *skipped*. Chuckles murmured down the line of chairs before the doors closed again, leaving her to her thoughts.

She wouldn't be alone for long.

Chris promised.

She didn't have to do anything alone now. And hadn't he proven that he always kept his promises?

Soon, the song changed behind the closed doors, and Valeria dragged in a heavy breath. Lifting her head to smile, the doors opened wide open to expose her waiting behind them.

Every guest stood.

Valeria smiled wider behind her veil.

She should have taken the time to admire the way the decorations had come together in the hotel's hall where they chose their venue. All the reds and whites, melding together with the roses as accents, and centerpieces. The silk aisle runner dotted with red and white rose petals, compliments of her daughter. The event planner and the small army she brought in to decorate the place had worked so hard to get it ready for this moment.

She looked over the people, noting familiar faces; some she had only recently met, and others she had known for months now, smiling back at her.

And then, she stared forward.

At *him*.

Chris waited at the end of the aisle, his twin at his left, wearing a custom, tailored tux he filled perfectly. It reminded her how lucky she was to have this gorgeous man waiting on her—smiling *for* her. Well, he reminded her of that every time he woke her up in the morning, and each night before she fell asleep with him next to her. His white silk vest and tie was a stark contrast to the red set his twin, and other brothers wore for the day.

The chiseled line of his jaw softened when his grin deepened, and his dark gaze drifted down her dress to take her in. The proud glint in his eye said he liked what he saw waiting for him. Just like that, she was the only woman in the world, and he was the one man made for her. She'd been careful to do that for this day. Ensure he didn't see her dress—that it would be a complete surprise.

Chris had been more than willing to play along.

Whatever she wanted.

He loved her too much.

She understood.

She loved him the same.

From all the way across the room, she sensed his stare. The way he drank her in and appreciated her. *Adored* her. He never hid it. Not from her, or from anyone else. She couldn't wait to spend the rest of her life being loved by this amazing man.

Maria waved at her mom from her spot next to Haven, reminding her they still had a whole ceremony to get through. Valeria stopped wasting time standing at the end of the aisle when where she wanted to be next to Chris far more.

That's where she belonged.

Forever.

EPILOGUE

"Whatever it is," Chris said when he answered the ringing phone while heading up the stairs, lest it wake up his sleeping wife or Maria, "make it good, and fast. I have better things to do this morning than talk on the phone."

"Is that how you greet your father?"

"Well ... no."

"Good," Gian said, "I was worried you forgot your manners in your new married life."

"I've been married almost two months. You don't think it might take longer?"

Gian made a noise under his breath. "I'll be honest, I might as well have forgotten the rest of the world existed for the first six months of mine and your mother's marriage. That was a wonderful time."

"And that's enough of that," Chris muttered.

"Anyway," Gian said, "I called for a reason. Happy birthday."

"Who did you tell first this year, me or Corrado?"

"Both of us," came the new voice on the call.

A three-way call.

Nice.

Chris chuckled. "Ah, Papa got smart this year."

"Wouldn't want either of you feeling left out," Gian returned, his amusement clear.

A long running joke between Chris and his twin on their

birthday was whoever got called first by their parents—
mother or father—was clearly loved the most. It was only a
couple of years ago that their parents caught onto the joke
which they didn't find all that funny. Or rather, their mother
didn't find it as cute as they did.

Their father played along.

They couldn't say the same for their ma.

"And now can I go back to bed?" Corrado mumbled. "It
was way too early for this."

Chris checked his watch. "It's nine."

"Thank you for that information. I will let a *very* pregnant
Ginevra and an extremely anxious Alessio know that their
nightly habits of walking the halls and worrying about every
little thing isn't an acceptable excuse to keep me awake until
two in the morning. Care to be here while I do that, brother?
Or to lend me a couch when they kick my ass out?"

Gian laughed.

Chris was quick to say, "No, you're on your own there."

"Thanks for that, really."

"I do what I can," Chris replied.

"Go back to sleep, Corrado," Gian said, "and call your
mother later. Alessio isn't the only anxious one lately."

"Right, right. Later."

One call clicked off, and Chris knew he was left with only
his father. During his conversation, he had climbed the two
levels of stairs in his three-level home and stood in the
doorway of their master bedroom. Across the large space,
Valeria slept happily under gray and white striped sheets,
only a peek of her bare shoulders and a splash of black hair
could be seen on her pillow.

God.

He loved this woman.

So much.

More every day.

"Someone asked Ginevra who the father was when she went to the salon the other day with your mother," Gian said.

Chris frowned. "What?"

"The boys were *very* angry."

"I mean ... I understand the curiosity someone might have," Chris said, "but not the ignorance to outright *ask*. That's nobody's business."

From the moment his twin had announced Ginevra's pregnancy to their family, the expectation of how to act and receive it was undoubtedly clear. It was *we* are pregnant. It was *they* were expecting a baby. *Their* daughter. From the start, neither Corrado nor Alessio had differentiated, and Ginevra was the same way.

Everyone fell in line because, sure, while the circumstances of a poly relationship might be strange to some, it was his twin's everyday *normal*. What was Corrado's life didn't have to fit into everyone else's box—they didn't have to live it. They did, however, have to respect it.

"What did Ma do?" Chris asked. "You said she was there, right?"

Gian chuckled. "Had all her future appointments cancelled and found a new salon before lunch."

"Easy when her last name is Guzzi."

"Easy when she is who she is, you mean."

"That, too."

"Nonetheless, I thought you might want to know for later today when we're having the birthday dinner at the mansion," Gian said. "In case they're sensitive about the baby and the pregnancy, that might be why."

"Yeah, thanks. I'll let Val know."

"And how is she, hmm?"

"Pardon?"

"Valeria. How is she?"

"Perfect. She's perfect."

"I bet. I know she's been busy prepping for the fall semester to start. Has she settled on a major after her bachelor's?"

"Not yet," he said, "but she's got all the time in the world."

Chris had promised her that.

He intended to keep it.

"Well," his father drawled, "I will let you get back to your morning. I'm sure you have plans, and I didn't mean to interrupt them. Living that good life, huh?"

Maria was still sleeping.

Valeria, too.

Still, his father wasn't wrong.

He wasn't sure what that *good life* was his father spoke about, or if this was it, but it was the perfect life for Chris. That's what mattered most to him.

"I will see you later, Papa."

"You, too. Happy birthday, son."

Oh, it was about to be *very* happy.

"Oh, my *God*."

Chris's dark chuckles whispered along his wife's naked skin as he raised from between her thighs, dropping hot kisses to her trembling stomach, up to the valley between her breasts, and finally along the damp column of her throat.

Valeria's heavy breaths, thick from her orgasm, panted into the bedsheets. There was nothing he liked more than waking this woman up by loving her. Usually, with him between her thighs because *fuck* …

That was a win-win for him, too.

Her taste was still tart on his tongue, and she all but sucked the flavor of her arousal off his tongue when he kissed her. Her soft moans were swallowed by his kiss, but he was already lost in the way she had widened her legs for him. The slickness of her pussy grinded against his bare length while her fingernails dragged burning lines down the muscles of his back.

"*Fuck*," he breathed.

"Yes, yes."

He was a lucky fuck.

Every morning, this woman was in his bed.

She arched into his hands that slid down her body, and he leaned up to hover above her while she licked her lips. Sinful and inviting. *Begging* and ready.

God, he loved it.

His fingers flexed around her waist, loving that he knew this woman never missed a fucking meal. He was fit, and toned, but her curves drove him crazy. From the expanse of her hips, to the roundness of her ass when she was backing into his thrusts. Every part of her was perfect, and he wanted her to know it every morning she woke up, and each night before she fell asleep.

That was his job.

He did it.

"You want that dick, huh?"

Valeria laughed breathlessly. "So bad."

See, and now he had wakened her up with his tongue between her thighs, it only made her want more. That was the *win-win* for him.

It was only once Chris slid home inside Valeria's clenching pussy, feeling her tightening around him in the best way, that he kissed her again. He loved to feel the way her lips trembled against his when he stretched her open one inch at a time, slow but so fucking good, too. She was always so shameless, her hips rising to meet his while her hands pulled him closer to her.

"*Stop teasing …*"

Because she knew.

And he loved that, too.

His control snapped when her heels dug into his back, and her fingernails found the best spot to dig in along his sides. He couldn't fuck her hard enough, then, or *fast enough*. He would never get enough of this woman, no matter what.

But wasn't that the beauty of it?

Chris lost himself in the way Valeria worked her body against his, fast to seek her own bliss while he was chasing his. Her noises muffled against his kiss until he felt that climax rush through her again as she froze beneath him. He followed soon after, holding her tight as he thrust deep, and came hard.

"*God, I fucking love you.*"

Valeria's laughter, so high and sweet, was better than a morning prayer. Hell, maybe it *was* his new prayer. He tangled his arms around her, flipped them over so they were both on their sides, and he could bury his face into the mess of her hair, and *sighed*.

"Happy birthday," he heard her say. "I love you, too."

"Best fucking birthday yet."

"You wait," she whispered, "it will get *way* better."

He didn't know how.

Chris was willing to find out though.

"Can I get it for Daddy now, Mamá?"

Hearing Maria call him *daddy* never failed to make Chris smile. It didn't matter if she was saying it because it annoyed her that he refused to let her wear her pink, sparkly running shoes on a rainy day, or because she was asking for five more minutes of storytelling at bedtime. He wasn't sure when she thought of him as her father, but he vividly remembered when she asked if she could call him that.

You're kind of like my daddy, right?

Kind of?

It's all he wanted to be.

She all out refused to call him papa or father, and Chris understood why. She related those titles to a man whose name they didn't speak because it upset her, and of a time in her life which was still all too recent, and traumatic.

So, instead, he got to be her daddy.

That was better.

Because her daddy didn't let her down.

Ever.

Her daddy loved her unconditionally.

No exceptions.

"Okay," Valeria said, "you can go get it, but hurry before Uncle Les gets up there to take his bat."

Chris shot her a look across the backyard of the mansion where she sat beside Cara and Ginevra. There, they could watch the rest of the Guzzi men—well, most, as the younger Guzzi twins had been sent off to Chicago after their twenty-first birthday—and the other guests who wanted to join from their birthday dinner play their game of baseball from a safe distance. Valeria *pretended* like she didn't see Chris glancing her way with his questioning stare about just what she was hiding from him, but he knew she did.

Alessio came up to bat after Maria darted for the back of

the mansion, and from the spot they'd chosen as the pitcher's mound, Corrado grinned. "You want that curve ball, Les?"

The man tapped the metal bat against the heel of his shoe before pointing it at Chris's twin, saying, "I'm up for whatever—you know that."

"*Right.*"

Sitting on third base, Chris just wanted to hit home so he could sneak over to Valeria and find out why Maria disappeared into the mansion. She had already given him a birthday present earlier after they cut the cake. A damn nice Rolex, custom-made with the Guzzi *G* designed in diamonds on the face.

What else was there?

"I mean, we've already won," Corrado added. "There's no way you will get those two runs, and this is your last bat."

"Stop gloating," Alessio returned. "That's your one warning."

"That's what makes it *fun.*"

"Throw the goddamn ball."

"Language," Cara called out.

"Sorry."

Corrado threw the pitch when he thought he distracted Alessio with his apology, but he should have known better. He got his two runs when the metal bat connected with the ball and sent it flying past the tree line on the back property— their designated space for a *home run*. Because no one wanted to go searching for balls in the small patch of forest.

Alessio only stepped off the home plate as Chris came jogging across it, tossing his bat so it flipped around in the air before landing back in his waiting palm. He pointed the bat at Corrado, smirking wickedly.

"I think I'm gonna *walk it*," he said. "Remind you who you're trying to better, yeah?"

Corrado shook his head, grinning. "Who's gloating now?"

"And who likes it, huh?"

Chris would have enjoyed the banter between his twin, and Alessio, but he was already heading toward Valeria who was smiling his way.

"Where did Maria go?" he asked his wife.

Valeria peered up at him. "In the house. And congrats on winning."

"Why?"

"Because you won the game."

"No, why did she go in the house?"

"For a surprise."

"For me?"

"Since when are you nosy?"

"Just because it's your birthday, son," his father called as he crossed the backyard with Maria skipping at his side, "doesn't mean you get everything you want … or does it?"

He might have questioned his father on that statement, but he was more interested in his girl, and the gift in her hands. A white box, maybe twelve inches long, and wrapped with a big, golden bow. She held onto it like it was a lifeline.

"What's this?"

Maria smiled. "It's for you. And me."

Chris shot Valeria a look.

She only shrugged.

"Open it?" Maria asked.

Chris took the chair his father pulled out so he could sit beside his wife, with his mother on the other side of him. Gian came to stand behind his chair while Maria placed the box in his lap. Sweet as could be, she bounced on the spot while she waited for him to reach for the gift.

"Any hints?" he asked Valeria.

She shook her head. "It's better if you … understand all at once, I think."

"Definitely," Gian added.

His brow dipped. "They know what it is?"

"We needed help with—"

"Details," Cara was quick to interject. "Don't give him too much to go on."

Valeria laughed. "Yeah, that. Open your gift."

Well, okay.

Maria's excitement only grew like her huge smile when Chris pulled the satin ribbon from the top of the box. He gave her a laugh before opening the top, and then he looked down.

His whole world *stopped.*

Application for Adoption.

The papers were ready. All filled out, and it appeared a lawyer could file them anytime. It only needed one thing. A little arrow pointed to a space where his signature needed to go.

Chris grabbed a little tighter to the box, unable to speak.

Maria did it for him. "Because you're already my daddy, right?"

His father's hands found his shoulders and squeezed. Valeria reached over to stroke his cheek with her warm palm.

Yeah.

This was most definitely the best birthday of his life.

"Right?" Maria asked again, quieter the second time.

He looked up to meet her gaze.

Her smile never faltered.

"That's right," he said, keeping his tone level, although he didn't know how. "I promise."

Maria darted forward when he opened his arms to bring her in for a hug. Someone pulled the box from his lap just in time, so the papers inside didn't get crushed.

He didn't know who.

It didn't matter.

Everything he wanted was right in his arms and sitting beside him.

All around him.

His father had been right.

This was the good life.

BETHANY-KRIS

Bethany-Kris is a Canadian author, lover of much, and mother to four young sons, two cats, and three dogs. A small town in Eastern Canada where she was born and raised is where she has always called home. With her boys under her feet, a snuggling cat, barking dogs, and a spouse calling over his shoulder, she is nearly always writing something ... when she can find the time.

Find Bethany-Kris at her website:
www.bethanykris.com

Sign up to Bethany-Kris's New Release Newsletter here:
http://eepurl.com/bf9lzD.

BOOKS BY BETHANY-KRIS

Always

Revere

Unruly

The Companion

Naz & Roz

Guzzi Duet

Unraveled, Book One

Entangled, Book Two

DeLuca Duet

Waste of Worth: Part One

Worth of Waste: Part Two

Donati Bloodlines

Thin Lies

Thin Lines

Thin Lives

Behind the Bloodlines

The Complete Trilogy

Filthy Marcellos

Antony

Lucian

Giovanni

Dante

Legacy

A Very Marcello Christmas

The Complete Collection

Effortless

Inflict

Cozen

Captivated

Dishonored

Find more on Bethany-Kris's website at www.bethanykris.com